What Others Are Saying About
Loree Lough and *Currency of the Heart*...

Loree Lough's books are filled with complex characters, heart-tugging stories, and unexpected curves in the road. This is what we, her readers, have come to expect from her, and *Currency of the Heart* does not disappoint. Readers will love Shaina and are certain to become invested in this story from page one as she strives to survive despite the death of her husband. They'll love Sloan, too, as he tenderly helps her rebuild her life.

—*Sandra D. Bricker*
Award-winning author of 20-plus novels, including the series
Another Emma Rae Creation

One of my favorite go-to authors, Loree Lough has again captured my imagination with *Currency of the Heart*. I am amazed by her ability to engage my emotions and my thoughts as she spins her wonderful, heartwarming tales. Each of her more than 100 books has become an old friend, like a cozy quilt or a trusted confidante. And I suppose that's why I keep coming back to her again and again.

—*L. G. Vernon*
Author, *The Wilderness Road*

Once again, prolific author Loree Lough gifts her readers with a sensational romance. Set in the 1880s in booming Denver, Colorado, *Currency of the Heart* will transport readers from the plains of the Midwest to the splendor of the Rocky Mountains, from bustling city to peaceful ranch. I was swept away into the world of Shaina Sterling and Sloan Remington, and my curiosity was piqued by this stirring tale laced with secrets.

—Rita Gerlach
Author of the series The Daughters of the Potomac

I had read man   orary romance novels by Loree Lough before discovering her a   ies. Loree draws her readers right back in   m experience the sights, smells, soun   heroes and heroines are believable and likeable, all of them having backgrounds and secrets, trials and tragedies, that keep us wondering how in the world there could ever be a satisfying ending. *Currency of the Heart* does not disappoint!

—*Robin Bayne*
Award-winning author of 20-plus books, including
The Artist's Granddaughter

Warning! Once you pick up a Loree Lough novel, you won't be able to put it down until you've come to the end. *Currency of the Heart* is warm and romantic, filled with characters you'll care about and remember long after you've put down the book. You'll feel as though you're right there with them, enduring joy and heartache, coping with the challenges of the past, and feeling the true spirit of people who aren't perfect but who learn that a Spirit-filled life is the only true life. There's a reason Loree has sold more than 100 books! This one's another can't-put-down book you'll treasure.

—*Barbara Cameron*
Award-winning author of the series Amish Road and
Quilts of Lancaster County

Currency of the Heart is a regular page-turning event, a clash of circumstances involving money that will either join two people at the heart or create a great divide. Characters Shaina Sterling and Sloan Remington carry secrets neither is willing to divulge. When their strong wills butt heads and the truth unravels, it will be God's divine intervention that makes all the difference. Loree Lough hits this one right out of the ballpark!

—*Sharlene MacLaren*
Author of 14 award-winning novels and four series, including reader
favorite Tennessee Dreams

Loree Lough always delivers a fabulous read, whether it's a heart-tugging romance or heart-pounding adventure. In this case, it's both! *Currency of the Heart* promises drama, romance, unexpected twists and turns, and, most of all, a satisfying ending that will leave you thinking about the story long after you've finished the book.

—*Carolyn Greene*
Author of 14-plus award-winning books, including *Unexpected Reunion*

CURRENCY OF THE
HEART

LOREE LOUGH

WHITAKER
HOUSE

All Scripture quotations are taken from the King James Version of the Holy Bible.

CURRENCY OF THE HEART
Secrets on Sterling Street ~ Book One

Loree Lough
www.loreelough.com

ISBN: 978-1-62911-275-6
eBook ISBN: 978-1-62911-276-3
Printed in the United States of America
© 2015 by Loree Lough

Whitaker House
1030 Hunt Valley Circle
New Kensington, PA 15068
www.whitakerhouse.com

Library of Congress Cataloging-in-Publication Data

Lough, Loree.
  Currency of the heart / by Loree Lough.
    p. cm. — (Secrets on Sterling Street ; Book One)
  Summary: "In Denver in the 1880s, a young widow and a prosperous rancher must learn to open up about their pasts if they expect to have a future together"—Provided by publisher.
    ISBN 978-1-62911-275-6 (alk. paper) — ISBN 978-1-62911-276-3 (eBook)
  1. Widows—History—19th century—Fiction. 2. Ranchers—Denver—Colorado—History—19th century—Fiction. I. Title.
  PS3562.O8147C87 2015
  813'.54—dc23

                        2014030896

1 2 3 4 5 6 7 8 9 10 11   W   22 21 20 19 18 17 16 15

Dedication

This book is dedicated to the almighty Father, who blessed me with an ability to type...and to string words together in ways that will draw people closer to Him.

Acknowledgments

A big, sincere thank-you to Sara and Barbara, the überhelpful ladies at the Denver Public Library, for their help with finding accurate 1880s-era maps of the city.

Special thanks to my dear friend Reverend Robert Crutchfield, from the Compassion Church of Katy, Texas, for allowing me to use portions of the eulogy he delivered when his beloved mother, Marilyn, passed. The words of the fictional Pastor Truett are so much more heartfelt as he presides over the funeral toward the close of the story because of Robert's Spirit-filled generosity. (By the way, Robert also wrote The First Responder's Prayer that was featured in all three novels of my First Responders series. I told you he was generous...and he's talented, too!)

I'm also grateful to my family for putting up with my goofy work schedule, with the messy table that holds research and interview notes, and with my tendency to talk nonstop about the characters who breathed life into *Currency of the Heart*.

"For God shall bring every work into judgment, with every secret thing, whether it be good, or whether it be evil."
—Ecclesiastes 12:14

Chapter One

November 7, 1882 · 6:20 p.m.

Will you just look at that," Elsie Wilson said, pointing. "Who does she think she is, Lady Godiva?"

Sloan looked up in time to see Jennie Rogers heading toward Sterling Street. There were so many things wrong with Elsie's question, he could only shake his head. For one thing, Jennie was dressed in bright blue, from her festooned hat to her high-heeled boots. For another, her ink-black hair reminded him of the years he spent with the Lakota-Sioux.

Elsie snapped her fingers, putting an end to the still-raw memories. "Sloan Remington," she scolded, "stop gawking at that woman!"

He didn't like being told what to do. Didn't like the way she said "that woman," either. What had Jennie Rogers ever done to her—to anyone in Denver, for that matter—to justify their poor manners toward her? No one had quirked an eyebrow when she offered to pay the new schoolteacher's salary or fund repairs to the courthouse roof, so it was mighty hypocritical of them to look down their noses at the way she earned enough money to do so.

If the truth about *his* past ever came out, would Elsie and others add his name to the list of citizens to avoid? *Of course they would*, he thought, frowning.

Elsie's expression softened slightly. "Good thing you're not a gambler."

He didn't have time for poker, and said so.

"Better practice a poker face, anyway." She wagged a finger near his nose. "Because that handsome face of yours is easier to read than a *McGuffey Primer*."

Sloan didn't know what she was babbling about. Even if Jennie owned a hat shop, she wouldn't have turned his head. As for how she earned her living, well, Sloan figured that was between Jennie and her Maker.

Elsie peered at her through the lace curtains. "Where do you suppose she's headed?"

"Don't know, don't care." Truth was, he had a pretty good idea. Several evenings ago, he'd seen Jennie headed in the same direction... and so had Rafe Preston.

Elsie snipped the final stitch, then used a pair of pointy tweezers to pluck it from his cheek.

"I declare, the woman doesn't have the sense God gave a flea. What's she thinking, parading through town, alone, when it's nearly dark?"

Well, she had him there. And the *ifs* began to stack up: *If* Jennie hadn't gone out alone that night.... *If* the sinister look on Preston's face hadn't prompted Sloan to follow him.... *If* he'd been a tick quicker, he could have averted the attack without sustaining a three-inch gash to his face. It wasn't likely Jennie knew what sort of mayhem had erupted after she'd slipped into Sterling Hall, for if she had, she wouldn't have made the trip again tonight.

Elsie grabbed a tiny brown bottle from the shelf above the exam table. Sloan read the label—Tincture of Merthiolate—and groaned inwardly. Clenching his jaw as she poured some of the orange liquid onto a cotton ball, he waited for the sting.

"You're lucky that ruffian didn't put your eye out," Elsie said, dabbing the cut.

Right again, he thought, doing his best not to wince. "Hey, take it easy, will you?"

Elsie seemed not to have heard him. "So now you'll have a scar for the rest of your life. And for what? Defending a woman like that?"

While she bandaged the wound again, the *should haves* piled up: He *should have* waited until Elsie left the room to tell Elsie's brother, Doc Wilson, what had happened that night. *Should have* gone straight home five minutes ago, when she'd said her brother was out, delivering the Pattersons' third child. *Should have* found a way to shut down Elsie's anti-Jennie gossip the instant it had begun.

She opened her mouth to say more, but a thunderous rumble stopped her.

Medicine bottles clattered on metal shelves as the doctor's wheeled stool rolled across the floor. It slammed into the glass door of the apothecary cabinet as the big pendulum clock crashed to the floor, its shattered face stopping with both hands on the number 6. The floorboards creaked and groaned as the ground beneath them shifted, throwing Elsie off balance, right into his arms.

"Wh-what's going on?"

A second, larger tremor rolled through the clinic, followed by two more in quick succession.

"Too close and too fierce to be some fool miner trying to dynamite gold from the mountains." Sloan knew, because he'd heard it as a boy, when his pa had dragged the family from Kansas to Aurelia to find a lode. He'd pressed his wife and their boys into manning a cradle strainer, and when that hadn't worked, he'd built a crude sluice box. But all they got was cold and wet and sick, and when May drew to a close, his ma and his brother were both dead.

"My guess is, it's an earthquake."

"Here? In *Denver*?"

Townsfolk had started reacting, as evidenced by the shouts and screams out on Broadway. Soon, some well-meaning citizen would barge into the clinic to check on Doc Wilson's unmarried sister. One look at Elsie, stuck to Sloan like a second skin, was all it would take to get the gossip mill churning. And since Sloan suspected that Abe Fletcher, one of his ranch hands, was sweet on her, he couldn't have that.

"The place is a mess," he said, holding her at arm's length, "but you're all right."

She looked around at broken vials and shattered jugs, then gave a helpless little shrug.

"Spunky as you are," he added, "you'll have this cleaned up before the Pattersons' young'un comes into the world."

He grabbed his hat from the hook beside the door. If the quake had caused this much damage here, how bad was it at Sterling Hall? More important, how had the women inside that big house fared? He pictured Jennie, taller than most men and strong enough to handle a four-horse rig. Unless a rafter had come loose and knocked her unconscious, she was fine. The widow Sterling, on the other hand, was barely bigger than a minute.

He took a Morgan silver dollar from his pocket and put it on the exam table. "Thanks, Elsie," he said, touching a forefinger to the brim of his Stetson. "I'll check in later to see if you need anything."

Outside, Sloan worked his way through the milling crowd, skirting around overturned barrels and stepping over fallen shop signs. If anyone were to ask where he was going in such an all-fired hurry, he didn't know how he would answer.

But he knew this: He had a powerful need to make sure the widow was safe.

Chapter Two

The tall brunette looked over her shoulder and smiled at her reflection. "I do believe I'll look gorgeous arriving *and* leaving in this pretty frock!" Turning, she faced her hostess. "One of my girls will have to alter it, of course."

Of course, Shaina echoed silently, remembering that the hem of every dress she'd sold Jennie Rogers had been at least eight inches too short, the bodices no less than two inches too tight.

"I'm thinking a wide band of satin will do nicely," Jennie said, fluffing the sea-green ruffle that accented the sweetheart neckline, "to match this one." She met Shaina's eyes, and her voice softened. "Are you absolutely sure you want to get rid of it?"

No, she didn't want to get rid of it, but Harper's pre-death spending had turned her into a near pauper. Shrugging, she pretended the gown wasn't one of her favorites and tried to forget that if she didn't sell it, she'd have no way to pay for groceries this week.

"Yes, I'm sure."

"Hmpf. That's what your mouth says, but—"

The floor shook beneath her feet as she watched Jennie peer into the flowery oval box that housed the matching hat. Shaina had never been the superstitious type, but this *was* the thirteenth outfit she'd sold to Jennie.

"But the rest of you says the opposite."

Shaina caught a glimpse of herself in the big oval mirror: chin up, spine straight, lips forming a taut line. She exhaled slowly and forced herself to relax. "If you buy the hat and matching stole, I'll throw in the hat pin for free. It's a genuine garnet, you know."

Jennie barely glanced at the bejeweled spike that pierced one side of the velvety bonnet, for she was too busy adjusting the small, flat hat that barely covered half of her dark, elaborate pompadour. "I like big, colorful hats with feathers and flowers and bows," she said, inspecting herself in the mirror. "I even have one or two with birds on them!" she added with a flourish.

Yes, Shaina had seen them. But, unlike the other women of Denver, she'd kept her comments about Jennie's showy attire to herself.

Instead, she said, "Spoon hats, like that one, were always perfect for the opera, so the people behind me wouldn't have trouble seeing over my head."

Laughing, Jennie waved the comment away. "As if that would be a problem, tiny as you are. And just listen to you, speaking as though you'll never attend another production at the Tabor Grand Opera House!"

In the first months after Harper's death, Shaina had attended a few productions. But tickets to the Tabor were far beyond her budget these days. She couldn't very well admit that, however—not even to Jennie Rogers, one of Denver's two most-recognized madams.

Was it her imagination, or had the rumbling under her shoes grown stronger? And louder? She'd experienced a similar sensation once, standing on the platform at Denver's Union Station as powerful locomotives steamed in. But the trains didn't run at this hour.

Outside, on Sterling Street, Shaina heard frantic shouts, high-pitched screams, and the terrified trumpeting of horses. Maybe John Iliff had corralled some of his cattle on the other side of town, and a careless worker had forgotten to latch the gate. But no, instinct told her that even an entire herd on the loose wouldn't shake the house this much.

Thrown off balance, she stumbled against the bookcase, feeling it move slightly behind her. Had Jennie noticed? Fear of exposing another secret vanished as the carriage clock crashed to the floor. It lay on its side like a fallen soldier, its silver pendulum unmoving, its opalescent face glittering in the firelight. "Happy Second Anniversary to the Love of My Life" read the silver plaque affixed to its base. Both curlicue hands pointed at the Roman numeral six.

Jennie's painted mouth formed a bright red O. "Shaina, I— I'm so—"

The words died on her lips as portraits rattled on the walls and tea-cups clattered in their saucers. Both women looked up, mesmerized by the half-inch diagonal crack snaking across the ceiling. Plaster rained down like brittle snowflakes, peppering their hair with gritty dust.

Blinking and coughing, Jennie dropped to her knees, oblivious to the trickle of blood inching down her forehead. Shaina grabbed the nearest piece of cloth—a table scarf that had been embroidered by Harper's mother—and gently dabbed at the gash.

Jennie relieved her of the fabric. "I'll take care of this," she said, pointing over Shaina's shoulder. "You need to take care of *that*."

Shaina followed the woman's gaze to the hearth, where the tremors had dislodged a miniature avalanche of hot coals, smoking and glow-ing on the wide-planked floor. Heart hammering, Shaina crawled closer, palmed the braided handle of the brass shovel, and quickly scooped them up. She whispered a heartfelt thanks to the Almighty, because just one second more, and the embers would have ignited the carpet fringe.

Ten minutes later, the women sat side by side on the dusty divan, staring at toppled lamps, broken figurines, and leather-bound books that had fallen from the shelves.

Jennie flicked a bit of plaster from her shoulder. She'd done her best to hide it, but Shaina had seen her many-ringed fingers trembling. She'd heard the quaver in her otherwise smooth voice, too.

"I appreciate your letting me stay and gather my wits."

"Believe me, I'm glad for the company." She was well aware that Jennie could have collected her things and hurried home. Instead, she'd decided to wait rather than take the chance that one of Denver's fine citizens would see her ducking out the back door of Sterling Hall and start the gossips' tongues wagging.

As Shaina tried to think of a way to express her gratitude, Jennie said, "I'll bet my brand-new parasol that we just survived an earthquake."

Shaina nodded. "I just read an article about the one in San Francisco. I must admit, though, the writer didn't come close to describ-ing it adequately."

Jennie laughed. "I'll say this for you, Shaina Sterling—when you're right, you're right!"

She didn't want to be right. She just wanted things to be the way they were before Harper died.

Jennie changed back into her own clothes and carefully folded Shaina's dress, then lowered it into a wood-handled brocade satchel. And although the hat wasn't her style and the stole wouldn't fit her, she added them, too.

Shaina hung her head. It had come to this, had it? One of the city's most notorious madams pitied her enough to buy clothing she didn't need and couldn't wear. It didn't seem possible to feel more pathetic.

"I'm sure one of my girls can wear these," Jennie said, placing the shoes atop the wrap. Then, getting to her feet, she rummaged through her beaded purse, grabbed Shaina's wrist, and pressed a wad of cash into her palm. Shaina didn't need to count it to know it was far more than the price they had agreed upon.

"Something tells me we'll be reading about this minor catastrophe in the *Rocky Mountain News*," Jennie said, closing Shaina's fingers around the money. "Now you listen to me, Shaina Sterling. That busybody Molly Vernon will likely pay you a visit, hoping to snag a quote from one of the city's elite citizens to add to her story. So you'd best start thinking of ways to keep her here, in the parlor. If she starts snooping around and adds two and two together...." Jennie picked up her things. "I have it on good authority she's trying to prove something to her tyrant of a father, in hopes that he'll start assigning her real news stories instead of making her write about garden parties and fancy weddings."

Shaina had never thought of Molly as a gossip, but Jennie's warning was clear: If the publisher's daughter figured out that Shaina had been impersonating a woman of means, then life as she knew it would abruptly end. Invitations to dinner parties and costume balls would stop. Worse, Denver's most privileged residents would cross to the other side of the street to avoid her, the way they did when Jennie and her girls were out and about. Before her marriage to Harper, Shaina wouldn't have cared what they thought. But she cared now.

She followed Jennie into the kitchen, where the curtains had fallen from their wrought-iron rods and now lay in lacy puddles on the pine floor.

"Well," Jennie said, giving her a sideways hug, "look on the bright side. You sold the most valuable stuff before disaster struck."

So it *was* possible to feel more pathetic.

"Oh, don't look so glum." She gave Shaina a playful shove. "You still have a roof over your head and plenty of pretty frocks in your armoire. And, unless I'm mistaken, you have just enough Limoges porcelain in that sideboard so you can serve tea and crumpets when your fancy friends stop by."

Shaina nodded dumbly, because Jennie was right—things could be worse. A terrifying childhood memory flashed in her mind, and she blinked it away as the pretty young madam opened the back door.

Despite the cold blast of wind and snow that blew into the kitchen, Shaina's cheeks burned with shame. She was no better than the stuffy, self-righteous women who turned up their noses at this good-hearted woman. Only a hypocrite would accept her generosity in the dark, by way of the back door! Jennie might not earn a living in the most reputable way, but at least she treated others with honesty and respect.

"Good thing I rode Acorn tonight, 'cause I'd freeze my toes clean off, walking a mile in this windy mess," she mused. "Plus, I can avoid all the busybodies." Laughing, Jennie pulled her cloak tighter around her throat, then hesitated a moment on the top porch step. "I'll send a couple of the girls over here in the morning to help you put the place back together."

Shaina shook her head. "Oh, no. Thank you, but you've already done far too much. Besides, you know better than anyone that the parlor is the only fully furnished room in the entire house. I'll have things cleaned up in no time."

Jennie returned Shaina's feeble smile, then hurried down the steps and untied the horse. After climbing into the saddle, she tugged on a pair of leather gloves and picked up the reins. "I hope I won't see you soon," she said with a wink.

Shaina understood perfectly: A visit would mean that she needed to sell something else because she'd run out of money. Again.

"Take care going home," she told Jennie. "Those articles about the earthquake described aftershocks that could spook a horse."

"If Acorn were easily spooked, he would have run off during the earthquake." She gave a click of her tongue, and the horse moved forward. "Get on inside before you catch your death. Last thing I want to do in this miserable weather is attend a funeral."

Leaning against the closed door, Shaina fought tears. Over the years, Harper had spent thousands of dollars on things that gave the appearance of material success. And he'd gambled on Sterling Manufactory's future profits to keep the money train chugging. She hadn't personally squandered away their fortune, but by accepting his extravagant gifts, she'd contributed to their financial demise.

She would *not* cry, because she hadn't earned pity.

Not even her own.

Chapter Three

Sloan tethered his horse and shook his head. *Leave it to Harper to fritter away good money on a row of bronze hitching posts,* he mused. *Maybe if you'd spent your money on sensible things, instead of spoiling your pretty little wife....*

The image of Harper standing motionless in the alley beside the saloon, the silver barrel of a Collier flintlock pressed to his chest, made him cringe. It had been more than a year since that dreary morning, yet Sloan still wondered what he could have done differently to prevent Harper from firing that .50-caliber round from the chamber.

"Don't tell Shaina I died a coward," Harper had wheezed when Sloan reached his side. He'd rambled nonsensically for a moment, and then, with his last breath, he'd said, "Promise me...you'll be the one to tell her.... Promise me you'll look out for her...."

Promise me. The exact words spoken by Harper's dying father, right here at Sterling Hall, nearly two years earlier: *"Promise me you won't let my boy destroy everything I've worked a lifetime to build."* In the presence of a stiff-backed lawyer, the man had pleaded with Sloan to sign documents making him a silent partner in the company. "You saved Simon's ranch, and for the sake of every man who counts on me for a salary, I'm counting on you to save Sterling Manufactory, too." It was only because Sloan knew most of those men—and the wives and children who relied on their salaries—that he'd signed.

Now, Sloan climbed those same brick steps and stood on the porch. Heart pounding, he stared at the big bronze door knocker, wondering if it was a dragon or a lion or both, as he had that dismal morning. He hadn't wanted to come here that day, and he didn't want to be here now. But he'd given his word.

Sloan swallowed. Hard. Then he reached for the knocker.

He lurched when the door swung open.

Shaina hadn't expected to see him, either, as evidenced by the way she plowed right into him. Her dustpan and whisk broom clattered to the bricks, and if he hadn't wrapped his arms around her, she would have ended up down there with them.

It wasn't the first time he'd held her this way. In response to the news about Harper, she'd crumpled like a marionette whose puppeteer had let go of the strings. He'd been in no hurry to let go of her that day, either.

Was it her heart, beating hard against his chest, that made it seem the ground was quaking beneath his boots? Or was it the earthquake's aftershocks?

She stepped back and cupped her elbows. "Sloan Remington, you scared the stuffing out of me! What are you doing out here on my porch—in the dark, alone, and at this hour?"

"The, uh…." He shrugged and ran a hand through his hair. "The earthquake. Just checking to, uh, to make sure you're all right."

"As you can see," she said, arms akimbo, "I'm perfectly fine."

Oh, you most certainly are. Backlit by the glow of the foyer sconces, she reminded him of the painting of an angel he'd seen years ago on the wall of an old church. Sloan resisted the urge to pluck bits of plaster from her straight, dark hair. He smiled and softened his tone. "Then how 'bout I have a look inside…make sure the ceilings won't cave in on you?"

He'd witnessed a holdup once, and the terrified bank patrons had looked exactly as Shaina appeared now, eyes wide and unblinking, body trembling from head to toe, lips parted slightly. He understood her fear: By letting him into the house, she risked his finding out that she was flat broke. If he'd known that Harper's personal holdings were more knotted up than the company's, he would have helped there, too. His challenge—after witnessing a few late-night exchanges between Jennie Rogers and the widow Sterling—was coming up with ways to lend a hand without her finding out what he knew.

"Everything inside is fine, too." She stooped to retrieve her cleaning tools. "Some books fell off the shelves, and a few curtain rods came loose from their brackets." On her knees, she swept up the spilled debris. "But I can handle it."

"With some help from Broze and Hilda, you mean."

And there it was again—that look of quiet desperation—and he felt a pang of guilt for having caused it. He knew full well that the caretaker and his wife had been let go nearly six months ago. "Nigh onto thirty years at Sterling Hall," Broze had growled when Sloan had run into him and his wife at the edge of town, "and all we get are two old nags and a rattletrap wagon." Hilda had shown Sloan the letter of introduction Shaina had written to her friends who owned the prestigious Peck House Hotel in Empire, and he'd pieced together the rest of the story: Finding them employment, housing, and reliable transportation out of town was the only way Shaina knew to protect them—and also to keep them from spilling the beans about her sorry financial circumstances.

She lifted her chin a notch. "I know you see me as spoiled and pampered, but I'm quite capable of cleaning without their help."

Spoiled and pampered...pretty much what he'd been thinking right before her front door had flown open.

"I'm sure you are. Capable, that is. And I'm sure Broze and Hilda are enjoying their, uh, *visit* in Empire."

"Well, of course they are. Why wouldn't they be?"

Her indignation prompted a grin, but he choked it back. He'd already caused her enough upset for one evening. "No reason. No reason at all."

His words seemed to relax her, and he felt a little less guilty about having riled her. It couldn't have been easy, running a place this size all by herself. But rather than risk being shunned by Denver's high and mighty, she'd done it. The odd mix of valor and vanity brought a Bible verse to mind.

"'Pride goeth before destruction,'" he quoted, "'and an haughty spirit before a fall.'"

She narrowed her eyes slightly. "While I'm impressed that a man like you can quote Proverbs...."

A man like him?

"You don't know me well enough to make such assumptions."

He resisted the urge to say, *"All right, then, Mrs. Sterling—how 'bout we use 'spoiled rotten,' instead?"*

"May I ask you a question, Mr. Remington?"

"Sloan, please."

"Fine. Sloan."

He grinned. "You can ask, but I can't promise to answer."

"What happened to your face?"

Instinct made him touch the fresh bandage. "Long story," he said, "and it's clear that you're freezing out here in this cold wind. So if you're sure everything is all right, I'll just be—"

"I have nothing but time," she said, "so come inside and tell me all about it by the warmth of the parlor fire."

Her visit with Jennie, cut short by the earthquake, must not have satisfied her need for companionship. Compassion made him follow her into the foyer. Made him hide the pity aroused by the sight of it, too. The last time he'd entered Sterling Hall, a crystal vase of flowers had glittered atop a round mahogany table in the entryway, and behind the door, a mirrored hall bench had reflected an elaborate umbrella stand. Sloan remembered it well, because, in his rush to catch Shaina when she fainted, he'd kicked it, and the clatter had roused her from unconsciousness. Life-sized portraits of Harper's parents once flanked the arched doorway leading to the dining hall. It wasn't likely anyone had bought the paintings, but the frames must have been worth something, because, like everything else, they were gone. How did Shaina explain the stark décor to her snobby friends?

"Can I fix you some tea?" Her voice echoed in the empty room.

She'd extended the same invitation a year ago. Then, as now, his response of "I'd like that" surprised him, because he'd never been overly fond of the stuff.

"Do you mind joining me in the kitchen?"

Once there, she struck a match and lit the oil lamp that hung above the trestle table. "Please make yourself comfortable while I stoke the fire."

"How about if I do that while you fix the tea?"

They both reached for the poker at the same time. Her small hand all but disappeared beneath his. He felt the calluses that had formed on her palms, proof that she wasn't as delicate, or as spoiled and pampered, as she appeared.

When she released the poker—and freed her hand from his—he found himself wishing she hadn't.

While he crouched to stir the coals in the stove's belly, she pumped water into the kettle. From the corner of his eye, he could see her placing teacups on saucers, tucking embroidered napkins beside them on the table, as he blew air across the dying embers.

Straightening, he dusted his hands together. "Lots of clouds up there tonight. Let me carry in a few armloads of wood while we wait for the water to boil." He walked toward the back door. "Out here?"

"Yes, I put a stack beside the porch, right after I—" She stopped and cleared her throat, telling him without words that she had not only put the wood there but chopped it, too.

It didn't take long to confirm: No two logs were the same size. *Oh, to be a bird in the trees,* he thought, *watching her heft the ax.*

"Thank you for saving me a trip outside in the dark later," she said as he laid the logs in the old crate beside the stove.

"Happy to be of service."

Smiling, Shaina pulled out a kitchen chair. "Please, have a seat. The water didn't take long to boil, because I brewed a pot earlier for—"

She pretended that her sentence was cut short by her concentration as she poured water into the flowery teapot. What had really silenced her? Humiliation born of the methods she'd chosen to keep the wolf from the door? Or shame at having chosen one of the town's most disreputable residents as her buyer? Not the latter, Sloan hoped, because he was beginning to admire how well she'd handled adversity. And he liked thinking that if Shaina discovered the truth about his past, she would accept it, just as she seemed to have accepted the truth about Jennie.

Sloan sat and glanced around the room. Half a dozen place settings of delicate porcelain were neatly displayed behind the glass doors of the china closet. How many more had the hutch held before hard times necessitated their sale? He supposed the sideboard housed matching serving pieces, along with flatware, tablecloths, and napkins like the ones she'd laid beside their cups. Unless she'd sold those, too.

When he noticed the fine lace curtains on the floor, he got up and snapped the rods back into their wrought-iron brackets, then made a clumsy effort to tidy the window coverings.

A small smile lifted the corners of her mouth. "You're just all kinds of helpful, aren't you?"

"It's the least I can do," he said, nodding toward the table.

She peeked inside the teapot. "Sorry I can't offer sugar or cream. I ran out. This morning. And haven't had time to...to have more delivered."

Did she think no one noticed her daily treks to the edge of town, where she loaded her tiny pink-lined basket with a loaf of bread, an egg, and enough milk to fill a small jar?

He shrugged. "I prefer it black, anyway."

Several weeks ago, he'd been in the back of the grocer's when he'd overheard the preacher's wife, Tillie Truett, ask Shaina why she had sold her chickens and dairy cows. Even from that distance, he'd seen her cheeks redden as she explained, "With Broze and Hilda gone, I just can't take care of them all by myself."

Tillie, evidently unsatisfied with the answer, had pressed for more information. Broze and Hilda wouldn't be gone forever, she'd said; couldn't the young fellow who maintained the lawns and gardens pitch in until they returned? Sloan had saved Shaina from further embarrassment by stepping up to make small talk with the older woman.

Shaina sat down across from him and pointed to his bandaged cheek. "So," she said, folding both hands on the table, "were you in a knife fight?"

The accuracy of her guess surprised him. "Uh, I—" Sloan cleared his throat. "Sort of."

She laughed, and the delightful sound sent a tremor up his spine.

"You were *sort of* in a knife fight?" She made another musical giggle. "I hope I didn't exercise poor judgment, inviting you into my home."

"You're safe with me, Mrs. Sterling."

Simon Remington, the man who had rescued Sloan when the rest of his family died that cold, bleak spring, had taught him to lead an upright life. Lessons learned at the knee of that good man had, in part, inspired Sloan's promise to her dying husband.

Shaina hid her chafed hands in her lap. "I hope I'm not exercising poor judgment," she said, meeting his eyes, "admitting that I believe you...*Sloan*."

He had a notion to say, "*It's your own fault, sitting there, looking lovely despite your soot-streaked cheeks and plaster-peppered hair.*" Instead, Sloan sipped his weak, lukewarm tea. He didn't like the stuff, no matter how it was served; yet he smiled, in no particular hurry to empty the cup.

She tilted her head slightly and returned his smile. "And please, let's dispense with the 'Mrs. Sterling,' shall we? It's just plain Shaina."

"Shaina it is, then," he said, studying her lovely, big-eyed face. *Though, if you ask me, you're anything but plain.*

Chapter Four

Sloan hammered the last brace into place while James walked the spool farther down the fence line. The men had another hour or two of backbreaking work ahead of them, repairing posts that had shifted during the earthquake.

"I can almost taste Mable's sourdough biscuits," James said, mostly to himself. "Think she put them green apples you brung her into a pie?"

"Hope so." Sloan threaded barbed wire around the winder stick.

"She don't cook fancy less'n you're here," James added. "Sure do wish you'd come round more often."

Sloan pictured Mable, who ran Remington Ranch with the precision of a drill sergeant. He'd been months shy of his ninth birthday when Simon—the only person on earth who'd known the truth about him—had rescued him from the side of that cold, bleak mountain and brought him to his ranch. Right from the start, Mable had taken Sloan under her wing and showered him with unspent maternal affection; and the brokenhearted boy, who'd watched helplessly as fever had drained the life from his adopted family—his ma, his brother, and finally his pa—had soaked it up like a dry sponge.

James spat a wad of tobacco over the top rail. "You gonna stand there woolgatherin' till the sun goes down or help me fix this busted fence?"

It wasn't the first time James had meted out a fatherly admonishment, and, God willing, it wouldn't be the last. They'd come close to losing him after a fall from the hayloft had left him with a broken neck. Doc Wilson had predicted that if James survived, he would spend the rest of his days flat on his back. Sloan grinned, remembering James's own diagnosis: *"Gonna take more 'n a stiff neck to keep this ill-tempered ol' fool abed all the livelong day!"* By year's end, the man was back on his feet, and the following spring, he could saddle a horse and ride for miles. These days, the only evidence of the fall was a slight hitch to his step.

"Awright," James growled, "who is she?"

Sloan returned the man's good-natured grin. "Who's who?"

"Your feet don't fit a limb." He did a fair-to-middling imitation of a barred owl before adding, "The li'l gal what's got you all addlebrained, that's who."

It didn't make a lick of sense that Shaina Sterling came to mind. Shaina, whose voice had grown husky with regret as she apologized for serving him weak, unsweetened tea. Shaina, whose ice-blue eyes had flashed in the lamplight as she complained that the disreputable politicians were sure to destroy the Denver she'd come to think of as home....

"How long have you known me, James?"

"Sixteen, seventeen, years...purty much your whole life, I reckon." He squinted one eye as another gob of tobacco hit the dust. "But since when does Mr. Straight Talk answer a question with a question?"

"Since you forgot that all it takes to make me addlebrained is talking about women."

Nodding, James stroked his thick mustache. "Awright, then, we'll leave it be." He winked. "For now."

An hour later, their chore complete, Sloan, James, and four ranch hands gathered around the kitchen table. The big stew pot was half empty when Mable said, "Last time you fellas were this quiet was the day you lost the herd that was grazing in the north pasture to a gang of rustlers." She exhaled a shaky sigh. "I still have nightmares, thinking about what they did to poor old Harlan Brooks."

James frowned. "Just 'cause a man wants a little peace with his biscuits don't mean somethin' bad happened."

"What if it hasn't happened yet?"

He guffawed. "You boys seen anythin' suspicious?"

Abe Fletcher, the youngest, only shrugged.

Will Tomkins shook his head, and so did Noble Burke.

The newest hire, Leo Blevins, stared into his stew and said, "Not me."

James gave a satisfied snort. "See there? Nothin' to fret about."

"If you say so." Mable's voice, stance, and stern expression told Sloan she wasn't buying it.

And neither was he.

"What is it with women," James began, "always lookin' for trouble where there ain't none?" Sopping up the last of his stew with a broken biscuit, he added, "Worryin' only accomplishes two things."

Mable sighed and closed her eyes, as if praying for the patience to hear him out.

"It gives small things big shadows."

"And what's the second thing?" Abe wanted to know.

"Puts gray hair on a man's head."

Grinning, Sloan leaned back in his chair. "From the looks of things, you've spent the better part of your life worrying."

While the men chuckled, Mable folded both arms over her chest. "I declare, you boys are so backward, it's a wonder you can see where you're going! So, if it isn't missing cows, why *is* everyone so quiet tonight?"

"Don't know 'bout these pups," James said, "but this old dog is plumb wore out."

Grunts and growls of agreement harmonized with spoons scraping against stoneware bowls.

"Not too tired for apple cobbler, I hope." She patted his bony, work-scarred hand, and winked at Sloan with a look that said, "*I baked it 'cause it's your favorite.*" Mable darned socks and replaced missing buttons for every man, so if they noticed the little extras Sloan received, they probably chalked it up to the fact that he owned the place. But he hadn't owned anything more than the clothes on his back when she'd begun doling out the special treatment.

While James and the hands discussed tomorrow's list of chores, and Mable dished up apple cobbler, Sloan pondered the sense of foreboding that had enveloped him. He'd felt the same way before those rustlers had killed Harlan and stolen a hundred head of cattle, as well as the night when a field fire had distracted Sloan, Simon, and the hands from the bandits who'd driven off every newly rounded-up mustang corralled near the barn. As soon as supper ended, he aimed to single out each man and find out if he shared his suspicions that something was off.

He picked at his cobbler, which drew Mable's attention.

"I've never known you to dawdle over dessert," she said. "I heard in town there's a fever going round." She pressed the back of her hand to his forehead. "You just being your usual, backward self, or are you feeling poorly?"

Sloan got to his feet. "Only thing wrong with me," he said, patting his belly, "is my weakness for your biscuits."

And before she got a chance to remind him that his face was easier to read than a book, he headed for the back door. "Gonna walk off that stew of yours."

He grabbed his hat and jacket from the hooks behind the door. "Walk with me, kid," he said to Abe.

The younger man stuffed his mouth with the rest of his cobbler and was still shrugging into his coat when he caught up with Sloan. The men leaned on the corral fence, watching as James's horse nibbled at the straps that kept its turnout in place.

"Guess ol' Sally doesn't realize it's for her own good," Sloan mused.

The mare, like several of the ranch's saddle horses, preferred the outdoors to the confines of the barn. Abe was one of the few who understood that even the sturdiest animals were susceptible to deadly lung ailments that could spread from horse to horse in a matter of days. Sloan would rather laugh off the ribbing of fellow ranchers who believed he treated his work horses better than most folks treated their young than watch even one more horse suffer and die.

Bending, he plucked a dry blade of grass from alongside the fence. "So how's that new fella workin' out?"

"Leo? He's all right, I guess."

What Abe lacked in years, he made up for in common sense. "You guess?"

"He don't say much." Abe glanced over his shoulder, then lowered his voice. "And he goes off on his own every chance he gets."

Sloan inspected the straw. "Where to?"

"Dunno." He shrugged again, then grabbed a straw of his own. "But, like Noble says, long as he does his share, ain't nobody's business where he goes when the day's work is done."

Propping a boot on the bottom rail, Sloan nodded. "Seen anything suspicious around here of late?"

Abe mimicked his boss's stance, seemingly content to watch the sun slowly disappear behind Mount Rosalie. "Nothing specific."

Sloan understood the younger man's hesitation to talk. If something Abe said got back to the others, they'd treat him like a pariah—or worse. Sloan had learned the hard way what that could be like.

"Whatever you say is just between you and me. You've got my word on it."

Abe studied Sloan's face for a blink or two, and then, apparently satisfied Sloan could be trusted, he said, "You know the way the air makes the hairs on the back of your neck stand up right before a storm rolls in?"

Heeding that very forewarning had, on many occasions, spared Sloan from nature's vicious disposition…and from the ill will of other men. If he'd honed it earlier in life, he might have evaded the wrath of his adoptive father, Ralph. When Ralph's wife, Kitty, had found Sloan on the side of the road, stuffing his face with wild raspberries, she'd taken pity on him and brought him home. Ralph hadn't wanted children; he'd barely tolerated Pete, the son born of his own loins, let alone a scrawny half-breed. That fact had never been more evident than when whiskey deepened his already foul mood. Sloan and Pete had been good for just one thing: Work.

Abe leaned an elbow on the fence and looked Sloan in the eye. "Well, that's the feeling I get when Leo's around."

"Why?"

"Dunno," he repeated, facing west again. "But I know this: When he's around, I make a point to keep my back to the nearest wall."

Sloan felt the same way about the man, who avoided eye contact and spoke with a curious accent. He'd seen Leo in town at Eyser's Saloon, sharing jokes and bottles of Tanglefoot with Rafe Preston. If there was any truth to the old saw that a man could be judged by the company he kept….

"Mind if I ask you a personal question?" Abe asked.

Sloan shrugged. "Just be mindful that asking doesn't guarantee an answer."

The boy returned his smile. "What happened to your face?"

"Why don't you save us both a lot of time and tell me what you think you know?"

Abe had been sweet on Elsie for some time. Any other nurse would have felt obliged to protect patients' confidentiality, but Elsie wasn't any other nurse.

"Your word to keep it between us still holds?"

"It does."

"Well, way I heard it, you called out Rafe Preston, on account o' his pesterin' Miz Jennie. If it's true that you gave as good as you got, I'd hate to see Preston's face."

"Never touched his face." And he hadn't. One roundhouse punch to the belly, and Preston had collapsed like an accordion with a hole in its bellows.

"Elsie said it took thirteen stitches to close up the gash he gave you. Said it's gonna leave a mean scar, too."

And it probably would. He absentmindedly stroked the thick pad of gauze.

"Guess you're hopin' it's true...."

Sloan sensed that Abe was itching to finish his thought. He had the height, muscle, and work ethic of a hand twice his age. When he learned that silence almost always topped talk, he'd be a fine man, indeed.

"...that gals think scars make a man interesting."

"Now, why in blue blazes would I hope a thing like that?"

You might want to take some of your own good advice to keep quiet, Sloan thought, pulling his Stetson lower on his forehead. He softened his tone as Shaina Sterling's soot-streaked face came to mind. "What kind of woman likes her men all cut up?"

Abe shrugged off the outburst—another sign he'd make a fine man one day.

"Mind if I ask another question?" Abe asked.

"Fire away." Sloan cut a glance at the boy. "But only if this is the last one."

"Word is you've been spendin' considerable time with the widda Sterling."

Considerable time? If he added up all the moments he'd spent in her company, the sum wouldn't total a full hour. Now, moments he'd spent *thinking* about her....

"She's a fine woman," Sloan said, choosing his words carefully. "Too fine for the likes of me."

"Aw, you ain't foolin' me none. I've seen you ride out of here in your fancy black suit. Only a handful o' places you'd go, all bow-tied and boot-polished thatta way. Seems to me if you're fine enough for those opera-goin', garden-party-throwin' townsfolk you rub elbows with—"

"Those shindigs bore the wadding out of me," Sloan interrupted. "Only reason I go is because those opera-goin', garden-party-throwin' townsfolk send lots of business to the manufactory."

But, much to Sloan's disappointment, Abe wasn't so easily distracted.

"Well, it still seems you're fine enough for Harper's widow."

Though Sloan had never learned to dance, it took some fancy footwork to avoid her at social functions. After her months of mourning, it had done his heart good to see her out and about, looking stunning in her beautiful gowns, smiling and laughing with friends. Coming face-to-face with the man who'd delivered the worst news of her young life would cast a shadow on her enjoyment, so once the polite "Thank you for coming" greetings were out of the way, Sloan always made himself scarce. If only they'd met under different circumstances....

Abe chuckled. "Bet you ain't bored rubbin' elbows with *her*!"

He paused, giving Sloan hope that he'd tired of the inquisition.

"So it's true?"

"That I spend considerable time with the widow? No, It isn't." *Oh, but I'd like it to be.*

"That's a sorry shame, boss. If you ask me, she's perfect for you."

Well, he hadn't asked, and he was about to tell the boy to mind his own business, when the wind kicked up, rousing the dozing horses. Ears pricked forward, they nickered and bobbed their heads, then moved to the corner of the corral, where the barn wall offered some protection from the cold blasts. All except for one.

Penny ambled over to Sloan and laid her head on his shoulder. Smiling, he ruffled her thick, dark mane. "You're sure not the scared li'l girl I brought here from Central City, are you." She gave a quiet snort, then nuzzled his shirt pocket in search of a treat.

"Think she'll ever grow hair over them scars?"

Sloan palmed one of the carrots he'd pinched from Mable's cutting board. While Penny munched, he stroked her slender neck, his fingers lingering where One-Eyed Pete had used barbed wire in a futile attempt to tame her wild streak.

"Not likely."

"Whatever happened to that fella you bought her from?"

He could tell from Abe's tone that he'd heard things, but Sloan saw no benefit in confirming or denying them.

"Last I heard, he went north." *Eventually*, Sloan added to himself.

After paying the man for an underfed bull and three scrawny calves, Sloan had offered a dollar for the paint that was clearly struggling to remain upright in her dark, dingy stall. Hearing that she wasn't for sale was all the proof Sloan had needed: Pete kept her around for his own twisted pleasure. Fiery rage had compelled Sloan to appoint himself judge and jury, and when he'd left Clear Creek Ranch that day, he'd had *five* animals hitched to his wagon, as well as the satisfaction of knowing that when Pete came to, he'd find an extra silver dollar in his torn and bloody shirt pocket.

"Never understood how a man could rough up a horse that way." Abe shook his head. "Any animal, for that matter. I say One-eyed Pete is lower 'n a lizard's belly."

Penny nickered and accepted a second carrot. Then, in the bat of an eye, she lifted her head, nostrils flaring and ears swiveling, and backed away from the fence.

Sloan recognized the signs of agitation, and so did Abe. Turning slowly, they faced the cause.

"Evening, lads." Leo tapped the brim of his bowler. "It's a bit cold to be standing out here in the almost-dark, isn't it?"

"Lads," indeed. First chance he got, Sloan intended to find out where the man had acquired his odd way of talking. He squinted into the smoke spiraling from the tip of Leo's neatly rolled cigarette. "We're just walking off Mable's stew," he said, watching Penny cross to the other side of the corral.

Leo nodded toward Penny, now huddled with the other horses. "I don't believe I've ever seen a mount that spooks easier than that one."

"Aw, she ain't spooked," Abe joked. "She's just tryin' to figure out why you've got a soup pot on your head."

"I'll have you know this fine chapeau cost a mere five dollars, significantly less than what you paid for your hat, I'd wager."

Abe's left eyebrow rose slightly, and Sloan could almost read his mind: A good Stetson could set a man back twenty dollars. But something told him it wasn't the price and style of hats that had drawn Leo outside. With any luck, he'd avoid eye contact now, too. It wasn't likely he'd overheard any of this spur-of-the-moment meeting, but even a glance could tip him off—an unsettling possibility.

"I'm goin' to bed," Abe said around a yawn. "James wants us to get outta here at first light to round up the runaways. That's a disagreeable time, even on the best days."

He was halfway to the bunkhouse when Leo said, "Good night, sleep tight, don't let the bedbugs bite. And if they do, then take your shoe, and knock 'em till they're black and blue."

The breath caught in Sloan's throat. He'd been eight, maybe nine, the last time he'd heard the rhyme. He couldn't say which stung more—hearing the words his mother had whispered to soothe him to sleep every night of their captivity with the Dakotas, or hearing them spoken by a man he didn't trust.

Leo dropped his spent cigarette and ground it into the loam with his boot. "It's been a pleasure working with that boy. He has a level head on his shoulders."

His wording made Sloan wonder if Leo was planning to quit.

"How old do you suppose he is?" Leo asked.

Just weeks ago, Mable had baked an apple pie for the boy's fifteenth birthday. If anyone else had asked, Sloan might have volunteered the information. Instead, he merely shrugged.

"I'm guessing sixteen…seventeen, at most. Does he have family in the area?"

Leo's sudden interest in the boy put Sloan on full alert. Was Leo baiting him? Because it sure seemed that way.

Well, no matter. Sloan had no intention of telling the man that after Abe's folks had lost their farm outside Omaha, they'd taken jobs in the city and sent their sons away to find work. He remembered finding the shivering, near-starved twelve-year-old during a cow-buying trip to Amarillo. Just as Simon had saved Sloan, he intended to do the same for Abe. From the start, the boy had proved himself equal parts hard worker and quick learner. Sloan would never admit it, not even to James, but the kid seemed more like a younger brother than a ranch hand. And because of that, Sloan felt duty-bound to protect him—although from what, he couldn't say, exactly.

He'd had enough of this small talk and was about to end the conversation when Leo said, "Think I'll follow Abe's good example and turn in, too. James isn't exactly the most pleasant chap when a man shows up late for work."

He was gone a full five minutes before Sloan started for the house. If he had a wife, the many peculiarities that described Leo Blevins were just the sort of thing he'd ask her opinion on.

What an odd thought.

Odder still that Shaina Sterling came to mind yet again.

Ridiculous, he thought. *You're totally unsuitable for marriage.*

How long, he wondered, before his conscience would set him free from the sins of his past?

Chapter Five

I'm so sorry," said Molly Vernon. "It's such a shame that you lost so many beautiful things in the earthquake." She clutched a brass-handled mahogany box to her chest. "With Hilda and Broze away on family business, it must have taken you hours to clear out all the debris."

If anyone had told Shaina that she would be grateful for a nature-born catastrophe, she would have called him insane. But the earthquake had provided the perfect explanation for the bare rooms throughout Sterling Hall.

"Oh, it wasn't so bad." And it hadn't been. Most of the rooms had already been emptied of lanterns, porcelain figurines, and furnishings of carved wood, so there had been precious little for the earthquake to destroy.

Shaina led the way into the parlor. "I did manage to salvage some of my china." Also true! Pointing at the silver tray on the marble-topped table, she added, "I've just brewed myself a pot of tea. Will you have a cup with me?"

"I'd love to." Molly removed her cloak and draped it over the arm of the sofa. After making herself comfortable, she pulled two small keys from her black velvet purse. "Isn't this just the most amazing thing?" she said, lifting a box onto her lap. "Mother sent all the way to England for it." She waved Shaina closer and inserted the first key. "See? It has places to store ink and pens and paper. I never carry ink, of course, because I'm afraid the vial might leak and ruin the lovely leather lining."

Inserting the second key, she giggled. "And look here—secret drawers, hidden behind this little panel!"

"What are they for?"

Molly withdrew a mechanical pencil. "Oh, I have no idea," she said, inspecting its tip. "Perhaps one day I'll get lucky and roust out a terrible secret someone is keeping. I could store my notes in one of the cubbies...until I sell the story to *American Magazine*, that is." Groaning, she added, "I could wring the neck of that old Greek—his name escapes me at the moment—who wrote, 'Let the women stay at home and hold their peace.' It's become Father's favorite quote, and if I hear it one more time, I might just scream!"

Shaina recognized the quote by Aeschylus. It did seem odd that words written by the Greek playwright in the fourth century B.C. still rang true in the minds of men like Daniel Vernon. Molly's mounting frustrations—being unmarried and childless, forced to live in her parents' home and to scribble entertaining little features for her father's newspaper instead of the gritty articles she wanted to write—gave credence to Jennie's earlier warning. Even if she'd come here today to roust a secret from Shaina's life, Molly wasn't likely to see her name above a piece in the *American*. But it would cause a big enough splash in Denver to make her the talk of the town—until the next scandal found its way into the pages of Daniel Vernon's newspaper.

"So, you're here on assignment?" Shaina asked as she poured the tea.

"Yes." Molly heaved a sigh of boredom. "I'm to document sprained ankles and broken mirrors and missing kittens, which will make absolutely no sense beneath a headline that reads, 'Rare Earthquake Shakes Denver to Its Core.'" She drew an imaginary headline in the air.

Shaina sat across from Molly and balanced her cup and saucer in her palm. "I'm so sorry that I can't offer any wafers, or even cream and sugar. With all that's been going on, I just haven't had a chance to buy more." And if she kept serving tea to everyone who stopped by, she'd soon be out of that, as well.

Molly waved away the apology. She hadn't asked any questions, and Shaina hadn't offered any information. What could she possibly be writing?

"I haven't been outside yet," Shaina went on. "Have you seen much destruction in town?"

The young woman looked up, frowning slightly. "Haven't been outside? Then where did you put all the things that were broken during the earthquake?"

"Why, in the cellar, of course." Yet another fact to be thankful for! In separating the items that could be sold from those that could not, Shaina had stored creaking chairs, worn linens, and cracked pottery in the food pantry beneath the kitchen.

"Yes, of course. It was rather cold that evening, wasn't it? I don't suppose I would have gone out, either, for fear that something might topple and render me unconscious. Especially if I lived alone, as you do." Molly tilted her head and smiled sweetly. "It's a shame about Porter, isn't it?"

What an odd point in the conversation to insert that question, Shaina thought. She'd made provisions for Broze's assistant to work for one of Harper's cousins up in Boulder. How Molly had come to find out that Porter had left was only one of the reasons Shaina's heartbeat had doubled. If she knew of that, did she also know *why* Shaina had been forced to release Broze, Hilda, and Porter?

Molly tapped the nib of her pencil against the paper. "I seem to recall seeing Sloan Remington here that night."

There was a certain "cat got the canary" look on the young woman's face.

"Oh, yes," Shaina said quickly. "He stopped by to see if I needed any help. And when he saw that I didn't, he left."

For months now, she'd managed to answer every well-intentioned inquiry about her house, her absence at social affairs, and her suddenly reclusive behavior. The earthquake had indeed provided a perfect cover story for her missing furniture and knickknacks, but it had also given Molly an excuse to stop by. How much longer could Shaina respond truthfully to the woman's questions if she kept poking and prodding?

Molly sipped her tea. "He's very handsome, don't you think?"

Shaina pictured Sloan. He was taller than any other man she'd ever met, with collar-length hair that gleamed like black satin and arms that could hoist hundred-pound sacks of grain and also provide gentle support. He didn't smile often, but when he did, it was like sunshine piercing a flinty sky. And his commanding voice, which could tame unruly horses, also had the power to comfort the brokenhearted and calm the frightened.

Molly laughed. "I'll take your dreamy-eyed silence to mean you agree."

Shaina forced a smile. "I expect every woman in Denver would agree."

Nodding, Molly added something to what she'd written. "Why do you suppose a man like that never married?" she asked without looking up. Then she fixed a thoughtful gaze on the bookshelf behind Shaina. "Is he hiding something? Or running from something...or someone?"

A few months before Harper's death, he and Shaina had sat in front of two regulars at the opera house who'd raised the same questions. *"Ignore the old biddies,"* her husband had whispered in her ear. *"They're just jealous because they know Sloan wouldn't give them the time of day."*

The pastor's wife had once described Molly Vernon as a handsome young woman, which Harper had interpreted to mean "three feet south of pretty." Shaina had disagreed then, and she would disagree now. Just because Molly chose to wear dark button-up dresses instead of ruffled gowns didn't make her any less a lady. If anything, her belief that smiling and laughing in public was the reason modern-day men agreed with Aeschylus is what made her appear less than feminine. If Sloan gave Molly the time of day, would he turn her head? And so what if he did? It shouldn't matter to Shaina.

So then, why did it?

Shaina felt her cheeks redden as a pang of guilt shot through her. She'd never understood how some widows could remarry mere months after losing their husbands, so it made no sense that, for a fleeting moment, she imagined herself on the arm of Sloan Remington.

She glanced at the framed tintype likeness of Harper on the mantel, recalling that she could braid her hair in half the time it took him to groom that droopy mustache. During their first months of marriage, they'd shared countless hours discussing books, attending the opera, and dining with friends. All too soon, however, he'd started spending more and more time at his office. She wasn't the only woman in their social circles whose husband seemed married to his work, and she had easily reverted to taking care of herself, just as she had before they'd met. It wasn't until the bill collectors had begun showing up, weeks after his funeral, that she'd realized Harper hadn't been working all those nights but playing games of chance—and only God knew what else—at The Palace Variety Theater and Gambling Parlor. The truth had hurt, left her feeling angry and insulted, but it had given her a certain freedom, too—and permission to stop missing him.

"How long has it been since you lost Harper?" Molly asked, as if reading her thoughts.

Shaina looked away from the photograph. "Too long," she said quietly.

"Do you miss him still?"

She didn't miss the duplicity that had bankrupted them. Didn't miss being asked to constantly assure her pale, reedy husband that she found him attractive, that she'd fallen in love with his big heart and sense of humor, not his bank account or position in town. It was an ugly secret—admitting that she'd married him for the security he would provide.

"Sometimes," Shaina began, "when I hear horses' hooves on Sterling Street, I wait for his key to turn in the lock." She sighed. "And then I remember…he's never coming home again." *And sometimes*, she added silently, *I'd rather face his disingenuous smiles and tall tales again than live this deceptive life I'm living now!*

"My apologies, Shaina." Reaching across the space between them, Molly grasped her hand. "I didn't mean to awaken sad memories, especially while you're coping with the aftermath of the earthquake."

Cracked plaster could be patched, shattered windows replaced. If only her broken life were as easy to put back together. At moments like this, Shaina wished for a friend who could be trusted with the truth, because she'd grown weary of pretending.

Molly began packing her writing case. "I should let you get back to"—she looked around the tidy room—"whatever you were doing when I stopped by, uninvited."

"Don't be silly. I'm glad you stopped by." Shaina helped Molly drape her satin-lined velvet cape around her shoulders. "I'm only sorry I couldn't help more with your article."

"You must be joking," Molly said as she headed for the foyer. "You were a *big* help!"

Long after the teacups were washed and put away, Shaina paced through her nearly empty house, going over every word that had passed between them. Hours after that, as she lit the lanterns and stoked the fire for the night, she still didn't understand Molly's parting comment. If she had blinked, Shaina would have missed the quick glance at Harper's photograph and the self-satisfied smile that had brightened the reporter's face.

Chapter Six

Sloan had added everything humanly possible to make his suite of rooms more welcoming—a four-poster bed, several over-stuffed chairs, a private water closet—but not once in the years he'd divided his time between The Remington Hotel and his ranch had he felt truly at home here.

Facing east on his private balcony, he could see an array of three- and four-story buildings that were becoming the norm. To the west were Mount Silverheels, Bald Mountain, and other peaks of the Rockies' Front Range. Workmen for the Denver, South Park, and Pacific Railroad were on the ridgeline right now, finishing up work on the tracks connecting Breckenridge to Como. Somewhere up there, he, his adopted brother, and Ralph had taken shelter in a ramshackle cabin near Quandary Creek. Miraculously, Simon Remington had found him, blubbering like a baby after breaking his shovel trying to bury them both in the rocky, near-frozen ground.

Quiet knocking pulled him back to the present, and Sloan opened the door to young Bridget Sweeny, peeking at him over a stack of sheets and towels.

"Would y'like me t' change yer linens now, Mr. Remington, sir?"

Her melodious brogue never failed to lift his spirits. "I was just leaving for the office," he said, "so this is the perfect time." He pointed at the small, burled-wood dining table near the balcony doors. "Mable made me some sugar cookies, but I'll be heading back to the ranch this evening. Will you help me out by taking them with you?"

"'T'would be my pleasure, Mr. Remington, sir. It'd be a sorry shame t' see 'em go to waste!"

Sloan strapped on his gun belt. "I should be back in a few days," he said, grabbing his hat. "Tell Colum he's welcome to best you in a game of chess while I'm gone."

"Best me, indeed. Only place that'll happen is in m'brother's dreams!"

Chuckling, Sloan stepped into the hall.

"Safe travels, Mr. Remington, sir. Be sure t'thank Mable for the cookies."

He winked, then pulled the door shut behind him. If he had a daughter, he'd want her to be like Bridget, right down to the sparkling blue eyes that were so like Shaina's.

He groaned under his breath as he stared down the stairs. Maybe by the time he made it from the third floor to the lobby, he'd figure out why it seemed Shaina was always on his mind. As he reached the first landing, he pictured her—tiny and spunky, kindhearted yet fierce when she had to be.

Weeks earlier, he'd assigned Colum the task of painting numbers above the doors leading from the stairwell to each floor. When he rounded the next corner, Sloan saw the number "Two," and he began compiling a mental list of things that came in pairs. *Socks. Boots. Gloves. Husband and wife.*

The latter pair so rattled him that he nearly crashed headlong into Caitlin Sweeny, who ran the front desk of The Remington Hotel.

"*Oh, m' feabhas, cad é do hurry!*"

Seeing that he had no idea what she'd said, Bridget's mother laughed. "Forgive me, Mr. Remington, sir. It's a habit I need to break, revertin' to Gaelic when…." She paused, as if searching for the right word.

"When some buffoon nearly knocks you down the stairs?" he finished for her. "I'm the one who's sorry, Mrs. Sweeny." He bent down, picked up the envelope she'd dropped, and handed it to her. "Are you all right?"

She tucked the envelope into her apron pocket. "It'd take more than a wee surprise to slow me down," she said. "But where *are* you going in such a hurry, sir? If there's somethin' I can help y'with, just say the word."

He opened his pocket watch. "I have a meeting at the bank in ten minutes. Lunch with the mayor after that." He snapped the watch shut and dropped it into his vest pocket. "Is there anything you need before I leave for the ranch?"

"I'll ask the mister, and if he thinks of somethin', I'll have him find you. God be with you as you travel, sir!"

As he headed out the door, he pictured her husband, Fergus Sweeny, the hotel manager. He had the brawn of a bull, the brain of a genius, and the standards of Aristotle. He, his wife, and their children didn't know the meaning of the word *lazy*. With a combination like that, no wonder the hotel ran like clockwork. This Christmas, Sloan would be sure to find a special way to thank them for their reliability.

The weather was raw, making the three-block walk to the bank a miserable experience. Penny would have to brave the cold soon enough, he thought as he passed the blacksmith's shop. Old Willard was shodding a few horses from the fire department, so at least Sloan's favorite mare was in good company.

Sloan turned up his collar and dug his hands deep into the pockets of his coat. Funny how quickly things could go from calm to chaotic. Earlier, the skies over Denver had glowed bright and blue, and a light yet steady wind had stretched the clouds into wispy bands of white. Now, an umbrella of gray had opened over the town, and the gusts blew hard enough to rattle windows and slam shutters. If it didn't snow tonight, he'd eat his Stetson.

"Well, well, well," Charlie Carlson said when he walked into the bank. "Look what the wind blew in."

The men exchanged pleasantries as the banker led Sloan to his office. Once there, Carlson opened the rosewood cabinet that stood beside his desk. "Can I interest you in a Cabañas?"

Sloan held up a hand. He'd never been fond of cigars, but if he was going to smoke, it surely wouldn't be something grown in Cuba.

"Coffee, then? Or sarsaparilla?" Carlson knocked on his top desk drawer. "Got a bottle of Old Crow in here," he whispered. "Got two glasses, too...."

"No thanks." Sloan propped his ankle on his knee and hung his Stetson from the toe of his boot. "I'm meeting with the mayor when we're finished here. Last thing I need is bourbon breath."

Carlson bit the tip off the cigar spat it onto the floor. "The mayor, eh?" he said, lighting a match. "Any relation to what we're talking about today?"

Sloan had come here to speak as a character witness for Doc Wilson, who, convinced that the proper equipment and sterile conditions were essential to a patient's post-operative health, hoped to secure a loan that would enable him to add an up-to-date surgical suite to his little clinic.

"Nope. Just wondering if you've decided whether or not to approve Amos Wilson's loan."

Carlson lit the cigar, then sat back, puffing until a thick ring of smoke encircled his bald head. "You know I can't discuss the particulars of my meetings with Amos."

"Yeah, I suppose that would be like me going around town telling folks the names of men who rent rooms at The Remington with ladies who aren't their wives." He gave the banker a moment to let that sink in before tacking on, "Something like that would be real bad for business."

The pudgy fingers of Carlson's free hand tapped his ponderous belly, keeping perfect time with the pendulum of the silver clock on his desk. "Yes. Yes, it most certainly would."

"Only reason I asked about Amos's loan," Sloan continued, "is to let you know I'm willing to act as cosignatory."

"Cosignatory?" Carlson echoed. "But the man can barely make ends meet. Why would you do something so foolhardy?"

When he'd first heard Doc Wilson's idea, Sloan had offered to fund the clinic improvements, but the doctor's pride wouldn't allow it. Now, sitting here in the banker's smoky but well-appointed office, it dawned on him that *he* could put together an agreement that wouldn't offend Doc Wilson's sensibilities. If he repaid the loan, fine. And if he couldn't, Sloan would consider it an investment in the betterment of Denver. There were a dozen reasons he didn't trust Charlie Carlson—among them, the man's allegiance to the Law and Order League, the secretive committee whose crude form of justice was always at odds with the police.

"Sorry to have wasted your time, Charlie." On his feet now, Sloan nodded toward the window. "It's looking mighty ugly out there. Take care to get home before the storm sets in."

He didn't wait for a reply. Instead, Sloan buttoned up his coat and plowed into the wind. With any luck, Doc Wilson would be in his clinic rather than out on a call somewhere, delivering a baby or tending one of the many people suffering with consumption. If he presented his idea well, the doctor would accept his help without losing face. At least, he hoped so, because—

"Sloan? Sloan Remington, is that you?"

The voice was easy on the ears, and he recognized it instantly. He stopped, turned around, and waited for Shaina to catch up with him.

"What are you doing so far from home?" he asked her, aiming his thumb skyward. "Have you looked up recently?"

"Yes, I have." Glancing upward now, she grimaced. "Scary, isn't it?"

"Oh, I wouldn't worry about it. The storm is just as likely to blow north as it is to hit Denver."

"Well, we can hope you're right." Shaina smiled. "I wish my parents lived closer, so I could check in on my father and see if his bursitis is acting up."

It was the first time she'd mentioned her family in his presence. "Where do they live?"

The sweet smile faded when she said, "Missouri."

Sloan wanted to hear more, but her teeth were chattering. "Let's get in out of this wind." He slid an arm around her waist with an aim to lead her across the street. He half expected her to issue a polite rejection, so it was a pleasant surprise when she complied without complaint. "I doubt The Windsor will be very busy this time of day, especially with the threatening weather ahead."

"That's because anyone in his right mind is at home, shuttering the windows and doors."

As he opened the door, he saw their reflection in the glass: himself, taller and broader than his pretty companion, and smiling as if he'd just won a grand prize. In a way, he had, in the form of time alone with Shaina Sterling. How could he feel so grateful for something he hadn't known he wanted? *Who are you trying to fool?* he wondered as they scuttled inside and chose a table near the big stone fireplace. He slid out a chair for Shaina, and as she sat, he realized he'd owe the mayor an apology for missing their meeting. His talk with Doc Wilson would just have to wait.

Except for a black-jacketed waiter and the white-aproned cook at the end of the bar, they were alone in the restaurant.

The cook donned his puffy white hat. "Don't tell me," he said, smirking. "You're here to study my menu so you can duplicate it at The Remington."

Sloan chuckled. "We don't have a restaurant."

"So you say."

"Relax, Stan. I have no desire to compete with The Windsor." Granted, he'd considered adding a restaurant soon after buying the hotel, but when his research showed low profit margins, he'd rejected the idea. "So, what's on the menu today?"

"You're in luck—there's enough beef and barley soup back there to float a boat."

"May I bring each of you a bowl?" the waiter asked.

Shaina probably wasn't aware that she'd licked her lips. How long, Sloan wondered, since she'd had a decent meal? He didn't understand the guilt hammering in his heart. He wasn't a mind reader. His promise hadn't included checking to see whether or not she was taking proper care of herself. Or had it?

"Sounds good," Sloan said. "What else do you have back there?"

"Sage hen, liver and onions, ham steaks…."

"Any vegetables?" Produce was hard to come by—and harder to afford—in these parts.

"Yeah, but only root vegetables, I'm afraid."

Sloan nodded. "Then bring us soup and whatever you think goes best with it."

"I thought we were just coming in to warm up," Shaina whispered when the cook and the waiter had disappeared into the kitchen. "I haven't had time to make a withdrawal at the bank, so I'm afraid I can't—"

"I'm the last person you'd want to consult on matters of etiquette," Sloan interrupted her, "but unless I'm mistaken, the inviter pays the tab...and the invitee lets him."

In response, Shaina sighed and removed her gloves, as if resigning herself to her temporary fate. He'd more or less accepted his growing affection for her, but until that moment, he hadn't given a thought to how she might feel about *him*. The possibility that she merely tolerated him was more upsetting than he cared to admit.

"So what brought you into town on such a blustery day?" he asked her.

She hadn't been inside long enough for the fire's warmth to turn her cheeks rosy. Why would such a simple question embarrass her? Unless.... Unless she'd been headed to Jennie Rogers' to sell another household treasure.

While the waiter delivered their soup and filled two tall mugs with coffee, Sloan wondered why Shaina's social position in Denver had become such a point of pride. Didn't she realize how much easier her life would be if only she'd come clean? He couldn't very well point it out, at least not without admitting the he knew her secret. And only the good Lord knew how she'd react to that. Besides, how hypocritical would that be, considering his own past?

She wrapped both hands around her steaming mug. "To answer your question, I was on my way to visit Elsie Wilson. She sent a note by way of little Tim Ross, asking if I'd succumbed to consumption or some other horrid illness. It made more sense to show her I'm fine than to send a written reply."

When she shrugged, her knitted shawl slipped to the floor. She bent to pick it up, but Sloan beat her to it. Standing directly behind her, he draped it over her slender shoulders, letting his hands linger for a moment as he smoothed it into place. She seemed so small, so vulnerable, under his big hands, and it took a concerted effort to keep from pulling her to her feet and wrapping her in a protective embrace.

You're being ridiculous, he chided himself as he returned to his seat. This diminutive woman was stronger and more capable than most men he could name, as evidenced by the way she'd single-handedly kept

Sterling Hall from falling into ruin. Whether he should credit her strength of character or pure mulishness remained to be seen.

Her big, black-lashed eyes bored into his as he sipped his coffee. "You're quite the gentleman, aren't you?"

"I try." He met her gaze, blink for blink.

She was first to look away. "It really sounds as if we're in for quite a storm. Looks that way, too."

A powerful gust of wind lifted a cloud of road grit that peppered the windowpanes, and the whirlwind even tore some leaflets from the bulletin board near the bank's entrance. For a moment, they spun in the whorl, then skittered down the street before disappearing under wooden walkways and into alleys.

They would never make it home before the bad weather set in, and for the first time since splitting his time between the ranch and Denver, Sloan accepted that reality without complaint. Shaina didn't know it yet, but he had another gentlemanly surprise in store for her. When she finished a good meal, he aimed to make sure she got home safely. *Can't have a woman walking alone, especially in foul weather.*

He picked up his spoon and used it as a pointer. "Better eat up," he said. "Your soup is getting cold."

Chapter Seven

If he had to guess, Sloan would say the temperature had dropped ten degrees since they'd entered The Windsor. And the weathercock atop the granary was spinning fast enough to create a draft of its own. He was glad he'd insisted on escorting Shaina home to Sterling Hall. Tiny as she was, a gust might pick her up and deposit her in an alleyway.

He'd been taller than most folks for most of his adult life, yet he rarely paid much mind to his height. But walking beside Shaina made him feel ten feet tall, and not just because the top of her head reached only as high as his bicep. It felt good, having her right there beside him. Felt so *right* that he wanted to slip an arm around her waist, as he had when guiding her toward The Windsor.

A block or so ahead, a handful of men darted across the road, shouting and waving their arms. Shaina snorted indignantly. "I wonder if they made sure their wives and children were tucked in safe from the storm before scurrying off to the saloon."

It was the first time he'd seen her riled, and he nearly chuckled out loud. Yet he had no intention of fueling her ire by admitting that her complaint endeared her to him.

Another cold blast of air pummeled them. "Goodness gracious, sakes alive!" she exclaimed. "It takes your breath away!"

"Yeah, I guess the walk into town seemed shorter that the walk home."

Shaina mumbled something unintelligible, and he glanced down to see that she'd pulled her cloak up so high that it covered her lips. She was trembling, too, but what did she expect, with nothing but that woven shawl to keep her warm?

He shrugged out of his coat and draped it over her shoulders before she had a chance to protest. Her audible sigh of relief went straight to his heart, distracting him from the icy blasts that now sneaked under his own collar and cuffs. He gave in to the urge to pull her close, and for the second time that day, she surprised him by cooperating.

Shaina was the first to point out the smoke up ahead. Sloan had smelled it for blocks, but he'd chalked it up to the emissions of well-stoked fireplaces and cast-iron stoves. Thick black clouds churned above the rooftops, spreading, then fading as they melded with the ominous sky.

"Sweet Lord, please keep all my neighbors safe," Shaina prayed aloud as she quickened her pace.

A sense of dread roiled in Sloan's gut, telling him it wasn't the neighbors Shaina should be praying for. Sterling Hall sat a good two hundred feet from the road. The estate had once consisted of six hundred sprawling acres. But as the town had grown, and Mason had sold off more and more land in order to make investments in Sterling Manufactory, it had dwindled to a precious few acres. Two of the remaining twenty acres lay inside the ten-foot brick wall that surrounded the house and gardens, several sheds and lean-tos, a carriage house, and a six-stall barn. Most of the outbuildings stood empty, now that Shaina had sold the horses and dairy cows. For her sake, Sloan hoped it was one of those, and not the manor house, that was burning.

The clang of the fire truck's bell sounded behind them, followed by gruff shouts and the rumble of horses' hooves. The big rig reached the corner just as Sloan and Shaina did. Recognizing her, the driver bellowed something incomprehensible before the vehicle made a sharp left and disappeared into the thickening dust and smoke on Sterling Street. Now Sloan understood: The men hadn't been running toward the saloon. They'd been running toward the *fire*.

Shaina came to a dead stop and looked up at Sloan.

"What...what did he say?" she asked, gripping his forearm.

"I'm not sure." It wasn't a lie, even though he had a pretty good idea what Boonie Rourke had shouted. Shaina must have known, too, as evidenced by her wide, terror-filled eyes. In a matter of minutes, they would know for sure, and he needed every second to figure out how he'd comfort her if Sterling Hall was indeed burning.

"Did he…." She turned and stared into the still-settling dust kicked up by hooves and wagon wheels. "Did he say, 'Stay here—it isn't safe at your house'?"

Word for word, that was what Sloan thought he'd heard. But he didn't have the heart to admit it.

"We don't have to go down there, you know."

Shaina blinked. Swallowed. Then closed her eyes and rested her forehead on his chest. "*You* don't have to go down there," she whispered, "but I do."

"A team of horses couldn't keep me from going with you." He almost gave in to the impulse to draw her into a reassuring hug. Instead, he offered his arm, and she wasted no time moving forward once she'd taken it.

They were a city block from the property, but even from this distance, they knew which building was ablaze.

The entry gate hadn't been wide enough for the fire truck to pass through, so the men had used pickaxes and sledgehammers to broaden the opening. Shaina stood as still as a statue, looking at the piles of cracked bricks and crumbled mortar, at the arched bars and wrought-iron curlicue that spelled out "Sterling Hall."

Boonie ran up to them, wheezing hard, his face streaked with soot. He held up a smoke-blackened hand. "I wouldn't come any closer, Miz Sterling. Things ain't lookin' good, and you could get hurt bad." As if to emphasize the danger, a second-floor window exploded, showering the shrubbery below with shards of glass. A portion of the roof collapsed, sending the firemen scattering as it landed with an earsplitting crash. Red-hot embers rained down, their glow fading as they settled to the ground.

Shaina pressed closer to Sloan, whether seeking warmth or solace, he couldn't say. But if he felt overwhelmed by the sight, he could only imagine how it affected her. Yet there she stood, still and quiet, hands clasped under her chin.

The sharp scent of charred wood rode the murky wind. He could taste the bitter smoke that stung his nose, throat, and eyes. Yet something told him none of those things was the cause of the tears in Shaina's eyes.

She took a halting step forward. "Mr. Rourke, do you...do you have any idea what caused this?"

"Near as I can figure," he said, "it started in the chimney." Boonie pointed at what remained of the once-elaborate brickwork—now stained black—that had hugged the left side of the house. "Chair stuffin's, rugs, all them velvet curtains and lace doilies...the fire ate 'em up quicker 'n my young'uns gulp down rock candy." He paused, then added, "Too much wind, not near enough water...."

Shaina nodded, then bowed her head and buried her face in her hands.

Boonie met Sloan's gaze, then lifted his shoulders in a helpless shrug. "I'm mighty sorry, Miz Sterling."

She came out from hiding as Boonie joined the others. "They...they aren't packing up, are they?"

"Looks that way," Sloan said.

"But they can't! They can't just give up!"

She broke into a run toward the house.

It didn't take long to catch up with her. "Shaina, Boonie's right," Sloan said, blocking her path. "You need to stay back. It isn't worth the risk."

"Are you *mad?*" Eyes blazing, she tried to go around him. "Of course it's worth the risk! That's my *home!* It's all— It's the only thing I have left in the world!"

Boonie had been right about the danger, and he'd been right about something else, too: The massive, mostly wood house didn't stand a chance with all this wind feeding the fire. But Sloan couldn't bring himself to state the ugly facts.

He grabbed Shaina by the wrist, pulled her close, and held on tight. "You're wrong," he whispered into her hair. "That old house isn't the only thing you have left." *"You have me,"* he wanted to say. "You have folks in Missouri," he said. "And, most important of all, you're safe."

The fire engine crunched over the gravel drive, stopping when it rolled up beside them. "Me n' the boys, we done all we could," Boonie told Sloan. "Dug a perimeter ring round the place, and thanks to that big ol' wall, there's no danger the fire'll spread to the outbuildings or them trees out back." He cast a worried glance in Shaina's direction. "She gonna be all right?"

"She will," Sloan said.

He'd see to it, no matter what it took.

Chapter Eight

Getting back to town seemed to take a thousand times longer than the walk to Sterling Hall. If not for Sloan, Shaina didn't know how she would have gotten through those horrible, harrowing moments. She did her best not to close her eyes, for when she did, visions of the fire, greedily consuming the house, sprang into view.

In the lobby of The Remington, Sloan guided her to the small parlor that doubled as a library and, after wrapping her in a soft patchwork quilt, told her to stay put while he rustled up some hot tea and warm biscuits.

"Stay put"? she thought to herself. *Where would I go?* She might have laughed if the question weren't so disturbingly valid.

Shaina looked around at the fireplace, crafted of river rocks, and the thick oak mantel that displayed several pewter candlesticks and a burl-walnut-encased clock. Even from this side of the room, she heard the steady tick that kept time with her heartbeats. Seated in one of the two brocade-upholstered tulip chairs, she smoothed the crocheted doilies that protected the arms from stains and wear, then admired the plush bloodred Persian rug beneath her feet.

Until then, she hadn't noticed the ashy coating that clung to her high-button boots. Instantly, her gaze traveled the path she'd taken to get here. Grateful that she hadn't tracked soot across the floor, Shaina opened her drawstring purse and took out a lace-edged handkerchief she'd embroidered with "SAS"—for Shaina Ann Sterling—then leaned forward to dust off her boots. The stains would probably never wash out of the cloth, but no matter. There were dozens more just like it in the chiffonier in her room.

Correction—there *had been* dozens just like it.

Sloan returned a few minutes later, trailed by several hotel staff. She'd seen them in town but would have been hard-pressed to recite their names. Sitting up straighter, Shaina stuffed the soiled handkerchief back inside her purse, then smoothed her windblown hair into place as Sloan's employees stood shoulder to shoulder, facing her.

Resting one hand on the back of her chair, Sloan said, "Shaina, I'd like you to meet the Sweenys. Without them, The Remington could not conduct business."

Fergus and his son, Colum, he explained, kept the grounds well-groomed and made repairs when needed, while Caitlin ran the front desk and Bridget kept the guest rooms clean and tidy.

"Any one of them will be more than happy to help you in any way possible." He winked at the Sweenys. "Isn't that right?"

"Aye, Miz Sterling, ma'am." Bridget smiled and curtsied, then took a small step forward. "Whether you'd like tea and biscuits or fresh towels for your room, y'need only to ask."

The others echoed the girl's offer, and then Caitlin moved closer. "Lost me own childhood home to fire, back in Killorglen. M'heart aches for you, ma'am, but sure as I stand here, I promise y'won't always feel this lost and afraid."

Shaina didn't know what to say. And even if she did, it wasn't likely she'd be able to speak past the aching sob in her throat. Nodding, she bit her lower lip and prayed for the strength to hold fast to her self-control. *Oh, Caitlin, I pray you're right.*

"We're blessed to have two suites on the third floor," Sloan was saying, "and if you're ready, Bridget will take you to yours." He winked again. "You'll be happy to hear it has indoor plumbing."

Harper had always taken care of the hotel bills when they'd traveled. Was the daily rate of a suite one dollar or ten? There were two silver dollars and a five-dollar buffalo greenback at the bottom of her purse. If she put the money toward a train ticket, how far from Denver could she travel? Home to Missouri, perhaps, where only a handful of family members knew her? Where no one would look right through her because she no longer had the means to live as she once had?

"We want you to know that you're welcome to stay as long as you need to," Sloan added.

She could probably afford *one* night's stay and a train ticket. "Thank you, but I'll be here only until morning," she said, rising. "Do you happen to know the train schedule?"

"Hate to be the bearer of bad news," Fergus said, "but y'won't be goin' anywhere for days. By mornin', the tracks'll be covered, and I have it on good authority the railroad won't take the risk of an accident like the one in Kansas a year or so back."

She'd read in the newspaper about the derailment, and she'd been in Denver long enough to know how severe the mountain winters could be. Still, Shaina looked to Sloan for confirmation. *Please tell me Fergus is mistaken....*

"I'm afraid Fergus is right," Sloan said with a shake of his head. "The snow has already started."

"Good inch on the ground already," Colum confirmed.

Shaina glanced out the window. Thousands of nickel-sized flakes made it impossible to see across the street.

"For the time being, at least, you're safer here," Sloan pointed out, "where you can take your time sorting through your options."

Options? With seven dollars to her name and no hope of raising the sum?

"You look a mite peaked," Caitlin said. "If you'll just follow me, we'll get you settled upstairs."

Shaina forced a smile as the woman said, "Bridget, be a dear and fix Miz Sterling a tray of tea and scones, will y'please?"

The smiling, freckle-faced girl quickly disappeared as Shaina fell into step behind Caitlin.

At the top of the winding staircase, the woman paused and produced a huge key from her apron pocket. "Your room key is inside," she said as the tumbler clicked beneath the cut-glass doorknob.

Inside, a small but welcoming sitting room boasted a small settee with a cushion of wine-red velvet, flanked by deep-seated wooden rocking chairs big enough to accommodate even the largest of traveling salesmen. Lace curtains at the windows were topped by swags of burgundy silk. The low shelf unit beside the door housed well-worn leather books, and the round table in the middle of the room held a marble chess board. Underfoot, a rug festooned by maroon medallions softened mahogany floorboards.

"The bedchamber's right this way," Caitlin said as she opened a pair of wide, curtained glass doors to reveal a brass bed angled between two windows draped in pale blue satin. An imposing wardrobe stood against one wall, a drop-leaf writing desk against the other, and both bedside tables held white-globed lanterns.

Caitlin opened a second set of curtained doors. "What is it the French say when they've found something incredible?"

It took only a brief glance into the water closet to bring the phrase to mind. "*Pièce de résistance?*"

"Yes, that's it!"

A copper tub gleamed against the dark wood wainscoting, and across from it, a porcelain washbasin rested in a marble-topped cabinet, both of them equipped with enamel knobbed faucets.

"Hot *and* cold running water?"

"Nothin' but the best for Mr. Remington's guests. And he doesn't charge extra for the luxurious touches, I'll have y'know. Men like that are rare, indeed. Especially in these parts. And *especially* these days!" Caitlin opened the tall, narrow wardrobe that stood beside the basin cabinet. "Soap, towels, and scrubbin' cloths. If y'find yourself in need of something that isn't here, just give that a tug"—she pointed to a black braided cord with a tassel that hung beside the tub—"and one of us will come runnin'."

"I—I don't know what to say," Shaina admitted. "Thank you."

Bridget entered with a soft knock, balancing a silver tray in her free hand. "This ain't the prettiest teapot," she said, "but it keeps the water hot longer than the others."

"It looks beautiful to me. Thank you." Shaina looked at each woman in turn. "Thank you both for your hospitality."

"Don't thank us," Caitlin said, laughing. "'Tis Mr. Remington made all this possible." She walked quickly to the door. "Now, if you'll excuse me, I need to get supper on the table for m'husband and hungry children."

Bridget started to follow her mother but hesitated in the doorway. "Don't quite know how to put this delicately," she began, "but I'm guessin' that, thanks to the fire, y'don't have a nightgown, or a dress to wear tomorrow, either."

"You're right," Shaina acknowledged. The clothes on her back were all that she owned, and they reeked of smoke.

"I'm happy to bring a few things from my closet, if y'won't be insulted."

"Why would I be insulted?"

The girl's freckled cheeks turned bright red. "Well," she began with a shrug, "yer a fine lady, and I'm just a lowly servant girl—"

"What! Why, you're lovely and sweet and generous, is what you are!" Shaina took her hands and gave them a gentle squeeze. "I'm touched and grateful that you're willing to share your clothes with me, Bridget, and I shall wear them with pride."

The girl flashed a smile that warmed Shaina's heart…and shamed her to the soles of her dusty boots. Had her efforts to rub elbows with Denver's elite left "ordinary folk" with the impression that she considered herself superior?

Bridget stepped into the hall. "I'll be back quick as a wink with some things y'can wear. While I'm gone, better drink yer tea, or ye'll think me a liar, saying that old stoneware pot holds the heat better than the pretty porcelain ones!"

Shaina took her advice. Seated at the table, she filled her cup. It wasn't until she reached for the silver spoon beside it that she noticed the sugar bowl. She hadn't sipped sweet tea in months, and she happily added a spoonful to her cup.

Her hand froze mid-stir as a shocking question arose in her mind: What sort of silly, shallow fool had she allowed herself to become? Her house had burned to the ground, along with the few things she had left to call her own, yet her eyes were welling with tears of gratitude…for *sugar*?

Something Sloan had said the night of the earthquake echoed in her head. He'd quoted from Proverbs: "*Pride goeth before destruction, and an haughty spirit before a fall.*"

Using the lace-edged napkin, she dabbed at her tears, then straightened her spine and drew back her shoulders. She hadn't always been this way. And, God willing, it wasn't too late to get the old Shaina back.

It wouldn't be painless, for it would require coming clean with everyone she'd duped—starting with the man who'd been there every time life had attempted to flatten her.

Chapter Nine

Over supper that night, the Sweenys discussed Sloan's sanity—or, more accurately, the possibility that he'd lost his mind. They didn't say it in so many words, of course, but he got the meaning, loud and clear.

"Woman like that will self-pity us out of house and home," Fergus predicted.

"Yeah," Colum put in. "We already got more to do around here than we can handle, just the four of us."

"Regular guests know what's expected of the staff," Caitlin put in, "so I think yer pa's right. Miz Sterling is accustomed to being waited on, hand and foot."

Sloan reached for a biscuit, wanting to remind them that he'd been sitting there all along, listening to their complaints.

"We'll do our best t'make her feel welcome and comfortable," Caitlin quickly added.

"Of course you will," Sloan agreed, looking at each of them in turn. "I'd expect nothing less." But he wasn't smiling when he said it, and they quickly dropped their gazes to their bowls of stew.

"Well, I think she's lovely," Bridget blurted out. "And thoughtful and kind. I don't believe for a minute that she ever lay about, like some princess in a tiara, demanding to be waited upon!" With all eyes on her, she blushed. "Say what you will. That's my opinion," she said quietly, crossing both arms over her chest and frowning. "Y'might consider givin' the poor woman half a chance, especially after all she's been through." She paused, but only for a heartbeat. "It's the Christian thing t'do!"

While her brother and parents stared in silent awe, Sloan chuckled. "With a heart like yours," he said, patting her hand, "I predict that in a few years, you're going to make some lucky man a very happy husband."

While her brother snickered, she blushed again, more deeply this time.

"Hush, Colum," Caitlin scolded. "Bridget's right. Miz Sterling does seem nice enough."

"Ain't what they're sayin' in town...."

Now, all eyes were on Fergus, the stern, no-nonsense manager of The Remington.

"What're they sayin', Da?" Colum asked.

"They say she's a snob. Thinks she's better'n most. That she'd rather rub elbows with the cream of the crop than say a courteous hello to common folk like us."

"It's all gossip, Colum," Caitlin said, "plain and simple. And if I hear-tell of you repeatin' it, son...." She aimed a forefinger at him. "Let's just say you're not so big that I won't tan yer hide."

Colum groaned, and Fergus pushed back from the table. "Yer ma's right about the gossip. I'll not give another moment's attention to the rumors." On his feet now, he leaned near his wife's ear. "But there *is* somethin' odd about that lass." He kissed her cheek. "And now I'm off to batten the hatches."

Once he was gone, Bridget carried the dirty bowls and flatware to the sink. "I didn't mean to stir up a hornets' nest, Ma." She met Sloan's eyes to add, "Sorry if I spoiled yer supper, Mr. Remington, sir."

"You did nothing of the kind, dear girl. The stew was delicious. And so were the biscuits. Another wonderful meal, Caitlin."

She smiled and curtsied, as always. "Thank you, sir." Then to Bridget and Colum, she said, "Get to bed now, both of you. Ye'll need yer rest, 'cause there'll no doubt be snow and ice to scrape in the mornin', or we'll have guests and passersby slippin' and fallin' left and right." She shooed them from the room, then sat down across from Sloan. "I hope ye'll accept my apology, sir, for Fergus's thoughtless mutterin'."

The family squabble had jarred Sloan more than he cared to admit, but he hid his unease behind a smile. "No harm done, especially since Mrs. Sterling wasn't around to hear any of it."

"*Dia do aisling*, Mr. Remington, sir."

That particular Irish wish, he'd heard before. "May God bless your dreams, too," he said as he stood and left the kitchen.

In his tiny office behind the front parlor, Sloan paced from the door to the window and back again, head down, hands clasped behind his back, repeating Fergus's words in his mind. The man had earned his respect by performing his duties with uncomplaining levelheadedness and by doing so whether Sloan was at the hotel or away at the ranch. He spoke the truth and didn't sugarcoat things. And so his opinion of Shaina was unsettling, to say the least. Had he overheard or witnessed something to inspire the comment that there was "something odd about that lass"? Sloan didn't think so. To his knowledge, he alone knew the truth about her financial situation. Surely, she had a better reason for going to such extremes to protect her social standing than maintaining the approval of Denver's privileged few, because his own instincts told him that beneath the pretense beat the heart of a good, decent woman.

He had to pass Shaina's suite on the way to his own. Knowing Caitlin and Bridget, they'd provided her with everything she needed for a comfortable stay. But it had been a harrowing day, and if Shaina was anything like him, she'd be up all night, fretting about her future. That would explain the light spilling into the hall from the transom above her door.

In the off chance she'd managed to doze off, he rapped quietly.

A second, perhaps two, passed before the key turned in the lock. She opened the door a crack, and when she saw him, she opened it wider.

"Sloan," she whispered, "it's after ten."

"Just thought I'd make sure you have everything you need before I turn in."

She gave him the barest hint of a smile. "You really *are* quite the gentleman. Thank you, but I'm fine."

Fine, indeed, he thought, taking note of her puffy, red-rimmed eyes. She'd bathed and washed her hair, probably hoping to rinse the stench of smoke down the drain; but from the looks of things, the Sweeny women hadn't thought to bring her a comb. She looked younger, tinier, prettier—if that was possible—in her borrowed calico frock. Had Caitlin and Bridget forgotten to offer her a nightgown?

He pointed at the dress. "I'll ask Bridget to fetch a—"

"She brought me a gown and a robe. Slippers, too. But it made no sense to put it on."

"Why? You're not likely to sleep well in a dress."

"I'm not likely to sleep at *all*, so I thought I'd save her the bother of laundering and pressing it."

It sounded like she planned to leave tomorrow. But where would she go? And how would she pay her way? "Tomorrow night, then?"

Shaina sighed, and after a quick glance toward the ceiling, she said, "I was planning to tell you this in the morning, but…." She opened the door all the way. "Please come in. We wouldn't want to wake your other guests."

She sat on the edge of a rocking chair, hands folded primly in her lap, feet planted flat on the floor, waiting for him to take a seat. But Sloan wasn't at all sure he wanted to hear what she meant by "this."

"It's freezing in here," he said, rubbing his palms together. He crouched by the hearth and stoked the fire, adding a few logs to the grate. He took his time with the bellows and the poker, mostly to buy time to prepare himself for whatever plan she'd been hatching in the hours since declining his offer to join them for supper.

"Thank you," she said when he sat. "I didn't trust myself to do it."

Instantly, he understood: Boonie had said a chimney fire had likely sparked the blaze at Sterling Hall. Instead of faulting the fierce wind, aging mortar, crumbling bricks, or any one of a dozen other possible causes, Shaina had decided to blame herself.

"How many times do you suppose you built fires in that old fireplace, and in the kitchen stove?"

He could almost hear her doing the math in her head: No less than once a day for the six months since she'd dismissed the help.

"Arithmetic was never my strong suit, but I'm guessing two hundred times, give or take a few." She met his eyes. "Why would you ask such a silly question?"

"It's a good thing I'm not easily offended," he said, grinning. "Here's another silly question for you: How many times have you checked the fire before leaving the house?"

"Ah, I see where you're going with this." A small smile turned up the corners of her mouth. "I suppose you're right."

"You *suppose*? Ask anyone—I'm rarely wrong!"

"It's just that, considering every other bad decision I've made lately, it was natural to assume it was my fault."

Every other bad decision?

"It's peculiar, isn't it, how we frail humans can convince ourselves that we're doing the right things for the right reasons?"

She stared straight ahead, and it seemed she was thinking out loud more than sharing a sliver of her past with him. Still, it pleased Sloan that she trusted him enough to unburden herself in his presence. He sat back and waited for her to continue.

"A tornado destroyed the family farm in Portage Des Sioux. It happened in February of seventy-six—a lifetime ago, though it sometimes feels like yesterday. It demolished most of downtown St. Charles, and…and my fiancé was found in the rubble. I believed a lie of my own invention—that if I found work in a nearby town, I could send money home to help my parents rebuild, as well as help myself get over Evan's death. Bad decision number one…."

She worried her lower lip and clenched and unclenched her hands. Sloan wanted to say or do something to comfort her. He wanted her to continue, too, but his conscience wouldn't allow him to press for more information. If Shaina had a mind to, she'd tell him in her own good time.

"Then the train stopped at Union Station, and the conductor said, 'Pay up or get off.' So I disembarked. Bad decision number two. I had just enough money to rent a small room in Five Points, and while I was depositing the rest, robbers came in, and…."

"And that was the night Harper was shot."

She nodded. "I'd helped out a little at the clinic in St. Charles, and when he went down, I did what came naturally."

"Bad decision number three?"

"No," she said around a smile. "That came later. I never lied, mind you," she added, raising her hand as if taking an oath, "but when people jumped to the conclusion that I was a certified nurse, I didn't correct them. When Mason asked me to take care of Harper, I saw an opportunity to do some good *and* earn enough to keep the wolf from the door, as well as to send a few dollars home every month." She met Sloan's eyes. "*That* was bad decision number three."

"But you helped out at home, and Harper got well under your care. How can you say it was a bad decision?"

"The answer to that is all mixed up with bad decision number four: I knew Harper was confusing gratitude for love, yet I did nothing to set him straight. I enjoyed living in that big house, where, for the first time in my life, I had a room of my own, servants to launder the pretty dresses he bought me, and so much food that I never went to bed hungry. So, when Harper proposed, I told myself he was a good man. That, in time, we might fall in love. That, even if we didn't, we'd enjoy a satisfying life, like the thousands of couples over the centuries whose marriages were arranged by well-meaning relatives."

It didn't surprise him that Shaina chose "satisfying" to describe her marriage to Harper. Sloan had seen them together at numerous functions, and while they'd treated each other with polite decorum, it would have been a stretch to call them a loving couple. It couldn't have been easy, going through the motions every day of her loveless marriage, and yet she'd honored her vows.

"You must think I'm a horrible, heartless woman."

Sloan frowned. "I don't think anything of the kind. Why would you say such a thing?"

"Because just now, you looked as though you'd peeked into my soul and seen every bad decision-induced stain written there."

"May I be honest with you, Shaina?"

Her delicate eyebrows disappeared beneath a veil of dark, wavy bangs. "I suppose."

"I've often been told that my face is an open book." Resting his elbows on his knees, he leaned forward, putting his face inches from hers. "What you saw was admiration—"

"Admiration! Of me?" She hid a quiet laugh behind one hand. "So you're a gentleman, a savvy businessman, and a humorist, as well!"

He ignored the sideways compliments. "I was thinking about the strength of character it must have required to remain true to a man—a good man, for the most part—you didn't love." *He didn't love you, either,* Sloan thought. If he had, how could he have betrayed her in so many ways?

Shaina's brow furrowed slightly. "I was quite fond of Harper, because, as you so astutely pointed out, he *was* a good man...for the most part."

Harper's dependence on alcohol, gambling, and ladies of the night had left her in far worse financial shape than when they'd met. His addictions had nearly destroyed Sterling Manufactory and had sent his brokenhearted, disappointed father to an early grave. That she'd remained a devoted wife in spite all of that told Sloan everything he needed to know about her. It also helped him better understand why she'd fought so hard to hold on to the status and material possessions provided by her marriage.

"Laugh if you must," he finally said, "but I do admire you."

She smiled, but only barely. "Then you, sir, are too easily fooled."

The remark sat him up straight and inspired a quiet chuckle from deep in his chest.

"I hope you'll forgive me," she said. "I'd planned to explain a few things, and I'm afraid I got a little carried away. But it's your fault—"

"My fault?"

"You're very easy to talk to."

He shrugged one shoulder. "I try."

It wasn't true, and he knew it. Sloan had never been one to pry. And when others chose to share tidbits of their past with him, he'd always found an ingenious way to change the subject. Only a fraud could have listened without divulging the secrets of his own dark past. Or someone who wasn't aware of how people still felt about Indians and half-breeds.

Her smile, sweet and genuine, warmed him to his toes and left him feeling addlebrained. It reminded him of the day he and James had been repairing fence posts and his old friend had asked him the name of the woman to blame for his inattentive behavior. A woman wasn't to blame, he'd insisted; and at the time, it had been true. *If you know what's good for you, you'll pay attention around James from now on,* he chided himself.

He believed she'd invited him in to say thank you…and good-bye. Sloan didn't need the first, and he didn't want to hear the second. There were a dozen reasons why she should stay. High on the list was his growing attraction to her.

Sloan yawned. Stretched. Got to his feet. "Well, I'm about done in."

"But…but I…I…."

Half in, half out the door, he said, "See you at breakfast." Simon had taught him never to run from a problem or avoid a challenge, but he hadn't included lessons on coping with disappointments of the heart.

Moments later, Sloan found himself pacing in the kitchen. As he waited for the coffee to percolate, he thought of the young ladies he'd escorted to the opera, political events, church socials, and town festivals. For the most part, their topics of conversation had revolved around the latest fashions, and pointing out women who'd chosen not to follow trends—women like Shaina, who daringly discussed politics and the latest inventions.

Even now, relegated to borrowed petticoats and a plain housedress, she stood apart from the rest. When poverty had sent her to Denver, she hadn't complained about her situation, nor had she used feminine wiles to coax some poor sap into rescuing her from her plight. Instead, she'd rolled up her sleeves and gotten to work. Sloan didn't believe for a minute that guarding her secret had been the sole motive behind her actions. And he simply couldn't let her leave. Not without exhausting every effort to convince her to stay.

He poured himself a mug of coffee and carried it upstairs.

As usual, Bridget and Caitlin had prepared his room. Heat emanated from the belly of the cast-iron stove, and the lantern atop his bureau cast a soft, welcoming light throughout the suite. They'd turned back the bedcovers and draped his robe and nightshirt over the pillows.

The strong scent of charred wood still clung to his clothes, or he wouldn't have bothered with a bath. When at last he climbed into bed, Sloan knew he would rest well, because, despite the late hour and distressing events of the day, just knowing Shaina was right down the hall, safe and sound, would lull him into a sweet slumber.

Chapter Ten

Shaina woke to the scents of bacon and coffee and the sound of soft footsteps outside her door. Unless the clock on the mantel had stopped, she'd slept for five hours straight.

After washing up and tidying her hair, she hurried down to the kitchen, where Caitlin and Bridget had already set the table for breakfast.

"Well, good mornin'," Caitlin said, smiling. "It's good to see that y'rested. I prayed y'wouldn't stay up the whole night long, pacin' and worryin'."

"Your prayers were answered," Shaina said, smiling. "Thank you."

"My dress fits you well," Bridget observed. "Don't y'think so, Ma?"

Caitlin rested her fist on her hip. "That it does. Pink is a good color on you, Miz Sterling."

"Thank you. And I wonder…would either of you be offended if I called you by your first names?"

"Of course not, Miz Sterling!" they said in unison.

"Oh, I'm so glad. You've both done so much to make me feel safe and welcome here that I feel as though we're friends. But…."

Mother and daughter exchanged a quick glance, no doubt wondering what she'd say next.

"But that means you'll have to call me Shaina."

Bridget seemed ready to happily dispense with formalities, but her mother hesitated. Shaina prepared to emphasize the suggestion when Sloan walked into the room.

"I hope you'll have more success with that than I've had," he said to Shaina.

"But that's entirely different," Bridget put in.

He raised an eyebrow. "How so?"

"Well, yer our boss, for starters! 'T'would be impolite to call you...." She cleared her throat. "To call you...Sloan."

Chuckling, he poured himself a mug of coffee. "Was that really so hard to say?"

"No, but...." Bridget looked to her mother for help.

But before Caitlin could rescue her, Sloan said, "Let me ask you a question."

The women stood side by side, listening intently.

"Do you consider The Remington to be your home?"

"Oh, yes!" Bridget said. "We love living here!"

"Then, since we all share the house and the chores, we're like a family, wouldn't you say?"

"There's no denyin' that yer good to us," Caitlin allowed, "but you own this hotel and everything in it. We're as grateful as can be for our jobs and the generous pay y'give us each week...."

Shaina stood quietly, watching the exchange. Had Sloan's smile dimmed because he, too, expected Caitlin to offer yet another reason to continue calling him "Mr. Remington"?

"But yer our employer, sir." She lifted her chin. "Just wouldn't be right, addressing you by your first name."

Sloan looked at Shaina and lifted his shoulders as if to say, *"See there? You're fighting a losing battle."*

As owner of one of the biggest cattle ranches this side of the Mississippi, The Remington Hotel, and the majority of shares in Sterling Manufactory, he was one of Denver's wealthiest men. Why did it seem to matter so much *what* they called him?

Shaina clasped her hands. "I need something to get my mind off of...things. Is there anything I can do to help with breakfast?"

A loud knock at the back door interrupted Caitlin's reply.

"Looks like I need to make a bigger sign tellin' people to enter by way o' the *front* door," the woman said, moving to admit their visitor.

Abe brushed snow from his shoulders, then took one step into the kitchen. "'Mornin', all," he said, then turned to Sloan. "Been ridin' for hours. Snow's piled up deeper'n I ever recall." He removed his hat.

"Hate to be the bearer of bad tidings, 'specially so early in the day, but James sent me to fetch Doc Wilson. Asked me to fetch you, too."

"Dear Lord, what's happened?" Caitlin gasped.

"Mable tripped on the ramp to the henhouse."

"Dear Lord!" Bridget echoed her mother. "She weren't bad-hurt, I hope!"

"Looks like a busted leg to me, but we'll find out soon enough." Meeting Sloan's eyes, Abe said, "Stopped by Doc's place on the way here. He's already on his way to the ranch. You want I should wait and ride back with you?"

Sloan glanced at his pocket watch and frowned. "I have to reschedule two meetings at the manufactory before I can leave." He snapped the watch shut, then started for the door. "Why do I get the feeling you rode into town on an empty stomach?"

A slight blush was visible beneath Abe's weather-tanned skin. "It's downright unnerving when you do that," he said, grinning.

From the doorway, Sloan winked at Caitlin. "Make sure this boy gets a good meal before he heads out again."

"And what about you, Mr. Remington? Shall I wrap some biscuits and bacon for you?"

"Yes, please." He took Shaina by the elbow and gently led her into the drawing room. "I hate to impose, especially after all you've been through," he said softly, "but I'm wondering if—"

"I'm happy to help any way I can," she assured him.

He studied her face for a long, silent moment. "Mable runs the house, pretty much single-handedly, from dawn till dusk...."

His implication was clear: Are you sure you're up to this?

She smiled. "I wasn't always a spoiled socialite, you know. I can be trusted to cook and clean and take care of Mable." Holding up a forefinger, she added, "And it is *not* an imposition."

"Well then, we need to get you a few extra dresses on the way out of town."

Shaina started to protest, because she didn't want to feel beholden to a man she barely knew.

This time, it was Sloan who aimed his pointer finger toward the ceiling. "If it makes you feel less obliged, I'll deduct the cost from your pay."

Her pay? Had she heard him correctly? "My...my *pay*?"

"You'll be working long, hard days." He paused as a faint smile broadened his mouth. "You wouldn't want *me* feelin' indebted, now, would you?"

Well, he had her there. "No. No, of course not." She straightened her shoulders. "And you're right—I need to return this dress to Bridget, and I suppose I ought have more than just one of my own."

"Caitlin offered to wrap up some bacon and biscuits for us. We can eat on the ride to the ranch."

He was halfway to the door when she asked, "How far is it?"

"Oh, just ten miles or so. If we leave now, we can be there before dark." He gave her a sidelong glance. "You ride, right?"

Shaina remembered how, one by one, she'd sold the wagon, the buggy, and the teams that had pulled them. Harper's Arabian and favorite saddle had been the next to go. She'd held on to her beautiful bay for as long as she could, because few things made her troubles disappear like racing with Flame over the hillsides, the wind in his mane and her hair. It had broken her heart to sell him, but her parents had needed money, and she'd been running out of clothes and furniture.

"Yes," she said on a sigh. "I ride."

"Good. I'll have Eb over at the smithy's shop saddle two horses."

He left her in order to tie up loose ends at the manufactory, and while he was gone, she ate a slice of bacon and a biscuit to tide her over. She thought it odd that the fire hadn't haunted her dreams, as she'd expected, while images flashed in her mind nearly every time she blinked. Caitlin and Bridget did their best to make polite conversation, but she barely heard them. After a while, they gave up and spoke only to each other.

"I'm sorry to seem so rude," she explained. "It's just...." The last thing she wanted to do was appear like a weak, whiny female around these two hardworking women. "I know it seems odd, but I'm not concentrating very well this morning."

"It would be odd," Caitlin said, "if you *could* concentrate on anything other than the ordeal y'just went through."

"Don't y'worry, Miz—Shaina," Bridget assured her. "We'll have plenty of time to talk when y'get back from the ranch."

The ranch. Now *there* was something she could focus on.

"Tell me about Mable and James," she said. "Is there anything I should know? Because I truly want to help as much as I can."

"They're lovely people," Caitlin said.

"At first," Bridget put in, "Mr. James will seem cold and angry. But you'll soon find out that it's as phony as a tin penny. If you let him, he'll keep you spellbound with stories of his days with the Cavalry."

If Mable had indeed broken her leg, it could take a month or more to heal. Shaina nodded, relieved to hear she wouldn't be spending the next several weeks with difficult, hard-hearted people.

"And the ranch—what's it like?"

Caitlin smiled. "Ah, 'tis a beautiful place."

"It's big," Bridget said. "*Very* big. Why, I imagine 'twould take days and days to see it all!"

That made sense to Shaina. Cattle needed plenty of pastureland.

"The house is grand, too," Bridget continued. "Made of logs, all piled up higher, even, than The Remington!" She faced her mother. "D'you think Mr. Remington will put her in the west wing or in one of the upstairs rooms?"

"I'd imagine that'll depend on Mable. She won't be able to climb stairs, so I'm guessing he'll put 'em both in the west wing. It's big enough for him, and them, and all four of us!" Laughing, she took another pan of biscuits out of the oven. "Just listen to me, cacklin' like an old hen. Find yer da, girl, and the others, and tell 'em to get to the table quick, unless they want cold eggs."

Bridget darted from the room just as Sloan returned, and Shaina was suddenly struck by how handsome he was.

"The wind has died down, but it's still blowing," he said, draping a jacket over her shoulders. "This will keep you good and warm between here and the store."

Caitlin handed him a cloth napkin tied into a sack. "'Tisn't much, and it'll be cold by the time you eat it, but it'll tide you over till Miz Sterl—till Shaina can rustle up somethin' at the ranch house."

The next thing Shaina knew, Sloan was helping her onto the back of a roan mare.

"She's gentle as a lamb," he said, climbing into his own saddle.

They rode the short distance from The Remington to the store in silence. What would folks say if they saw him purchasing clothes for her? What would they think when they saw her ride off to his ranch, alone with him?

"Stop fretting. Your reputation won't suffer—not in the slightest. I'll tell folks you're doing me a favor," he said. "It's the truth, after all."

So, he was handsome and generous, and a mind reader, as well?

They were coming up on Sterling Street. "I wonder," she nearly whispered, "would you mind— Is it all right if— Do you think there's time…?"

He turned his horse to the right, and hers followed, all the way to the circular drive that led to what had once been the grand entry of Sterling Hall.

Shaina dismounted. "I'll be fine," she said, looking up at Sloan. "And I won't be long, so you needn't—"

He got down from his horse. "You're not going any farther without me." A leather-gloved finger lifted her chin until her eyes met his eyes. "Got it?"

Nodding, Shaina let him take her hand and lead her closer to the house. Immediately she stifled a gasp with her free hand. She'd expected it to be bad, but *this*?

Wisps of smoke spiraled from the blackened earth, and the acrid odor of scorched wood filled her nostrils. With her heart knocking against her ribs, she scanned the ruins of what had been her home. She began to tremble, and her ears started ringing, as a sweaty-yet-cold-all-over sensation enveloped her.

Sloan's strong arm slid around her waist. She couldn't tell if he had pulled her close or if she had leaned into him from a sense of helplessness.

He stepped in front of her, blocking her view, then crouched lower to study her face. "You all right?"

Eyes closed, she nodded. *You will not cry,* she told herself, *and you will not faint!*

"I'm sorry," she muttered.

Drawing her into a comforting hug, he kissed the top of her head. "Aw, darlin', whatever for?"

"For…for behaving like a spoiled little girl." She took a small step back. "For getting weak-kneed and teary-eyed." Pressing both palms against his chest, she looked up, into his kind and understanding face, then broke free of his embrace and plodded forward.

Heat warmed the soles of her boots as she stood ankle-deep in the debris. Everything, it seemed, had turned to cinders. She saw one tiny gilded shoe—all that remained of the few porcelain ballerinas she hadn't sold. Then she spied the tattered corner of a woolen shawl handed down through three generations of her mother's family. *"Take it,"* her ma had said, tucking it into Shaina's traveling case, *"so you'll have something to wrap around you when you feel homesick."* Even the silver-framed tintype of Harper was gone, all gone.

She was about to turn from the ghastly sight when the toe of her boot touched something. Going down on one knee, she dug through the soggy ashes. "My father's pocket watch," she said, rising slowly. "He gave it to me when I boarded that westbound train." Brushing the soot from its golden case, she remembered what he'd said as he pressed it into her palm: *"I'll be thinkin' of you with every tick."* Shaina held it out so that Sloan could read the inscription.

He cradled her hands in his and leaned in closer to read it. "'*See then that ye walk circumspectly, not as fools, but as wise, redeeming the time.'* Hmm. From Ephesians."

Shaina held her breath and snapped the lid shut. Then she exhaled a ragged sigh. "Well, I don't suppose there's anything more we can do here." She took a long, last look at what had been Sterling Hall, then turned on her heel and headed for the horses, tethered to one of the low-growing shrubs that lined the drive.

Chapter Eleven

When Shaina saw the wrought-iron sign that arced between two tall, rough-hewn posts at the edge of the road to the ranch, she thought her heart might leap from her throat. A combination of apprehension, doubt, and sadness fluttered inside her heart as Sloan climbed down from the saddle and opened the gates. Once he led her down that long, winding drive, her life would change, completely and forever, and the knowledge terrified her.

She didn't want to appear rude or ungrateful, so once the metal gates swung shut with a resounding clang, she forced herself to focus on everything he pointed out to her as they rode along: the house, barely visible atop a distant hill; the water towers he'd built to irrigate his fields; the herds of shaggy-haired, long-horned Highland cattle grazing in pastures that stretched as far as the eye could see.

"They're quite ingenious, aren't they, pawing at the snow-covered ground to get at their food?" She looked over at him. "What are they eating?"

"A mix of grass, hay, and alfalfa," Sloan said, slowing his horse.

She'd overheard people talking about his unusual white cows and his even more unusual grazing methods. Some admired his ingenuity, while others sounded envious that he could afford to experiment.

"It's healthier for 'em, especially during the hard winter months," he continued, "and I don't have to worry about losing them to the bloat."

"I see." She couldn't help but be impressed by his skill and knowledge, and the care he took to ensure the health and strength of his herd. If he took that much interest in cows, of all things, how much better would he treat a wife and children, if he had them?

She stifled a gasp, wondering what had inspired *that* peculiar thought. Sitting taller in the saddle, she focused on the gentle curves of the narrow drive, on the red-berried elders that grew waist-high alongside it. They'd crested a small hill, making the house easier to see. Caitlin and Bridget had said it was as big as The Remington, and as Shaina and Sloan moved steadily closer, she realized the Sweeny women hadn't exaggerated. She felt silly for having pictured a boxy, two-story log cabin.

A smaller version of the house was partially visible behind it. "Is that the bunkhouse?" she asked, pointing.

"No, that's the tool shed." He pointed to a similar building on the far right. "That's the bunkhouse." Moving his arm farther right, he added, "And that's the barn."

"And they're all constructed of logs," she said, mostly to herself.

"Well, Simon wasn't a man who believed in waste. When he first cleared the land, he put just about everything to use."

Shaina figured the name Simon Remington would be recognized by just about anyone from here to California. And from all she'd heard, the man had earned his reputation. If Sloan had learned his business and ranching acumen at the knee of that great man, no wonder he'd become a force to be reckoned with in his own right.

"That's an admirable quality," she agreed. "My pa loves to quote Benjamin Franklin."

Sloan smiled as, together, they said, "Waste not, want not."

Two corrals came into view, one large, one small.

"We use the big one when we've rounded up mustangs," Sloan explained. "The other one is where Penny, here, and her hate-to-be-cooped-up pals like to hang out when it isn't too cold."

"Penny," Shaina said. "A good name for a horse of that color. And what do you call this girl?"

"Angel Eyes."

She raised her eyebrows. "Angel Eyes?"

"For your information," he said, chuckling, "Mable named her, so you can wipe that look off your face that says, 'He doesn't *look* like one of those sissy fellers.'"

It seemed he had a talent for coaxing a smile out of her, and she could almost hear her ma saying, "*That boy will make a right-fine husband someday.*"

The observation puzzled her as much as the one she'd made mere moments ago.

"Hungry?" he asked.

Her stomach chose that exact moment to grumble beneath the sack containing the items he'd bought for her. Angel Eyes swiveled her ears back, and a slow smile turned up the corners of Sloan's mouth. Though she'd poked at her supper and nibbled the biscuit Caitlin had packed, Shaina hadn't eaten a real meal since Sloan had treated her to lunch at The Windsor. And, feeling nervous and shy sitting so close to him, she'd left more than half her soup and most of the roll.

He palmed his pocket watch. "I'll help you get supper on the table," he said after checking the time. "The men will be itchin' for a meal, and I'm sure Mable will be, too."

Just then Doc Wilson's buggy came into view. He slowed his team to a stop alongside Sloan and Shaina.

"Howdy, Doc," Sloan said, leaning on the saddle horn. "How are things with Mable?"

"As well as can be expected. She took a nasty spill. Broke her femur and tibia." He waved a gloved hand. "Sorry about that. In English," he said, smiling apologetically, "she broke her thigh bone and one of the lower leg bones. I've got her wrapped up good and solid, and she's sedated." He shivered, then fastened the top button of his coat. "James insisted on moving her bed into the library, so she's resting for the time being."

The doctor glanced at Shaina. "Elsie and I were very sorry to hear about the fire. Over breakfast, we discussed ways we might help until you're back on your feet." He paused to give her a gentle smile. "So I guess it's true that God works in mysterious ways, because almost the moment Mable finds herself in need of a caretaker, you find yourself in need of a place to stay."

Shaina felt ashamed that, until that moment, she'd been so busy wallowing in self-pity that she hadn't thought to thank the Almighty for providing for her. Later, she would ask forgiveness for her self-centeredness. Right now, Mable's well-being was more important.

"You're so right, and I'm grateful as I can be," she replied. "I'm also happy to help in any way I can."

"You know about her nursin' experience, don't you, Doc?" Sloan asked him.

"Of course," the doctor said with a nod. "Harper used to brag about the way you cared for him after he was shot in that bank robbery. If he said it once, he said it a dozen times—he might have died without you looking after him."

Shaina had to wonder why, at the mention of her husband's name, she had pictured the shattered glass and dented frame of his photograph, half hidden in the ruins of the fire.

"I'm sure you're aware that bones tend to heal more slowly for folks Mable's age," Doc Wilson said.

Shaina blinked to dispel Harper's image from her mind. She could feel Sloan watching her, and she didn't want to give him any reason to lose faith in her.

"Is there anything particular I should know? Or do? To make sure I take good care of Mable, I mean."

"I've left some laudanum for her. It's on the mantel. Give her a couple of tablespoons before she goes to sleep for the night. She'll fight you, but you must insist, because she needs her rest. During the day, give her one, maybe two more, spoonfuls, but no more than five a day."

Shaina heard the unspoken warning attached to his instructions, and understood what it meant. Once she realized how quickly Harper approached dependency on the drug, she'd devised all sorts of tactics to distract him from the pain. She had no qualms about being just as unbending with Mable, if need be.

Doc Wilson pushed his round gold spectacles higher on his nose. "Above all, make sure she stays off that leg, and keep her as quiet and as still as possible." He laughed quietly. "I've known Mable long enough to realize you're facing quite a challenge, but if even half of what Harper said about your nursing skills is true, you can handle it."

He lifted the reins and prepared to smack the horses' behinds. "You can stop looking so concerned, Sloan. Your housekeeper couldn't be in better hands." He winked at Shaina, then met Sloan's eyes again. "And neither could you and your ranch hands." As the buggy started rolling forward, he said, "I'll stop by day after tomorrow to see how she's progressing." And with that, he left them.

It took less than five minutes to reach the house, and they rode every second in silence. Was Sloan rethinking his decision to bring her here? Or wondering if she could handle all the housekeeping chores and tend Mable, as well?

The house came into view, erasing all questions from her mind.

Two thick stone chimneys stood, like twin sentries, on either side of the two-story center section. Shaina surmised that there was a third in the kitchen around back, for gentle puffs of white smoke rose from that area, as well. The same river rocks formed the foundation, and from it sprang a deep porch on which four bentwood rockers—two on either side of the massive carved-wood door—creaked back and forth in the wind.

Sloan reined Penny to a halt and dismounted. "Well, here we are."

"It's magnificent," Shaina said, climbing down from the saddle. As she grasped the brown paper bundle that held her new clothes, a deep voice startled her.

"Took you quite a bit longer to make the trip than Abe predicted."

She hadn't heard anyone approach, and neither had Sloan, judging by the firm set of his jaw.

"Gonna have to put a bell around your neck, Leo." He made hasty introductions and handed over the horses' reins. "Food and water and a good brushin'," he said, "then swap the saddle blankets for turnouts." With one hand pressed against Shaina's lower back, he led her to the porch, then turned to add, "When you're finished, come on inside so I can properly introduce you two."

Once or twice in the general store, she'd witnessed the friendly repartee between him and James, saw it again with Abe, just hours ago. How odd, she thought, that the instant he laid eyes on Leo, Sloan's entire demeanor changed—and not for the better.

"Would you like me to put the horses in the barn or the corral?"

Shaina tried not to show her shock. Harper had often teased her, saying things like, "Sometimes, I think you love those horses more than you love me!" and "Most folks don't pamper their young'uns the way you do these nags!" But not even she had ever blanketed a horse in its stall. Either Leo hadn't been a ranch hand very long, or he was deliberately testing Sloan's patience.

The latter, if Sloan's tight-lipped expression was any indication.

"Leave 'em outside," he replied before guiding her into the foyer and slamming the door behind them. "Have a look around and make yourself at home," he said before hurrying down the hall.

Shaina held the bundle of clothes so tight against her chest that the paper crinkled. She'd never seen a staircase that could best the one at Sterling Hall...until now. It was no less than six feet wide, and each tread had been carved from a log that still wore bark on its underside. Crisscrossing branches took the place of spindles, and a knotty, curved handrail had been sanded and polished to a smooth sheen.

She placed her package on a cushioned bench beside the door and entered the first room to her right. Here, the walls had been lined with books, some thick, others thin, bound in varying shades of soft leather. Two overstuffed sofas faced each other, and between them, a stacked-stone fireplace radiated welcoming warmth. There were no curtains covering the windows, but with that view of the Rockies, who needed them? She didn't need to see any more of the house to know that this was where she'd come if boredom ever took hold of her.

In the next room, Shaina found a substantial desk, a tufted leather chair, and more unadorned, many-paned windows. This fireplace, she guessed, stood back-to-back with the one in the library; and here, too, gentle heat reached her in soothing waves.

She would enjoy working in the kitchen, with its four-burner cookstove and water pump within easy reach at the sink. Glass-doored cupboards housed heavy stoneware plates and bowls, and a quick peek behind the blue-and-white-checked curtains covering the lower shelves told her she'd never want for a kettle or a pan. Matching curtains hung in the windows. When she pushed them aside, sunshine poured in, spreading across the floorboards like golden syrup.

A brass-and-hobnail glass lantern, suspended from a length of chain, lit the long, plank-topped table, and in the center sat a pitcher like her mother's. Sitting on the edge of nearest bench, she slid it closer to herself, eyes misting as her fingers grazed the white enamel.

The sound of boots striding purposefully down the hall put her back on her feet. After wiping her eyes, Shaina faced the door and smiled. "You have such a beautiful home, Sloan," she said.

But it was Leo, not Sloan, who stopped halfway between her and the door. She'd been inside all of ten minutes. How could he have fed, watered, groomed, and blanketed two horses in that amount of time? Whenever she and her brothers had rushed through their chores, he pa would say, "*Folks judge us by the work of our hands; take care not to give 'em an excuse to call you a careless fool.*"

"My apologies," Leo said, bowing slightly.

"You only just met the woman," Sloan said, entering behind him, "and already you're apologizing?"

There was a smile on his lips, Shaina noticed, but a hard look in his eyes. She wondered what Leo had done to inspire such mistrust in a man who'd knowingly welcomed a near stranger into his home to care for one of his dearest friends.

He stood beside her, putting the table between them and Leo.

"You've fed and groomed both horses. Already."

A statement, not a question, Shaina noticed. She also noticed that his accusatory tone wasn't lost on Leo.

"I thought it a better use of my time to let them eat in peace," he began, "figuring I'd brush them after you'd, uh, properly introduced me to this lovely lady."

If Sloan had waited until they were alone to ask her opinion, Shaina would have told him that she'd seen Leo staggering around town, bellowing like a bull moose. He'd gotten close enough—just once—to make her skin crawl as she'd recoiled from his foul stench of whiskey and of weeks without a bath. God willing, she'd see him only twice a day, when he sat at this table for breakfast and supper.

The clock on the shelf above the stove chimed three times, and she turned to Sloan. "I should probably get started on supper," she said, hoping he'd pick up on her cue to save the formal introductions for another time. "I left my things in the foyer, so...." To gather them up, Shaina realized too late, she'd have to pass the man whose very presence made her neck hairs bristle.

"Round up the boys," Sloan told Leo, "and meet me in my office in fifteen minutes."

Nodding, Leo backed out of the room, then disappeared around the corner without a word.

"Let me show you to your room, and then we'll pay Mable a visit," Sloan said to Shaina as he led her back toward the entry and threw open the double doors. "There's a water closet over there," he said, standing beside her, "and through that other door, you'll find a hall leading to the kitchen. It'll save you from traipsing up and down the main hall, and it'll provide a lot more privacy for you."

As in the other rooms, a stone fireplace dominated one wall.

"I'll build a fire, and have some wood brought in for you."

She thanked him, then counted seven globed candles on the mantel. On the bedside tables, she noted more brass-and-hobnail lanterns. The bedposts, bureau, and wardrobe had been pared from logs. The plump-cushioned settee and matching chair coordinated well with the colorful patchwork quilt, and she could tell that the deep-green curtains, when drawn, would make the room feel as snug as a cocoon.

"If you don't like it, you're welcome to stay in—"

"It's perfect. I feel right at home already." Shaina set her bundle of clothes at the foot of the thick mattress. "Is it all right if I check on Mable now?"

He smiled in a way she could only describe as tender. "Of course," he said, "but first, have I thanked you?"

He had. Several times. "I'm the one who's grateful," she told him. "Where would I have gone if you hadn't made this generous offer?"

"Something would have presented itself. The doctor and Elsie were discussing options just this morning, remember?"

"True, but—"

"Please, no buts. I'm breathing easier already, just knowing you'll be in charge." He grinned. "Why don't you change into one of your new dresses before we check on the old girl?"

"Good idea. This one reeks of smoke. If she's sleeping, it's liable to rouse her, just as sure as smelling salts would!"

Sloan lingered a moment, studying her face, and Shaina held her breath. It appeared as though he might kiss her. If he did, would she kiss him back? He gave her no time to answer. Stepping away, Sloan said, "You handle adversity better than anyone I can name."

She blinked, confused by his comment. "Adversity?"

His voice a husky whisper, Sloan explained, "Losing your husband, being forced to sell your favorite things to protect his good name, and then having your home destroyed by a fire...any one of those things would have crushed a lesser woman."

Is that what he thought—that she'd sold her possessions for money to salvage Harper's reputation? Shaina would have laughed if she could have found any humor at all in the real reasons she'd done those things.

"You give me too much credit." That much, at least, was true.

Sloan strode quickly to the hall, and as he pulled the doors closed, he said, "I have a feeling Mable is going to love having you here."

I hope so, she thought as the latch clicked into place, *but will you?*

Chapter Twelve

Sloan pulled a chair closer to Mable's bed and sat, watching her steady, restful breaths. Doc Wilson had done a fine job of stabilizing her leg—a good thing, because the woman didn't know the meaning of the word *rest*. If he had half a brain, he'd find Shaina before the woman roused from her laudanum-induced stupor and ask yet another favor of her.

It almost seemed orchestrated that she appeared at that moment. Seeing that Mable was still asleep, she pressed a forefinger to her lips and tiptoed to the foot of the bed. Sunlight slanted through the window and rested on her shoulders like a golden cape, reminding Sloan of every painting he'd ever seen of God's angels.

"Her cheeks are good and pink," she whispered. "That's a good sign."

"A good sign, yes," he whispered back, nodding like an imbecile as he took note of the way her new dress brought out the blue of her eyes. She'd donned her new boots and apron, and her thick dark hair was piled atop her head, with the soft wisps that had escaped her bun surrounding her face like a dark frame of curlicues. The sight was downright lovely.

"Well, since she seems to be resting comfortably, I think I'll get supper started," Shaina whispered. "I noticed onions, carrots, and potatoes in the root cellar."

When had she had time to go down there? But before he could ask, she said, "I found a chicken on the mud porch, too. I'm guessing Mable was plucking it when she fell. If I don't dillydally, we can have chicken stew with dumplings...."

She met his eyes, then hid a tiny giggle behind one hand. "Don't mind me. I tend to babble nonsensically when I'm nervous."

He got to his feet, took her hand in his, and led her into the hallway. "I have a favor to ask you," he said, pulling the parlor doors closed behind them.

"Anything. It's the least I can—"

Pressing a fingertip to her lips, he said, "You should hear me out first. It's a big favor. I wouldn't blame you in the least if you said no."

Shaina smiled, hands folded daintily at her waist, head tilted slightly in expectation.

Sloan's heart thumped wildly. He cleared his throat, hoping it would clear his head, too.

"Mable is a proud woman," he began. "You'd never know it by the no-nonsense way she behaves, but she's vain, too. Not in a baubles-and-beads way, mind you, but...well, being laid up and totally helpless is likely to drive her mad." He inhaled a deep breath, hoping to suck up the courage to continue. "So, I was wondering if—"

This time, it was Shaina who interrupted. "If she's more at ease thinking I need guidance and instruction, I'm only too happy to cooperate."

How had she known what he was about to ask? And why had she so quickly agreed to take orders from a woman she barely knew?

"I have a confession to make," Shaina said next.

Sloan tensed.

"I don't handle hard times nearly as well as you think. Being here, helping out, cooperating, even when it's only pretend, will serve as a diversion from...from everything." She exhaled a shaky breath. "It would be wrong to take credit for something I haven't earned."

"If you say so." He appreciated her attitude, regardless of what inspired it.

"Before I get busy in the kitchen, may I ask you a question?"

She looked so serious, standing as straight and tall as her five-foot-something frame would allow. Yet again, he felt duty-bound to protect her, to ease her discomfort, to assuage whatever was responsible for the faint frown now etched upon her pretty face.

"Of course you can. Any time. About anything."

Shaina glanced to her left, and out the window, Sloan saw Leo drape a blanket over Penny's back. "I could be mistaken, but it seems I know him from somewhere."

"Oh? Where?"

"I wish I could remember." An involuntary shiver shook her. "You know the feeling you get after walking through a spiderweb? As though you're covered in creepy-crawlies from head to toe?"

He'd encountered his fair share of webs. Unpleasant as the experiences had been, Sloan didn't recall anything to compare with her reaction.

"Yeah, I suppose...."

"That's how I feel when Leo is around. And I have no logical explanation for it." She giggled quietly, then rolled her eyes. "Am I not just *the* silliest person you've ever met?"

"'Silly' is about the last word I'd use to describe you," he assured her. Learning that the man made her ill at ease, too, was one more point in her favor, and it gave him hope that she could one day be trusted with a confidence. But for now, he'd err on the side of caution and keep his opinions about Leo—and the details of his past—to himself.

Shaina sighed again, then brightened. "Well, if I don't get busy, no one will eat tonight."

He watched her hurry down the hall and disappear into the kitchen. If she cooked half as well as she looked—

"Sloan! Is that you out there?"

"Yes, ma'am," he said, poking his head into the parlor. "It's me."

"Open that door, you ornery man."

He sat beside Mable's bed once more and wrapped her hand in his own. "So now that you're awake, little Briar Rose, maybe you'll tell me how you got yourself into this fix."

"Briar Rose?" Mable snickered. "Why, you silly man!"

"Don't tell me you haven't heard the story of the sleeping princess—"

"'Course I have. But I'm not little. Or young or beautiful. This isn't a castle. And you're sure as shootin' not a prince!"

She punctuated her speech with a laugh that belied her condition, telling Sloan that the laudanum hadn't completely worn off.

"Help me sit up a bit," she said, "so I can look you in the eye while you explain why I heard a woman's voice just now."

Sloan gathered several cushions from the sofa and tucked them behind her. "Let me fetch you some tea and a bite to—"

"Tea! Don't make me laugh. I'll have coffee, as always."

The label affixed to the laudanum bottle bore a ferocious-looking skull and crossbones beneath the word "POISON." Below that were the dosage instructions: "Adult dose: 1 tablespoon every one to two hours or as directed by the physician." When James had fallen from the hayloft, the doctor had cautioned against dispensing the drug on an empty stomach. And because of coffee's acidic nature and its tendency to keep a patient awake, he advised against that substance, as well. Sloan didn't envy Shaina's being charged with administering the painkiller to this mule-headed woman.

"I broke my leg, not my skull," Mable said. "You can't distract me that easily." She tidied her covers. "Who's in my kitchen?"

He sat down beside her yet again and, leaning his elbows on his knees, clasped his hands in the space between. "Before I answer, let me assure you she's hardworking and capable."

She made a face that said, *"We'll see about that,"* then said, "What. Is. Her. Name."

"Shaina. Shaina Sterling."

"Oh, stop. My leg hurts something powerful. I'm in no mood for your teasing."

"I'm dead serious, Mable. Shaina's chimney crumbled, and yesterday morning, when the winds were so brutal, Sterling Hall burned to the ground. She's homeless. Penniless. And—"

"Penniless, my big fat foot. Why, Mason and Harper could have bought up half the land between here and California if they'd had a mind to."

He'd never told her that Mason had solicited his help in cleaning up his son's messes, or what Shaina had been forced to do to keep the wolf from the door. So, he closed the parlor doors and told her ever gritty detail.

"Believe it or not, she has nothing, unless you count the threadbare dress and flimsy shawl she was wearing when her place went up in flames. She wouldn't let me buy her a few necessities unless I promised to deduct the cost from her pay. But you can't let on that I told you any of this, because pride is all she's got left."

Mable picked at a loose thread at the edge of her top sheet.

"Don't make me sorry I trusted you, old woman," he said, winking. "Give me your word that you'll keep the information under your nightcap."

"Can she cook?"

He shrugged. "We'll soon find out. She's making chicken stew as we speak."

"Lord help us all," Mable groused. "Bet she don't know the first thing 'bout darnin' socks or gettin' gravy stains outta the boys' shirts or beatin' dust from the rugs."

Sloan recalled that Shaina had come all the way from Missouri, alone, taking one odd job after another so that she could send money home to her folks. Based on that information alone, he had no doubt about her abilities to run the house or keep the men in line.

"If it turns out she never learned to sew or clean before she became a rich man's wife, I guess you'll just have to teach her," he finally said.

A woman like Mable had love and patience enough to raise a dozen children, and it was a shame she'd never been blessed with any. He could tell that she was softening, just imagining the prospect of taking another orphaned chick under her wing.

"Well, all right then," she said, feigning sternness. "But you'd better warn her that I won't stand for no sass."

"I'll tell her no such thing," he said as he got up and headed for the door. "I have no intention of being crushed between two stubborn, willful females."

"Have her make me a pot of coffee. It'll be a good test." Smirking, she added, "Woman who can't make coffee ain't of no more use round the house than…than some fancy knickknack."

"Even I know how to make coffee," Sloan retorted, "but it takes a special woman to beautify a room just by walking into it."

He had meant every word, but the instant he saw that discerning, maternal eyebrow rise on Mable's forehead, he regretted voicing his thoughts.

"Coffee it is, then," he said, ducking out the door.

He was halfway down the hall when he heard her laughing.

Chapter Thirteen

The low buzz of male conversation filled the kitchen as Shaina prayed, *Let them like the stew. And the biscuits. And especially the coffee!*

For the most part, the dinner discussion centered on preparations for the worst of the winter, which everyone knew would be upon them before they knew it: moving the herd to the south fields, where it stayed sunny on good days; sealing the cracks between drying logs of the house and outbuildings; replacing shingles blown away by high winds; checking for gaps between the windows and the sills; and making sure none of the mortar in the chimneys had deteriorated.

"There's so much to do," James said, "I feel like a short hog in tall grass."

"Well," Sloan drawled, "grass doesn't grow on a busy street." And when James opened his mouth to counter, he added, "You can't plow a field by turning it over in your mind."

It set him up for a round of groans and good-natured ribbing, and also told Shaina that her prayer had been answered. If the men hadn't liked the food, they would be grumbling about that instead of Sloan's long list of chores.

As an afterthought, she'd thrown together a cobbler made from apples she'd found in the root cellar. If her debut as the Remington Ranch cook wasn't good enough reason to dip into the supply, she didn't know what was. Sloan had pointed out the small orchard he'd planted near Mason's Pond, where two varieties of the hardy fruit grew. The trees looked strange and sad, cut back so severely for the cold weather; and when she'd said so, Sloan had quoted Isaiah 18:5 to explain the need for pruning. As she'd peeled and cored the results of his careful planning, Shaina wondered if being stripped of everything had been God's way of reminding her what was truly important in life.

She would work hard—that was what she'd do—to distract herself from every self-pitying thought that dared enter her head. Sloan had been right in reminding her that she had family back in Missouri. A roof over her head. What more could she ask for?

"Is the coffee ready, Shaina?" Sloan's gentle voice roused her from her ponderings.

Wrapping the handle in a potholder, she walked around the table and filled each raised mug.

"Smells good," James observed.

Abe took a swig, then looked at Shaina. "Hey, why ain't it bitter?"

"Is it supposed to be?"

"Well, 'course not," the young man said. "It's just the way Mable makes it."

James chuckled. "And no man seated here dared mention it."

His admission provided an opening for reviews:

"Like the hard biscuits."

"And salty stew."

"Runny eggs."

"Burnt toast!"

Growing up with two brothers and a father who believed flattering words were unmanly, Shaina recognized backhanded compliments when she heard them: In criticizing Mable, they were praising her. And she felt guilty.

"I had all afternoon to fuss over this meal," she explained. "I'm sure that if Mable wasn't so busy seeing to all your other needs, she would have the time to do just as good a job, if not better."

Abe snickered, then said in a loud whisper, "Women. Always in cahoots."

"Yes," Leo observed, "they do tend to stick together, don't they?"

"People who are right tend to do that," Shaina shot back.

James winked, and she read his expression as thanks for defending his wife. But his gratitude was dimmed by Leo's scrutiny. A shiver snaked up Shaina's spine as she tried to figure out why he seemed so familiar.

"What's that?" Sloan asked, pointing at something on the sideboard.

She returned the coffeepot to its burner, then carried the baking pan to the table and removed the tea towel she'd draped over it. "I thought I'd buy your approval with apple cobbler," she said, sticking a big spoon into the dessert.

Hoots and whistles of approval followed the pan as it was passed around the table.

"Don't get used to it, boys," Leo said. "Mable's a strong woman, and she'll be back in the kitchen before we know it."

No one knew how to react to that, least of all Shaina. Fortunately, the cobbler had sidetracked the men. All but Sloan, that is, who sent her a small, appreciative smile that quickened her heartbeat.

She hid her blush by pumping water into the big kettle. By the time it came to a boil, the ranch hands had retired to the bunkhouse. James refilled his bowl with stew and announced that he'd sit with Mable while she ate it. Sloan excused himself to finish some correspondence in his office. Shaina worked quietly, scrubbing pots and dishes, then returning them to the shelves behind the red and white checkered curtain that covered the lower cupboard. Being here felt good, felt right, and not only because it provided a haven from her troubles.

Troubles….

Leo's last remark echoed in her head. He'd been correct in saying that Mable's leg would soon heal, and when it did, she'd naturally want to resume her duties.

When that happened, Shaina would have to leave. So, she needed to save as much of her pay as possible. It would mean a little less in the envelopes she'd send home, but only until she found another job and a new place to live. Because back to Missouri was the *last* place she wanted to go.

She swept the day's grit and dust out the back door, then propped the broom in the corner.

It was evident, once she removed the big wooden tray from its shelf above the stove, that no one had used it in quite some time. After washing away a layer of dust, she draped it with an embroidered tea towel found in the top drawer of the kitchen cupboard. From all she'd heard about Mable, it wasn't likely she'd sewn those flowers and leaves onto it, but that didn't mean the woman wouldn't appreciate pretty things. Since the sugar bowl, milk pitcher, and serving plate bore the same design, she wondered who *had* stitched them into the fabric.

Shaina filled a mug with tea, added it to the arrangement, and decided that needlework might come in handy as a topic of conversation.

"One more chore," she muttered, lifting the tray, "and I can hide away until morning."

Halfway down the hall, Shaina sent a silent prayer heavenward, asking forgiveness for her selfish thought. Whether Mable would be an easygoing patient, as Harper had been, remained to be seen. But even if she behaved like Shaina's grandmother, who'd turned cantankerous and ungrateful in her later years, Shaina knew she must never view the woman's care as a chore.

She stopped just short of the parlor door and said another short prayer, this one for the insight to know how best to meet Mable's needs.

"There's not much you can do for me standing out there in the hall," said a gruff female voice.

With one last prayer—for patience—Shaina entered the room. The women had met in passing, at church socials and city festivals, but they had never exchanged more than a polite greeting. *No matter,* Shaina thought, smiling as she set the tray on a nearby table. All that was about to change.

"After you've taken your medicine," she said, "you can have some tea and cobbler."

"Don't need the medicine, don't want the tea," Mable grumbled.

If she didn't stand her ground now, she'd lose all hope of doing her job properly.

"Dr. Wilson was quite clear," Shaina said, lifting the bottle of laudanum from the mantel. "You're to take two spoonfuls at bedtime, because sleep is an important part of your recovery."

She uncorked the bottle and poured the smelly liquid onto the spoon as Mable made a thin, taut line of her lips.

"Oh, I see—you're waiting for me to tuck a napkin into your collar so you won't dribble the medicine onto your nightgown."

"Dribble, indeed! I'm not a doddering old woman!"

"Of course you aren't." She held the spoon nearer Mable's lips and prayed for a steady hand. One sign of weakness, and the woman would have full control of the situation, now and throughout her recovery. "If you cooperate with your evening dose, maybe I can sneak a little coffee to you every morning."

The only sound in the room was the tick of the mantel clock, until Mable exhaled a frustrated breath.

"Oh, all right," she finally said, opening her mouth.

She grimaced, and Shaina refilled the spoon. The second dose went down without a fight.

"When James was laid up, he said the stuff tasted sweet." Mable held out her hands, as if to push the spoon away. "He lied."

Laughing, Shaina capped the bottle and set it aside. Then, taking the two remaining pillows from the settee, she tucked one on either side of Mable's thighs.

"This will keep the tray from tipping this way and that," she said, arranging the tray on Mable's lap, "or from pressing too heavily on your broken bone." She stood back and added, "I wasn't sure if you liked your tea plain or with milk and sugar, so I brought both."

Mable sipped the brew and gave an approving nod. "It'll do. Not too strong, not too weak," she said. "If you make it this way all the time, I won't need either. But, just so's ya know, I prefer coffee."

"Duly noted, ma'am."

Shaina curtseyed as Mable took a bite of the cobbler. "*You* made this?"

"I did."

"Well, don't that beat all."

A compliment? Shaina truly couldn't tell. It seemed that, although she was surprised that a spoiled city girl could cook and bake, Mable approved.

"Before I became the pampered wife of a wealthy man," Shaina said around a grin, "I learned a thing or two."

Mable took another bite. "Do tell." She narrowed her brown eyes and, using the spoon as a pointer, said, "Just so we're clear on a couple of things, I'll take the laudanum at bedtime, and *only* at bedtime."

"Unless the pain gets unbearable during the day, right?"

"Pah," she said, waving away Shaina's comment. "And there's an order to doin' things round here. In the morning, bring me a pencil and paper, and I'll write you up a list."

"Thank you. That'll be a huge help."

"Now sit down there while I finish my cobbler," she said, pointing at a nearby chair, "and tell me all about your friendship with Jennie Rogers."

Shaina sat, wondering how Mable had found out about that, considering how seldom she came into town.

"Quit lookin' so perplexed. It's like I told you—I'm not a doddering old woman." She winked and added, "Believe it or not, that husband of mine gossips like an old hen!"

Once Shaina got started, the truth poured out quite easily; and by the time Mable had finished her tea and cobbler, the laudanum had taken effect. Shaina removed the tray and the extra pillows, taking care not to wake Mable, then dimmed the lights and tiptoed from the room.

She didn't know how many weeks it would take Mable to fully recover, but one thing was certain: Her days at Remington Ranch would not be boring.

Chapter Fourteen

Before leaving for Denver, Sloan stopped in at the horse barn. Satisfied that all was well there, he walked around back for a last look at his weather equipment. Knowing what Mother Nature might deliver could make the difference between life and death for all the livestock and could spare a ranch hand from being forced to take shelter in one of the five crude cabins Sloan had erected at strategic locations around his property. Just last week, Abe and Leo had restocked each one with the basic necessities. If a storm trapped a man, he'd find flour, lard, smoked elk, and deer jerky to keep his stomach from rumbling. He'd also have enough wood to keep a fire going to melt snow for water and to warm him until conditions improved.

The readings on the barometer told Sloan the air pressure was falling. According to the anemometer, wind speeds were picking up, and the hygrometer indicated a rise in moisture. He'd read Aristotle's *Meteorologica* from cover to cover, and although some of the theories had been debunked, Sloan found more than enough commonsense information among the pages to make educated guesses. The inch of snow that had fallen during the last storm had all but melted, and unless he'd read the gauges incorrectly, a similar system was on the way. The best method of verification, he'd learned, was to check with Smitty in Denver, to see if any weather reports had been transmitted by way of his telegraph lines.

The only thing left to do now was to saddle Penny and head into town. But first, he'd pay Mable a short visit to see how she was getting on with Shaina. He found her sitting up in bed, poking a fat needle through the circle of cloth stretched over her embroidery hoop.

"What's that going to be?" he asked, leaning in for a better look.

"A pillow cover," she said, then sniffed. "What's that I smell?"

Sloan straightened and ran a hand through still-damp hair. "Soap, I reckon."

"Hmph. Got business in Denver, do you?"

"Yeah. Need to check a few things at the manufactory and pay a visit to Smitty. And see Doc Wilson."

"Doc Wilson? Whatever for? He'll probably be here tomorrow to check on me."

"Might not be back by tomorrow." Sloan hoped that wasn't true. The more time he spent in Denver, the less he liked the city. "You been taking your medicine?"

"Only at night. Shaina made a good point—if I don't sleep well, I won't heal fast."

He noticed a tray on the table beside her bed. The empty plate and bowl told him that whatever Shaina had served for breakfast had passed muster with Mable.

"I see she's feeding you well."

She padded her ample belly. "Too well. I'd wager I'm ten pounds heavier than before I busted up my leg."

"I'm sure you'll work it off once you're back on your feet."

He pulled the side chair closer to the bed and sat down. "So, how much time does Shaina spend with you?"

Mable stopped sewing and gave the question a moment's thought. "Oh, I suppose it's safe to say she's in here a couple of hours a day."

"A couple of hours! How does she have time for everything else?"

"She's the one who insists on keepin' me company while I eat, and on rubbin' something called Braun's into my skin. Says it's to prevent bedsores. Takes my temperature, too; and, of course, forces that vile laudanum down my gullet." A faint smile lit her face. "She's a worker, that one. I wrote down a schedule, and it seems she's followin' it to the letter."

"So you like her, then?"

Mable turned back to her stitching. "She'll do."

A second of silence passed before she added, "That girl has quite a history for one so young."

"History?" Leaning forward, he rested his forearms on the edge of the mattress.

"Leavin' home when she was still a child, travelin' alone, takin' all manner of odd jobs to keep a roof over her head and her belly full...."

Sloan only nodded.

"Don't rightly know how she keeps a smile on her face, day and night, night and day, what with all she's been through." Mable shook her head. "Did you know she sends money back to her folks in Missouri?"

"I did."

She laid the sewing circle on her lap and branded him with a long stare. "You're not getting any younger, y'know. Don't you think it's time you started thinking about a wife and young'uns?"

Sloan picked up on her not-so-subtle hint. "There you go again," he said, chuckling, "beating around the bush."

"Pah."

Rising, he slid the chair back where he'd found it. "Well, I'd better get moving if I don't want to spend another night at The Remington."

"You take care," she said, wagging her forefinger maternally in his direction.

He pressed a light kiss to her forehead. "And you do the same."

As he headed for the kitchen, Sloan made a quick comparison between his mother—a tiny, slender woman whose pale skin and hair matched her delicate nature—and Mable, whose dark eyes and steely hair echoed her stature and personality. The only thing the two women had in common was his immense love for them.

He found Shaina out back, beating a rug she'd flung over the clothesline. There was just enough nip in the air to turn her cheeks a rosy pink, and just enough wind to fluff her dark curls. The loosened dust formed tiny twisters that rose up, then disappeared into the air. *She'll more than "do,"* he thought with a smile.

"Keep that up," he said, "and you'll pound the design right out of the weave."

"Goodness gracious, sakes alive!" she cried out, one hand to her chest. "I believe you just frightened away the last ten years of my life."

"I hear those are the worst ten, so you're welcome."

Grinning, Shaina hooked the beater over one slender wrist and tugged the rug down from the wire clothesline. "So, you're heading to Denver?" she asked as they walked together to the back porch.

"How did you know?"

She smiled up at him. "You're wearing your best leather jacket, and trousers rather than dungarees. Those are your 'do business' clothes." He held open the door, and as she passed by, she added, "Would you mind dropping something off at the post office for me? It'll take me only a minute to get it."

"Sure." A letter home, no doubt, along with most of the cash he'd paid her for last week's work. "I need to saddle Penny. Soon as I've finished, I'll meet you back here."

"I'll be ready."

He found Leo in the barn, brushing James's horse. Three weeks ago, before Mable's fall, he would have thought it odd, because his old friend didn't trust anyone with his pinto. Now that he was spending every spare moment in the parlor, it didn't seem quite so strange. And yet—

"How-do, boss? Off to the big city, I see."

"Just for a day or two."

"Unless old Mother Nature has something else to say about it."

"By my calculations, the weather won't turn for a few days yet."

"Unless old Mother Nature has something else to say about *that*."

Grinning, Sloan picked up his horse's blanket and saddle, threw both over his right shoulder, then grabbed the bridle and headed for the corral.

"I'll probably see you there," Leo said, patting his shirt pocket. "Soapy has arranged a few games of chance over at the Tivoli."

Sloan had heard all he cared to about "Soap Gang" and Smith's fake stock exchange. Though Soapy Smith had an unwritten pact with the town officials to leave the locals out of his bunco games, gambling, drinking fools like Leo Blevins and his pal Rafe Preston were anything *but* excluded.

"Just take care," Sloan said. "Rumor has it Big Ed and Texas Jack are in town."

Leo snickered. "I appreciate your concern, boss." He took a few steps closer to Sloan. Tossing the dandy brush between one palm and the other, he said, "Can I ask you a question?"

"You can ask...."

"Have you ever met a person and gotten the eerie feeling you know him from somewhere?"

"I time or two, I suppose."

"Well, it's strange—every time I'm around the widow Sterling, I get that feeling."

The hairs on Sloan's neck stood up. Shaina had said pretty much the same thing about Leo her first day at the ranch. If Leo had made the comment about anyone else, Sloan might have challenged him to confront the source of his eerie feeling. But it wasn't anyone else. It was *Shaina*.

He walked toward the door. "I'm sure you'll figure it out eventually," he said over his shoulder.

But as he saddled Penny and started for Denver, he hoped Leo wouldn't figure it out. At least, not before Shaina remembered why Blevins seemed so familiar to her.

Chapter Fifteen

Joe Michaels lifted his bearded chin, rested both arms on his ponderous belly, and planted his feet shoulder-width apart as he glared at Sloan through his wire-rimmed glasses. "Let's get something straight, right here and now, Remington: You got nothin' to say 'bout what I do on my own time."

Sloan made a note in Michaels' employee file, then calmly poked the pen back inside its holder and got to his feet.

"You're right," he said, moving to the other side of his desk.

Michaels took a step back.

"But I can and *will* have a say when you drag yourself into the plant half an hour late, still under the influence of the previous night's drinking."

"I ain't drunk, I'm tellin' you."

"Say what you will, but you reek of whiskey."

"Ain't my fault, is it, that Preston spilt a jigger of Red Eye on my shirt?"

If the man's rheumy, bloodshot eyes hadn't given him away, his slurred words and inability to stand still would have.

"You've had three warnings, Joe." Reaching behind him, Sloan took an envelope from his desk. "There's two weeks' worth of pay in here," he said, holding it out to him. "It should tide you over until you find another job. I hear they're hiring in the mines."

"You...you're firin' me?"

"I made myself clear the last time you were in here. I can't, in good conscience, allow you to work with tools and machines that are dangerous for a man who's stone-cold sober."

"You're *firin'* me."

Not a question this time, Sloan noted. "As I said, two weeks' pay should hold you over until you find other work."

Michaels took the envelope and turned on his heel. "You'll be sorry," he snarled, then slammed the door behind him.

Sloan went to the window to watch and make sure the man didn't leave any mayhem in his wake as he departed the manufactory. Michaels looked up, saw him standing in the window, and raised a fist.

"You mark my words, Remington," he bellowed, "you'll be sorry. I'll *make* you sorry!"

People in the street gave him a wide berth as he staggered left and right, probably on his way to the saloon.

In all his years of running Sterling Manufactory, Sloan had fired just one other man, for trying to break into the safe one rainy night. He hadn't expected Sloan to walk in on him. Hadn't expected to become the victim of the "bouncer's grip," either. But he'd gone peacefully, found work in Boulder, and never returned to Denver.

Sloan walked to the factory floor and sought out his foreman, Bud. The man's relief showed in his stance and his wide smile as he promised to post a notice on the bulletin board out front, letting it be known that there was an opening.

With his work up-to-date and the unpleasant task of Michaels' discharge behind him, Sloan headed for the clinic, hoping Doc Wilson would have the good sense to accept his help.

"Well, if it isn't Sloan Remington," Elsie said when he walked through the door.

"Ma'am," he returned with a tip of his hat. "Is your brother around?"

She sighed. "He's in his office, but I'll warn you—he isn't in a very good mood."

"Oh? Why's that?" Sloan asked as he followed her down the hall.

"Because he's trying to figure out how to make ten dollars cover a hundred dollars' worth of bills." She rapped on the door.

"What now?" Doc Wilson snarled.

"Pay him no mind," she whispered to Sloan. "He's all bark and no bite." She opened the door. "Sloan Remington here to see you, brother, dear."

Doc Wilson stood, looking more haggard than Sloan had ever seen him.

"That cut is healing nicely," the man said as he shook Sloan's hand.

"Yes, it is." He ran his fingertips over the ropelike scar. "But this isn't the reason I stopped by."

"Have a seat, then, and tell me why you're here."

Sloan waited for Elsie to leave, and because he knew she would listen through the closed door, he scooted his chair closer to the doctor's desk and lowered his voice.

"I know a good deal when I see it," he began, "and, as it so happens, this one is as good for the town as it is for you and me."

"You and me?" Wilson echoed.

"Hear me out," Sloan said, placing the envelope of cash on the doctor's desk. "That should cover the cost of adding to the clinic and purchasing new equipment, with money left over to pay all your creditors." He held up a hand to forestall any objections Wilson might raise. "When you start making a profit, you can begin payments. Ten percent of your profits...when there *is* a profit. Someday, if things go according to my plan, we can build a fully staffed hospital, with operating rooms and everything else you'll need to do your job properly. And this clinic will function as a place where people can come for stitches and whatnot."

Wilson picked up the envelope and ran a thumb over the stack of bills inside. "I—I don't know what to say, Sloan."

On his feet now, Sloan extended a hand. "Say, 'Have a safe trip home...*partner.*'"

And before Wilson could protest, he left, and nearly plowed into Elsie on the other side of the door. There were tears in her eyes as she said, "Sloan Remington, you're my hero!"

He laughed. "I'm nothing of the kind. Once that brother of yours gets things rolling, I stand to make a lot of money."

She snorted. "Please. We both know that isn't why you—"

"Will you do me a favor, Elsie?"

"Oh, yes, Sloan. Anything," she gushed.

"Keep all this under your bonnet—for your brother's sake, for my sake, for the sake of the town—will you?" He glanced at the closed office door. "I have a feeling his ego needs a boost even more than Denver needs an updated clinic."

She nodded.

"Then we're in agreement? You won't tell *anyone* about my deal with the doc?"

Elsie grinned. "What deal?"

He was still chuckling to himself when his boots hit the street. Hands deep in his pockets, he headed for The Remington. If he didn't stay too long visiting with the Sweenys, he'd have time to make a deposit at the bank and pay a visit to Detective Gus Anderson.

As expected, things were running efficiently at the hotel. He brought the Sweenys up to speed on the latest news about Shaina, and they sent him on his way with greetings for the young widow and Mable, too.

Gus wasn't in when Sloan stopped by the Pinkerton office, so he scribbled a note.

Need a big favor. Stop by the manufactory next week, and I'll tell you about it over supper at The Windsor.

After tucking the note into the leather triangle that held the man's desk blotter in place, he made his way to the bank.

Once his business in town was concluded, Sloan looked at the sky. It would be dark when he arrived back at the ranch, but at least he'd beat the storm. Penny seemed even more eager to get home than he was, and it took very little to persuade her to head west. As they cantered down Broadway, a cold gust ruffled awnings and set shutters to flapping. Shopkeepers waved a hasty hello as they hurriedly tied things down.

Sloan pulled up his collar and ducked as far into his jacket as he could without obstructing his vision. A familiar odor rode the wind and swirled around him. Red Eye and cigars, the same stink that Joe Michaels had dragged into his office earlier that day.

Moving only his eyes, he glanced left, then right, and spotted Preston and Michaels, leaning on opposite sides of the same support post, eyes narrowed, heads swiveling as they watched him pass by. Michaels flicked a half-smoked cigarette into the street, and it landed inches from Penny's hooves. Sloan knew she'd seen it, because her ears pricked forward, then swiveled toward the seedy twosome. Fortunately, she wasn't a horse that spooked easily, and she kept up a steady pace.

Was it his imagination, or was it some trick of the wind whistling past his ears, that made it sound as if Michaels had said, "Mark my words…"?

Sloan gripped the reins in his left hand, freeing the right to grab his sidearm, should the need arise to use it. *Six in the chamber*, he told himself, *six in your jacket pocket*. A small reassurance, since the two men were carrying the same—or more.

It wouldn't be easy, discerning between the sounds of trees creaking in the wind and the soft slog of horses' hooves clopping behind him through the snow.

Then he remembered something that calmed him a bit. Midway through the summer, as they'd ridden out to round up any stray calves, James had gotten an idea. *"If you find 'em, catch a ray of sun with this, and signal me,"* he'd said, and handed Sloan a small oval mirror. Then he'd tapped his pocket. *"And I'll do the same."*

Sloan slid a hand into his saddlebag and retrieved the mirror. Holding it just to the right of the saddle horn, he could see behind him almost as well as if he were looking over his shoulder.

In weather like this, Michaels and Preston would probably hole up in the saloon, where a blazing fire and cheap whiskey would keep them warm.

Probably.

One thing was sure: It would be a long, cold, nerve-wracking ride home.

Chapter Sixteen

With the soft glow of lantern light beckoning him, Sloan urged Penny into a canter and didn't rein her in until they reached the barn. She snorted quietly as he dismounted, knowing he'd soon relieve her of the hefty saddle.

Sloan walked her into the barn and lit the lantern on the tack bench. Before lifting the saddle from her back and slinging it over its stand, he unclipped the cinches and neatly threaded the keeper under the buckles to assure it would be ready for his next ride.

He stood Penny near the water trough and grabbed the hoof pick. Sliding a hand down her foreleg, he said, "Up," and Penny obediently lifted her foot. She'd earned a good grooming, and the truth was, the chore relaxed him.

Once he'd finished brushing the dust and dirt from her coat, he backed her into a stall and gave her some oats. She'd earned those, too, after their long, tense ride home. She munched contentedly while he returned the tools to their proper places on the tack bench. When he'd finished, Sloan slid a blanket over her back. And after securing its straps, he blew out the lantern and led her outside, latching the big double doors behind them. He hadn't even closed the corral gate before Penny joined her pals on the other side. "You're welcome," he said with a grin, then headed for the house, working the kinks out of his neck and shoulders.

He hoped a hot bath would help him sleep.

It did not. Every time he closed his eyes, Sloan saw the malevolent glares of Michaels and Preston. An eerie sixth sense told him they were cooking up trouble—and that he was the main ingredient in the pot.

Sloan headed for the kitchen to see what sort of leftovers he might scrounge up. The dim flicker of the lantern above the table illuminated a towel-covered plate. Peeling back the cloth, he found a crust of buttered bread and a slice of ham, and a note that said, "Just in case you're hungry."

Smiling at Shaina's thoughtful little surprise, Sloan took a bite, then walked to the sink and pumped himself a glass of water. It wouldn't be easy saying good-bye to her once Mable's leg healed. If he could talk the older woman into pretending she needed an assistant, could they convince her to stay?

Leaning forward, he parted the checkered curtains covering the window and peered outside. Moonlight sneaking through the high, thin clouds clung to the posts and rails that made up the corral, painting inky lines on the exterior wall of the log-and-board barn. The horses moved about, slow and calm, seeking tufts of grass and bits of hay on the loamy ground as warm vapor puffed from their nostrils. More beautiful, in his opinion, than any work of art created by man.

And then, something moving near the gate caught his eye— something that wasn't a horse or a lunar shadow. The defiant stares of Michaels and Preston flashed in his mind's eye. Just as quickly, the image vanished, as he realized it was one silhouette, not two, and far too small to belong to either man.

Shaina.

Curiosity lured Penny in for a closer look at whatever rested in Shaina's upturned palm. And curiosity compelled Sloan to put on his coat and go find out for himself what thoughtful surprise she'd offered his horse. He picked up the ham and bread and then, as an afterthought, grabbed Mable's shawl from the hook beside his Stetson; if Shaina caught a chill out there in the dark, he'd drape it over her slender shoulders, erasing any excuse she might have for returning too soon to the warmth of the house.

He made quiet clicking sounds with his tongue as he moved closer, so as not to startle her or Penny. The horse bobbed her head when he stepped up beside Shaina, as if to say, *"Don't distract her. Can't you see she has a handful of apple slices?"*

"I thought you'd be fast asleep by now," Shaina murmured.

The observation told Sloan she had heard him ride in earlier.

"I thought the same thing." He draped the shawl over the gate, held up the bread and ham, and took another bite. "Mighty thoughtful of you," he said after chewing. "What are you, a mind reader?"

"Maybe." She took another apple slice from her pocket and placed it in her palm. As Penny nibbled at it, she said, "Did things go well in town?"

He thought of the ugly scene between him and Michaels. "As well as could be expected, I reckon." But something about her tone made him think she had more to say. "Why do you ask?"

Shaina shrugged. "Oh, I don't know." She studied his face for a moment, then went back to stroking Penny's nose. "You just seem a tad...on edge."

She'd been as jumpy as a barn cat when he'd first brought her here, but the past weeks had erased all traces of nervousness. Clearly, Shaina drew comfort from hard work and wide-open spaces, and it pleased him that they had this in common. Sloan had come to respect her opinion; if he believed she could process the news about Michaels and Preston without returning to her formerly jittery self, he'd unburden himself, right here and now.

"Abe said you had to fire a man today."

He'd forgotten having shared that tidbit with the boy.

"That couldn't have been easy." Again, she met his eyes. "Does he have a family? The man you let go, I mean?"

"Far as I know, just a brother who's serving time in Canon City."

"Well, that's a relief. Not that his brother is in prison, of course, but that he doesn't have a wife or children who will suffer."

Sloan didn't know why, but he felt the need to defend his actions. "I warned the man on three separate occasions. To put it plainly, he pushed his luck one too many times."

"Oh, I hope it didn't sound like I was questioning your decision." She met his eyes. "I'm sure he deserved to be fired...and more," she said through clenched teeth.

Sloan didn't know how to explain the angry tremor in her otherwise musical voice.

She turned her attention back to Penny. "Too keyed up to sleep?"

That's putting it mildly, he thought, leaning both forearms on the gate's support post. And then he noticed the toes of her work boots, peeking out from the ruffled hem of her flowery nightdress. He grinned. Only Shaina would throw on a heavy coat and take a walk after everyone else had been tucked in for the night.

"So, what's keeping you awake?" he countered.

She sighed, and he watched the steam of her breath disappear into the night air, like the smoke from a spent match.

"It's nothing, really. Just...just family nonsense."

Sloan didn't want to pry, but if she had something to get off her chest, he wanted her to know it was all right to share it with him. He could almost hear Simon's deep voice saying, *"Honesty is the best policy."*

"Well, if you've a mind to talk about it, I've a mind to listen."

Shaina didn't respond at first, but when she did, she hung her head. "When Abe got back from town this morning, he brought me a letter from home." She patted her pocket.

Her folks had replied already? There were many things to dislike about the railroad, but from her manner, he had to assume the speed of mail delivery was not one of them.

"I hope no one is injured. Or ill."

"As coldhearted as it sounds, illness or injury would be preferable to the truth."

"The truth?"

"They've been bleeding me white for years. What Pa doesn't squander at the corner pub, Ma throws away on games of chance. They've both lost their jobs, and the landlord is about to evict them."

Well, no wonder she'd reacted with indignation to the news of Michaels' dismissal.

"Your brothers...?"

"In every letter, I ask about them, but Ma hasn't mentioned them in more than a year."

If they'd left Missouri in search of work, had they been sending money home, as Shaina had?

"She says what I'm sending isn't enough. That it has *never* been enough."

It had been his understanding that the money she sent would supplement their income, not support them entirely.

"Again, I'm sure I sound completely heartless to admit this, but my mother's letter came as a relief."

A relief?

"I've suspected all along they weren't putting the money to good use. Soon after Harper was mur—" Shaina stopped and cleared her throat before continuing. "After I realized what a financial mess Harper had left me with, I wrote to my aunt—Ma's sister—because the money I was sending home would have come in very handy. She responded right away, citing all sorts of things they were wasting money on, but I chose not to believe her."

Sloan could only imagine how she was feeling. Would she continue sending them money?

"I've been praying for guidance." She patted her pocket again. "It wasn't the answer I was hoping for, but at least now I know where I stand."

Which is…?

She looked up at him and smiled. "Oh, now, don't look sad on my behalf. I've been on my own for a long time. I'm fine."

Penny chose that moment to remind Shaina that it was time for another apple slice by nosing her, sending her stumbling into Sloan's arms.

"Yes," he said, gathering her near. "Yes, you most certainly are fine."

In the dim moonlight, her eyes sparkled like pale-blue diamonds, her skin having the look of fine porcelain. Was it as soft and smooth as it appeared?

Only one way to find out. Sloan pressed a palm to her cheek, fully prepared to kiss her.

She gasped. "Your hands are cold as ice!"

Shaina shivered, and when he drew her closer, she made no move to step back. Instead, she lifted her chin, as if waiting for his kiss. He could feel her heart beating hard against his chest. Felt her warm breath, too, puffing against his lips.

And then he heard *snick-snick*.

Nothing made a sound like that except for a Winchester 73. He knew, because it was his rifle of choice. In one smooth move, Sloan put Shaina behind him and squeezed the grip of his Schofield, thankful for the now-critical lesson Simon had drilled into his head: *"The only time you don't wear a sidearm in these parts is…never."*

He unholstered the revolver and prayed that the good Lord would protect Shaina, no matter what happened to him.

Chapter Seventeen

"For the love of all that's holy," Sloan grumbled, "you ought to know better than to sneak up on a man. Especially in the dark."

Frowning, James lowered the rifle. "And you oughtta know better 'n to prowl around when the rest of the world is sleeping."

Sloan reholstered the Schofield as Shaina came out of hiding. "You all right?" he asked her.

One side of her mouth lifted in a wry grin. "A tad flatter than I was a minute ago, but yes, I'm all right."

He faced James again. "So, why aren't *you* sleeping like the rest of the world?"

"Had a dream about Preston pullin' that short blade outta his sheath to carve up the other side of your face. Got up to walk it off, and heard noises."

Sloan pointed at the long gun. "You want to uncock that thing before you blow your toes off?"

James blinked, then slowly released the hammer. This time, when Sloan heard the familiar *snick-snick*, he exhaled a sigh of relief.

"Well, you two moony-eyed fools can stand out here in the cold if you've a mind to, but I'm goin' back to my warm bed," James grumbled. "It'll be light 'fore we know it."

Sloan and Shaina watched him head for the house, and when the screen door squeaked shut behind him, she said, "You know, it *is* cold out here."

Sloan picked up Mable's shawl. "And to think I hauled this out here in case you got cold." Draping it over her shoulders, he asked, "Too little, too late?"

114

She snuggled into the garment as they crossed the frosty lawn, and as soon as Shaina hung her coat on the peg near the back door, she stirred the coals in the belly of the cookstove. "There's enough for two mugs of coffee," she said, shaking the pot.

"Sounds good." It wasn't as though he'd get any sleep tonight, anyway, what with the foolishness in town and James's sudden appearance at the corral. *And who knows?* he thought with a grin. *Maybe we can pick up where we left off when—*

"I don't know how to thank you for what you did out there."

He chuckled. "Well, this is a first."

She cast him a puzzled glance.

"I don't think a gal has ever thanked me for flattening her against a fence before."

"Should I take it to mean those you *have* flattened were too unappreciative to express their gratitude?" The teasing smile waned as her delicate eyebrows drew together slightly. "You know very well what I'm talking about."

He looked into her beautiful blue eyes, glowing with gratefulness. Yes, he understood, and she'd been correct in assuming that if it had been someone other than James aiming that cocked-and-loaded Winchester at them, he would have taken a bullet for her.

But he couldn't very well say that, so he settled for, "I only did what any man would have under the same circumstances."

"Nonsense. I know better."

What did *that* mean? He tried to picture a man who'd do anything *but* protect her at all costs. Only one person came to mind: Harper Sterling.

Sloan opened the bread box, grabbed a corn muffin left over from supper, and sat down at the table. "Not sure why," he said around a bite, "but I just remembered the night we first met."

A wistful smile brightened her face. "At the Rothschilds' wedding. I don't think there has ever been a social function to rival it. Penelope looked so lovely in her gown."

Sloan chuckled. "As much as her pa paid for it, you could've wrapped a toad in that gown, and it would've looked lovely."

She laughed as she busied herself at the sink, hanging mugs on the rack and sliding pots onto a low shelf. "How would you know the cost of Penelope's gown?" she finally asked.

"Because I loaned him the money to buy it."

She hesitated for a second. With her back straight and her chin up, her stance reminded him of that night, when every other woman—including the bride—had taken a backseat to Shaina in the looks department. She'd been the vision of royalty in her simple gown of corn-flower-blue silk. She'd woven a ribbon of the same material through her dark waves and tied it in a small bow on top of her head. Rare pale-blue stones had glittered from her silvery pendant necklace and earrings, and a fur stole had been draped loosely over her shoulders.

"What kind of fur were you wearing that night?" Sloan asked.

"Beaver." She sighed, a muted, melancholy sound. "We'd hosted a dinner party, and as I fetched the guests' wraps, Harper caught me rubbing a friend's coat against my cheek. After everyone left, he wanted to know why I was fawning over sewn-together beaver pelts. I told him the truth: It was the softest, silkiest fur I'd ever felt. Three days later, I had one of my own."

Did she miss Harper still? He understood her loyalty, because for years after arriving at Remington Ranch, a sense of loyalty had dominated his every thought and action. He'd worked hard—harder than any ranch hand—to show gratitude to the man who'd saved him from abuse, homelessness, starvation, and worse. How like Simon to save him from feelings of inferiority, as well. *I didn't bring you home to serve as my footstool,* he'd said when Sloan had tried turning down the offer to fund his college education. *"Will you ever realize that you're the answer to my prayers for a son?"*

Prayers....

It dawned on Sloan that he'd forgotten to seek the Almighty's guidance on anything related to Shaina, starting the moment he'd promised Harper that he'd look out for her. Well, that would change—starting tonight. And, God willing, someday she'd see him as someone other than the man who rewarded hard work with hard cash. Because the good Lord knew he didn't see *her* that way!

"Was the stole a birthday present or an anniversary gift?" he asked, though he knew the answer.

"It wasn't for a special occasion. It was just Harper's way." She sighed. "I often wonder...would he someday have come to understand it wasn't necessary to buy my affections?"

A loaded question if Sloan had ever heard one. She'd as much as admitted to having married Harper to guarantee a roof over her head. As time had passed, had she found bona fide reasons to love the man? Or had she become his wife out of a sense of pity? Maybe, Sloan thought, it was a bit of both.

Sloan draped an arm over the back of his chair and did his best to look indifferent about her life as another man's wife.

"Furs, jewels, fine art, a mansion and grand estate..." he said. "A body might have mistaken you for a spoiled-rotten child."

The flash of surprise on her face was quickly supplanted by a wry grin. "You haven't seen me angry. Under the right circumstances, I can throw a tantrum to outdo any spoiled-rotten child."

If losing her husband, her fortune, her position in Denver society, and her home, all in the span of two years, hadn't prompted a fit of temper, Sloan didn't know what would. But he smiled and thanked her for the mug of coffee she placed in front of him.

She bent slightly to study his face. "Your wound seems to be healing up nicely."

As her fingertip traced the still-raw area, he closed his eyes and inhaled the faint scent of flowers clinging to her hair. Did she understand how much self-restraint it required to keep from pulling her into his lap and smothering her beautiful face with kisses?

It seemed she'd read his mind, for Shaina chose that precise moment to sit in the chair beside him.

"Have you seen Rafe Preston since...since he did that to you, I mean?" she asked, wrapping both hands around her mug.

Sloan nodded. "Couple of hours ago, matter of fact, as I was leaving town." *And if looks could kill, I'd be toes-up and six feet deep right about now.*

She rested an elbow on the table and propped her chin on a fist. "Jennie told me how—or should I say *why*—it happened."

"I wasn't aware she knew anything about it."

"She doesn't miss much, that Jennie."

Sloan only nodded.

"Jennie said she would have thanked you publicly, except that it might have caused your reputation more harm than good. Last I heard, she's working on a secret plan to show her appreciation."

"Appreciation for *what?*"

"For saving her life, of course. She says you're a hero. And after what you were willing to do outside just now, I'd have to agree."

Hero, indeed. In the weeks before the fever squeezed the life from his adopted family, his so-called mother had all but forced food down his throat. Simon later explained what Sloan had been too young to realize at the time: She'd done it in hopes that at least one of her slavish sons would survive. All these years later, he still hadn't shaken the notion that if he hadn't been such a greedy young boy—if he'd shared the weak broth and crusts of bread—it might have provided just enough strength to save his brother.

"You know what I wish Jennie would do? To thank you, I mean?"

Sloan shook his head. "She doesn't owe me anything. Not even a thank-you."

Shaina studied his face, then said, "Humility is a good thing if it doesn't go to extremes. You risked your life to protect Jennie from that horrible, horrible man. Only God knows what you spared her. And because you did, you'll wear that scar for the rest of your life." She brightened. "Why, it's like a badge of honor!"

He could only shake his head again and hope for something—anything—to distract her.

"I wish she'd stop *talking* about building a hospital and just *do* it," Shaina went on. "I've always dreamed of working as a nurse again. If she owned the place, well, it would be like a dream come true for all of Denver *and* for me."

He thought of his plan to make that very thing possible. "It's a good idea," Sloan conceded. And then he faked a yawn. "I believe I'll hit the hay. James was right—the sun will be up before we know it."

He bid her good night and hurried to his room. It wasn't likely he'd sleep a wink, but if he did, he hoped his dreams would be filled with a bighearted, bright-eyed beauty named Shaina, rather than the doubts that had plagued him all these many years.

Chapter Eighteen

Rafe Preston tossed back a jigger of whiskey and wiped the back of his hand across his lips. "Did you see his eyes bug out when we stared 'im down?" he said with a snicker.

"Did my jobless heart good to see *somethin'* take the place of that better-'n-everybody look on his face." Joe Michaels banged his empty glass on the bar. "Smitty, another round for me an' my friend, here."

Friend? Preston bristled slightly as the barkeep finished polishing a clean beer mug. After adding it to the pyramid of steins above the cash register, he met Michaels' eyes in the mirror.

"Thought I heard you say you're tapped out," Smitty said.

"Aw, your mama musta tied your apron too tight. I never said nothin' of the kind."

Liar, Rafe thought.

Michaels made a move as if to unholster his revolver, and Preston froze. The man spent most of his waking hours looking for trouble. And these days, with the mines reducing production and honest work so hard to come by, trouble was far too easy to find.

"Bring us another round," Michaels growled, "'fore I do somethin' you'll be sorry for."

One eye squinting into the fog of his cigar, Smitty turned, slow and smooth, and reached under the bar. "You don't want to do that," he said, thumb on the hammer of a Colt Peacemaker. "You're completely drunk. Go home and sleep it off, and I'll forget about your bad manners."

The piano no longer plinked, the high-pitched giggles of dance hall girls faded, and cards stopped shuffling as a dangerous kind of quiet settled over the saloon.

Preston got down off his stool and laid a hand on Michaels' shoulder. "Easy, Joe. You wouldn't want Smitty, here, to lose his job for pourin' free drinks, now, would you?" He looked at the barkeep. "It's nothin' personal, ain't that right, Smitty?"

Michaels laid both hands on the counter, a reluctant but noticeable surrender.

"I'll buy your last round," the bartender said, putting the pistol away.

A collective sigh of relief was quickly drowned out by bawdy laughter and the clink of poker chips as Smitty refilled their shot glasses.

"But that's the last one," he said, slamming the cash register drawer.

Michaels glared as Smitty walked to the other end of the bar. "I've a mind to plug 'im right where he stands, just on principle."

The maniacal look on his face made Preston think he might just do it.

"Aw, you got your free drink. What's your beef?"

He muttered something under his breath, then picked up the glass. "Yeah, well, a man oughtn't have to endure two humiliations in the same day."

Preston downed his whiskey in one gulp. "Yeah, well, it wasn't Smitty who fired you."

Michaels gave that some thought, then polished off his whiskey and staggered toward the exit.

Smitty went back to swabbing the counter. "See you tomorrow, boys."

Michaels glared over his shoulder. "For two bits, I really would plug 'im, just to damper that know-it-all mouth of his."

"Easy, pal," Preston said, patting Michaels on the back.

"Keep your hands to yourself, *pal*, unless you know a way I can come up with rent money before the weekend."

"Matter of fact, I do. Go home and get some sleep. Tomorrow, when you're sober, I'll tell you all about it."

As Preston walked toward his room behind the feed and grain, an idea began percolating. He'd already agreed to partner with the illegitimate sons of two legendary outlaws. Leo and Jimmer had ridden with their notorious fathers just long enough to learn the art of ambush.

Their well-thought-out plan to derail the Central Pacific in the tunnel at Altman Pass would make them all rich.

While Preston took care of the Pinkertons who had been hired to protect the gold and silver bars intended for delivery at the Carson City Mint, Jimmer would toss the cache to Leo, who'd be waiting on the old wagon road below. They were one man short, and Preston intended to recommend Joe Michaels to ride ahead and dislodge the track, then head down to help Leo with one of three mule teams. He pictured the short-tempered blowhard with his slate-gray eyes, scruffy beard, and long, yellow teeth. Desperate for money, he would agree to clean up after the mules…until that hair-trigger temper got the better of him. Sooner or later, he'd say something to rile the others, and end up carrying lead in his sagging belly instead of his loading his share of gold and silver into his saddlebags.

For two bits, Rafe thought, *I'll plug 'im myself.* Not in the canyon, where they'd divvy up the loot. No, he'd find an excuse to stick with Michaels after they headed in four different directions to confuse the law. It would mean more weight for his horse to carry, but he could easily afford another.

Preston entered his sparsely furnished room, tossed his hat and coat onto the bureau, and toed off his boots. After unholstering his revolver, he inspected the chamber, counted six cartridges, and snapped it shut. The door didn't lock, and he slept easier with the double-action Colt under his pillow.

He stretched out on his squeaky cot, smirking as he recalled how he'd come to own the .38. Just last week, he'd been in the saloon when a stranger had slid onto the stool beside him. It had been worth the price of a bottle of whiskey to find out why the grizzled fellow had looked so familiar. Wanted for a brazen holdup in Leadville that had cost three bank employees their lives, he'd hidden $40,000 under a lodgepole pine near Clear Creek. "When the heat's off," the drunkard had boasted, "I'll fetch it. Won't never have to work another day in my life."

How hard could it be, Preston had wondered, to find a tree that normally grew at higher altitudes? A wanted man himself, he couldn't collect the bounty, so he'd paid himself with the Colt and the sixty dollars he'd found in the outlaw's pockets.

Preston pictured an imaginary chalkboard on the ceiling and wrote $100,000.00 with his fingertip. Leo and Jimmer would no doubt squander their $25,000 on whiskey and women. But he'd invest his share—$37,500—on that little plot of land near Clear Creek. And after he found the old man's stash, *he'd* never have to work another day in his life.

The comforting thought was all it took to lull him to sleep.

Chapter Nineteen

The church was one of Shaina's favorite buildings in Denver. When the morning sun hit the façade this way, the fragments of mica in the granite cornerstones glittered, and the stained-glass windows winked with rainbow hues. The tall, slender steeple glowed bright and white, leading the eye to the copper cross, covered in verdigris, that reached toward heaven like a child with arms open to receive its father's embrace.

Shaina hurried through the black wrought-iron gate that surrounded the front courtyard, then raced up the brick steps to prop open the entry doors. Sloan and Abe carried Mable inside and settled her in the front pew as James confiscated a padded bench from the altar. It was so good to see her out and about that Shaina's eyes misted with tears of joy. She choked back a sob, too, because no one, not even Doc Wilson, understood why Mable's leg was taking so long to heal. After concluding his last exam at the ranch, the doctor had sworn Shaina to secrecy before telling her that if the woman wasn't up and about by Easter, he'd have no choice but to perform exploratory surgery in hopes of finding the cause.

James sat on the aisle to Mable's left, and Shaina took the seat to her right.

Sloan rested a hand on the back of the pew and leaned in close enough to whisper into Shaina's ear, "Save me a seat."

As she laid her purse in the seat beside her, Mable frowned at Sloan. "Where are you off to?"

"If you must know, I'm going to help Abe move the horses and buggy round back."

"Whatever for? You'll just need to move them right back again when the service ends."

He smiled in a way Shaina could only describe as paternal.

"True enough. But in the event someone else needs to be carried into church, we wouldn't want to block the walk, now, would we?"

Mable chuckled as he walked away. "I wonder," she said, leaning into Shaina, "if that man will ever figure out how much fun it is to tease him."

They'd shared the same house for nearly two decades. Surely, Mable knew that Sloan was on to her—

"Well, well, well. If it isn't Shaina Sterling."

Instantly, Shaina tensed. She would know that voice anywhere. Turning slightly, she smiled over her shoulder. "Good morning, Priscilla."

"You look"—Priscilla Macmillan's gaze skimmed Shaina's plain blue dress—"lovely. And I see you've forgotten your bustle, as usual."

"I've never worn a bustle, and, God willing, I'll never have to." Shaina forced a cheery smile and leaned back for a better look at Priscilla's outfit, a close-fitting burgundy velvet jacket with a wide panel of shimmering satin on the bodice that flared out at the waist, accenting the billowing folds of the matching skirt.

"You look lovely, as well. How are you today?"

"Never better. But the question is, how are *you*?" Priscilla tucked her green velvet gloves into a matching drawstring purse.

Due to the harsh winter weather and her personal situation, Shaina hadn't been to church in many months. She'd missed walking up the aisle on Harper's arm, nodding polite hellos to neighbors, and singing along with the choir. But being scrutinized by women like Priscilla? She hadn't missed that at all.

Priscilla adjusted the green mesh veil of her jaunty hat and turned to her husband, a thin, pale man with muttonchops and tiny round spectacles.

"I can't remember the last time we've seen Shaina here at church, can you, dear?" she asked him.

"I haven't the foggiest notion," came his bored reply, "but it's good to see you, Mrs. Sterling." Then he went back to talking to the fellow behind him.

Priscilla leaned forward and laid a hand on Shaina's shoulder. "I'm so, so, *so* sorry about what happened to your beautiful Sterling Hall. Why, you must have been positively heartbroken to lose it!"

Shaina didn't know how to react.

"Were you able to salvage anything?"

"Only the clothes I was wearing at the time."

Priscilla sighed. "Ah. Well, that explains it, then."

When Sloan had taken her shopping that day, Shaina had been only too mindful of the fact that she'd insisted on repaying him for every item. The blouse and skirt, with the matching short-waisted jacket, had made perfect sense, since each piece could easily be paired with others to look like different outfits.

"I'm sure it'll take a while to replace all your lovely gowns. If I can help in any way...."

"Oh, I doubt I'll bother," Shaina said. "But thanks all the same."

Sloan chose that moment to return. "Mrs. Macmillan," he said, tipping an imaginary hat at Priscilla. Then he scooted in beside Shaina and whispered, "Do you need my handkerchief?"

"Your handkerchief?" She sat back just far enough to study his face. "Whatever for?"

"Why, to slow the bleeding, of course."

"The bleeding?"

Facing forward, he muttered out of the corner of his mouth, "Her sharp tongue precedes her."

Shaina hid her giggle behind her hand as the preacher waved Sloan to the altar.

"What do you suppose that's all about?" she asked Mable.

"My best guess is, the good reverend is fixin' to ask Sloan to sing."

"I had no idea he could—"

"Oh, darlin' girl, are you in for a real treat."

His speaking voice was pleasant enough, and he was certainly easy on the eyes. As usual, he stood like a well-trained soldier, boots shoulder-width apart, shoulders back. His dark trousers skimmed muscular legs, and the matching coat partially covered his sidearm. Unlike so many others, he hadn't topped off the collarless shirt with a puffy tie or one of those double-breasted brocade vests so popular in men's fashion these days.

He took a step closer to the reverend, one hand resting on his pistol's grip, the other on Meb Truett's shoulder. What were they talking about, she wondered, to inspire such serious expressions?

Priscilla leaned forward and almost rested her chin on Shaina's shoulder as she whispered, "Unless you want the congregation to think you're sweet on your *boss*, you should probably stop ogling him that way."

Ogling? And why the emphasis on "boss"?

She bristled as the heat of a blush crept into her cheeks, not because the comment embarrassed her, but because she'd allowed herself to react at all. On too many occasions, she'd heard Priscilla take aim at some poor soul's least attractive trait. After learning that Harper had left her flat broke, she'd gone out of her way to avoid being a target of that sharp tongue. If she happened upon Priscilla while running errands, she'd say, "Hilda is polishing silver today," or "Hilda is busy sewing new draperies for the dining hall." The excuses had satisfied her snobbish friends, but once Broze and Hilda had left, Shaina had started avoiding the other women altogether by shopping during the early-morning hours, while they were still fast asleep. If it weren't all so sad and shameful, she'd laugh about how low she'd stooped to protect her "sterling" reputation!

"I hope he's paying you well to nurse Mable back to health," Priscilla added.

If she didn't come clean now, then when?

Shaina turned all the way around in the pew and faced Priscilla, fully prepared to tell her everything: that Harper had gambled them into bankruptcy. That if not for Sloan's intelligent management skills, the manufactory that employed many of Denver's heads of household would have closed its doors two years ago. That without the generosity of Jennie Rogers, she would have been homeless long before the fire. She'd be homeless now, if not for Sloan's bigheartedness!

But Mable groaned, prompting Shaina to sit back down. "What is it?" she asked, taking Mable's hands in her own. "Are you in pain?" She grabbed her purse. "I brought the bottle of—"

"I don't need laudanum," Mable grumbled. "I need you to hush." She gave Shaina's hand a firm squeeze. "Don't give that uppity hypocrite another moment of your time." She pointed at the altar. "*That's* where your attention ought to be."

The moment Shaina met Sloan's eyes, he smiled and motioned for her to join him.

"What do you suppose he wants?" she asked Mable.

"Only one way to find out." The woman crooked her forefinger, and when Shaina bent closer, Mable added, "And whatever you do, don't give Miss Priss the satisfaction of so much as a backward glance."

Nodding, Shaina took a deep breath and headed for the altar. Even as she lifted her skirt to climb the steps, she felt Priscilla's eyes on her. Heard her whispering, too, no doubt to ensure every other woman took note.

Pastor Truett took her hand. "So good to see you, Shaina. Sloan, here, has been telling me what a lifesaver you've been."

She glanced up at him, and upon seeing the proud smile on his handsome face, she sent a silent prayer heavenward. *Please, Lord, don't let me blush and gush like a moony-eyed schoolgirl!*

"Mable looks good, real good," the pastor continued, "and I know that's largely your doing. And according to Sloan, here, you've put just as much effort into running the house and meeting the needs of his ranch hands."

She was about to insist that it was Sloan who'd been the lifesaver, giving her a home when she had nowhere to go and a job when she needed it most. But Truett took her completely by surprise by saying, "Mason would be so proud."

Her father-in-law?

"Don't look so confused. You should know that he came to me on several occasions, looking for guidance on how to best handle Harper's recklessness." He glanced around the sanctuary, now filling with the usual parishioners, then gave her hand a slight squeeze. "He thought of you as the daughter he'd never had, and it distressed him to see how his son's indiscretions were hurting you."

She'd tried so hard to hide her true feelings. How had Mason known the depth of her concern over Harper's risky behavior? And why had the reverend chosen this moment, in front of God and Sloan and the entire congregation, to tell her about it?

"I'm sure you know that my father-in-law guarded his emotions carefully, so I'm touched to hear he cared enough to share that information with you," she told the reverend. "As for what I've done at the ranch, all I can say is, after everything Sloan has done for me, I only wish I could do more."

Sloan chuckled. "See? Didn't I tell you she'd react this way?"

"Yes," Truett said, "you most certainly did." He gave her hand another squeeze. "Sloan's confidence in you is the reason I'd like to talk to you privately—after the service—about a matter of great importance to me. To my wife, as well."

Shaina looked at Sloan, but instead of answers, more questions surfaced as she tried to discern the meaning behind the smile that warmed her all the way down to her toes.

"Shall I meet you in your office?"

"No, just stick with Sloan." He released her hand. "He knows."

She saw Mable, straining to pick up anything that might help her understand what they were talking about. Shaina gave a helpless shrug, because she didn't understand, either.

It was next to impossible to focus on the Scripture readings that preceded the pastor's homily. And though she tried to pay attention, her mind wandered during the sermon, because she couldn't imagine what the pastor wanted to discuss with her.

Pastor Truett asked the congregation to turn to Luke 24:29, then began reading aloud. "'They constrained him, saying, Abide with us: for it is toward evening, and the day is far spent.'" Pausing, he nodded and smiled before continuing. "'And he went in to tarry with them.'" Then he signaled the organist, who played the first rousing chords of "Abide with Me."

The first time she'd heard the hymn, Shaina had been a newcomer to Denver. It was a lovely piece that never failed to move her. But today, sung by Sloan's beautiful baritone, the lyrics held such meaning that goose pimples arose on her arms, rendering her unable to sing even one note.

"Told you so," Mable whispered near her ear. And when the hymn ended, she added, "I've always believed that if the Almighty allowed us to hear the angel Gabriel sing, he'd sound just like that."

Shaina had to agree, and her buoyant mood kept her afloat all through the rest of the service. Afterward, Sloan and Abe gently loaded Mable into the buggy, and as James took the reins, he promised that he and the young hand would look after her until Shaina and Sloan were finished speaking with Truett. A moment later, Shaina followed Sloan down the path connecting the church to the parsonage.

The pastor met them at the door. "I'd ask Tillie to serve some tea," he said as they stepped inside, "but she's, uh, still in bed."

"I'm sorry she's not feeling well," Shaina said. "If you'll show me the way to the kitchen, I'd be happy to brew a kettle. Might be just the thing she needs to settle her stomach."

Truett and Sloan exchanged a glance. Was Mrs. Truett's illness the reason for this meeting?

"Right this way," Truett said, leading them down the hall. And while Shaina prepared the tea, Sloan and the pastor talked quietly.

"I heard you and Abe will be going to Cheyenne in a few weeks," Truett said.

"You heard right," Sloan affirmed. "This winter was hard on the oldest bulls. We lost two during the January blizzard, so the first chance I got, I wired a friend who raises Galloway cattle. He claims their shaggy coats make them perfect for Colorado's cold winters, so we're going to put 'em to the test."

Truett nodded. "Long ride to Wyoming, though. How long do you think the trip up and back will take?"

"Weeks…if we were riding. But we're taking the train. Easier on the cows, and a sight easier on us, too."

It was the first Shaina had heard about the trip. Apparently, Sloan and Abe had made these plans earlier that week while rounding up the newborn calves. She wished that the pastor would ask how long the journey would take by train. They hadn't even packed yet, and already she missed Sloan.

You're being ridiculous! she chided herself. Handsome, successful, and powerful, Sloan Remington could have any eligible woman in Denver. In Colorado. In the country! What would a man like that want with a needy, penniless widow?

There was an atlas in Sloan's library, she remembered. Hopefully, one of the maps would tell her how many miles separated the ranch from Cheyenne. She uncovered a loaf of bread, carved off three slices, coated them with butter and honey, and served a slice to each man. After delivering mugs of tea to Sloan and Truett, she filled a third and set it beside the third slice of bread on a napkin-covered tray.

"If you're thinking of bringing that to Tillie," the pastor said, "don't waste your time."

Both his tone and the look on his face were troubling, but she didn't ask for an explanation. Instead, she carried the third mug to the table.

Once she sat down beside Sloan, the pastor said, "Do you remember a few years back, when Tillie and I lost our son?"

How could she forget that long, heartbreaking day? She, Harper, and Mason had gone to the funeral service, then stood side by side in the icy wind as Truett croaked out a solemn, halfhearted graveside eulogy, after which they'd attended the somber reception.

"Yes," she said tentatively, "I remember it well." She also remembered the odd, inappropriate things people had said as they filed from the church basement: "There's more to this story than meets the eye," and "It's as though Tillie blames herself for the boy's death."

"Sloan is the only one I could trust when…." Unable to continue, Pastor Truett hung his head.

"I helped bring Tim home," Sloan said quietly, and the pastor's relief was palpable.

Brought Tim home from where?

As though he could read her mind, Sloan mouthed, *"Tell you later."*

The pastor exhaled a long, ragged breath. "You see, it was Tillie who found Tim. Found him hanging…from a rope slung over the basement rafters. It changed her. Changed me, too. But I quickly learned that it helped if I lost myself in work. I made improvements to the church, met the needs of the congregation, studied the Word like never before." He stared straight ahead. "Tillie…Tillie lost herself in a bottle."

"Lost" was the perfect word to describe the way Tillie had looked at the funeral, and ever since. Just when it seemed she'd pulled herself together, she would collapse in a wailing heap. Shortly before the fire, Shaina had overheard two men at the grocer's, discussing Tillie as if she were a squeaky hinge rather than the woman who, for years, had cheerfully served her community. "If Truett can't get his wife under control after all this time, how can he run the church?" asked the first. The second man had not only agreed but even suggested convening a meeting to discuss replacing the pastor with "someone man enough to keep his woman in line." How much worse would it have been if they'd known about the drinking?

Suddenly, Shaina understood. Maybe they *had* found out and issued the pastor an ultimatum. And a deadline. But if he thought Shaina held any sway with the men in charge, he was seriously mistaken.

"Have you heard the rumors? About my Tillie, I mean."

"No, I haven't." She'd heard nothing about the drinking, if that's what he meant. "In truth, I've been out of touch with society for quite some time."

He leaned forward and clasped his hands on the tabletop. "And I suppose we're fortunate that her problem is still our dirty little secret."

And he was right. Because, to the sanctimonious men who'd hired him, bankrupt widows, ladies of the evening, and God-fearing grieving mothers like Tillie were cut from the same cloth…and just as dispensable. If they *had* gotten wind of that dirty little secret, the Truetts would already be gone.

"I miss our boy, too. But Tillie?" The pastor sighed yet again.

"We all grieve in our own ways, and in our own time," Sloan said.

Spoken like a man who knew the pain of loss, Shaina thought.

"I think it just takes longer," he added, "for some to realize and accept that the one we've lost is in a better place."

Truett nodded. "After the doctor diagnosed Tim with cancer, he grew despondent. He wouldn't let us pray over him. Said that if God was capable of performing a cure, He should have prevented the disease before it ever seized him." Again, Truett hung his head. "So I must disagree. Tim is *not* in a better place."

Sloan looked as helpless as Shaina felt, and they both sat in stunned silence as Truett quoted from Scripture: *"Know ye not that your body is the temple of the Holy Ghost which is in you, which ye have of God, and ye are not your own? For ye are bought with a price: therefore glorify God in your body, and in your spirit, which are God's."*

"Yes, I know it well," Shaina said. "First Corinthians six, verses nineteen and twenty. I must have recited the passage a hundred times after I learned the truth about Harper's death."

The pastor met her eyes as Sloan said, "What do you mean, the truth about Harper's death?"

It seemed that God had intended this Sunday to be a day of confessions.

"A few months before the fire," she began slowly, "I went through the house, looking for something of value I could sell to keep the pantry stocked. Most of the furniture and art had already been sold. The only piece of jewelry I had left was my wedding band, and I couldn't bring myself to part with it. I hoped to find something of worth in Mason's library."

Her hands began to tremble, and she hid them in her lap.

"I found a journal. Harper's journal, to be precise." Shaina remembered how the careful script had deteriorated into a sloppy scrawl as the page numbers increased, how the very last entry had been practically illegible. She could almost smell the sharp scent of the brandy that stained the pages, and she could feel the sting of tears as she closed her eyes and narrated his final lines: *"My father was right: I'm hardly worth the oxygen required to keep me alive. So I've bought shiny new bullets for my gun. After tonight, I'll no longer waste perfectly good air. God forgive me."*

Chapter Twenty

She'd known the truth for months, yet she'd kept Harper's secret? Sloan had never met a woman like Shaina. Even now, she seemed determined not to wallow in self-pity. Was she too good to be true, or had she simply perfected the art of subterfuge?

"So you see, Pastor Truett," she was saying, "I don't believe for a minute that Tim isn't in heaven right now, waiting for you and Tillie to join him."

Truett shook his head. "The sixth commandment is quite clear, Mrs. Sterling: *'Thou shalt not kill.'* I don't presume to know the mind of God, but if I had to guess, I'd say that He meant we are not to take a life, not even our own."

"I believed that, too…at first," Shaina said gently. "I went searching for verses in the Bible that would make me feel better about how much I'd lost, and I found some comfort in First Corinthians ten, verse thirteen, where God promises not to test us beyond our capabilities, and assures us that when things seem impossible, He'll provide a way out of our troubles."

"Only 'some comfort'?" Truett asked.

"I'm ashamed to admit it now, but I judged Harper harshly. When I first learned he'd taken the coward's way out and left me alone to clean up his messes, I hated him. I needed to understand, and in looking for answers, I found seven references to suicide in Scripture."

Calmly, self-assuredly, she listed them: King Saul and his armor-bearer. Also Abimelech, Samson, Ahithophel, Zimri, and, of course, Judas. She cited the corresponding references, too, surprising Sloan and the pastor alike.

"Don't look so shocked, you two. Studying the Word is the only thing that spared me from living my whole life feeling sorry for myself. The good Lord knows I had ample time to read the Bible!"

And ample time to practice the art of deception?

Shaina continued, "Don't we all go to the grave with a few unnamed, unforgiven sins? A person who takes his own life is out of his mind, wouldn't you say?"

"Yes, I suppose you could say that," Truett allowed.

He seemed to have more to say, but before he could come up with a biblical rationale to rebut her question, Shaina tacked on, "Do you really think that God, in His infinite wisdom and mercy—which means He knew that both Harper and Tim weren't in their right minds when they took their own lives—would turn them away?"

The pastor sat back, crossed both arms over his chest, and stared at the ceiling. "I don't know. But it's something to study and pray about, I'll give you that."

Shaina helped herself to a slice of honeyed bread. "But surely you didn't invite me here to discuss Scripture passages."

Truett cleared his throat. "Ah, yes. That." Hands clasped on the table once more, he said, "You see, Mrs. Sterling—"

"Please, call me Shaina."

"Very well. You see, Shaina, I had hoped that a change of scenery might be good for Tillie. Some new faces. Some honest hard work to keep her hands occupied, and a good old friend—Mable—to occupy her mind."

He *had* hoped? Sloan wondered if it meant the pastor had changed his mind.

"In light of all you've told me today—about Harper, that is," Truett continued, "I think...perhaps...." He scrubbed a hand over his face and started over. "I believe it would be unfair to expect you to run Sloan's house, care for Mable, and watch over Tillie, as well."

The man made a good point, and Sloan might have said so, if Shaina hadn't drilled him with a wide-eyed stare.

"Is that what you think, too? That by coming clean, I've somehow proven myself incapable of shouldering the load?"

"Nothing could be further from the truth," Sloan assured her. "You're one of the most capable human beings I've ever encountered."

He sat, mesmerized by the big, long-lashed eyes that searched his face for...duplicity? Insincerity? Sloan didn't know what she hoped to find written there, but oh, what he wouldn't give for the power to read that quick, amazing mind!

She shoved her chair back from the table and got to her feet. "Well then, Pastor—not that my opinion matters all that much in the grand scheme of things—you should know that I completely agree that a change of pace and a switch of scenery will probably do Mrs. Truett a world of good. I give you my word that I'll keep her just busy enough to forget the dirty little secret that she believes brings her comfort."

With that, she headed for Tillie's room.

"Where are you going?" Truett asked.

Shaina stopped just short of the hall. "Why, I'm going to talk with Tillie, of course. I'm sure you'll agree that if I explain how overwhelmed I am at the ranch, and how much I'd appreciate her assistance—temporarily, of course—she'll be more receptive to the idea."

She must have read his silence to mean he *did* agree, because Shaina smiled before disappearing down the hall, leaving Sloan and Truett to stare at their mugs of now-cool tea and a plate of uneaten bread that was quickly growing stale.

"I can hardly believe the things I shared with her," the pastor said. "Why, I told her things I've never told anyone, not even you." He stared at the doorway. "She is a remarkable young woman."

"I couldn't agree more."

"And you're sure she can handle things all by herself?"

"But Meb, Shaina is anything *but* all by herself. She has Abe and James, and, in some ways, even Mable." Sloan sat a little taller. "And of course, she has *me*."

The admission inspired a dry grin from the pastor. "I suspected as much."

"Suspected? What do you mean?"

"You stand taller when she's near. Speak more softly. And that look on your face—"

"Good grief, man." Sloan hoped his nervous laughter didn't give him away. "You sound like Professor Norton, who taught Medieval Lyrics…the college course I nearly failed."

Calm down, he thought. Meb Truett's seminary education had included sessions in philosophy and psychology. What other explanation was there for his ability to see and hear things that weren't there?

Or was Sloan merely suffering from a massive case of denial?

"So, you're telling me it isn't necessary to block off a date on the calendar for a wedding, then?"

He cared for Shaina, about her well-being and happiness, but caring and love were two very different emotions. He'd spent countless hours watching over her, and yet he couldn't say that he really *knew* her. He had so many questions, but how could he hope for answers when she guarded so many secrets? For every ounce of his respect she had earned while deflecting life's blows, he had gained a pound of fear. Because what if, once she'd saved up enough money to get out on her own again, she returned to her former life in high society?

And then, there was the matter of his own past. What would the members of Denver's elite think of his crude beginnings?

"A wedding, indeed," Sloan muttered. He downed the mug of cold tea and grimaced. "Well, it's something to think on and pray about, I'll give you that."

The men shared a moment of quiet laughter before the pastor got to his feet. "I suppose I should go in there and see how poor Shaina is making out with Tillie. That wife of mine can be quite stubborn—difficult, even—when she puts her mind to it."

"I'm not a betting man," Sloan said, "but if I were, I'd wager Shaina is doing just fine."

Truett did not laugh. Didn't smile. Instead, his eyes filled with tears as he said, "Will you pray for me, brother? I need to hear the consolation of words, and I don't seem capable of speaking them at the moment."

Sloan had always been comfortable conversing with the Almighty in the privacy of his mind. But here and now, in the presence of a man of God?

Lord, show me what this good man needs to hear. Then he bowed his head and said, "O heavenly Father, we thank You for friendship, for homes and food and all the good things that come from Your benevolent hand. We ask that You would keep us aware how fragile life is, and remind us often that each day is a gift. Give us the wisdom to accept the trials of this life that we do not yet understand, and the heart to forgive those who confuse and confound us. You have charged some of us with the care of others, and we ask You to bless us with hearts and minds that are open to You, that You might show us how to gently guide them, and teach us how to lead by example. We ask these things in Your most holy name, amen."

Truett looked him square in the eye. "You have a good heart, Sloan Remington."

"And I couldn't agree more."

Both men turned toward the feminine voice.

Sloan didn't know whether to see her as a nosy spy or a pleasant diversion. "Shaina. How long have you been standing there?"

Hands clasped at her bosom, she said, "Exactly long enough. That was…beautiful."

You are beautiful, he wanted to say, and immediately he censured his traitorous heart. *She's an enigma*, he reminded himself, *and until and unless she trusts you enough to reveal those secrets she's harboring, you'd be wise to keep your guard up.*

And if she shared her secrets, would he share *his*?

Tillie stepped beside her.

"Meb, dear, I'd hide my clerical collar if I were you"—she pointed at Sloan—"because that boy can pray!"

Shaina slid an arm around the woman's shoulders. "Tillie has agreed to do me an enormous favor…if it's all right with you, Pastor Truett."

For a preacher, the man feigned surprise really well, Sloan thought.

"That depends, I suppose, on the favor."

Shaina explained the proposition he already knew: Tillie would ride home with her and Sloan to help out around the ranch. "I'm embarrassed to admit that I was married to Harper just long enough to grow spoiled and lazy," she said with a grin.

The Truetts had no way of knowing how far from the truth that was, but Sloan held his tongue.

"It'll be lovely feeling useful again," Tillie said, "and I'm ready to go when you are." She met her husband's eyes. "If it's all right with you, dear."

"Of course it's all right." He smiled. "I can pretend I'm a bachelor again, sleeping late and eating pie for supper, right out of the tin." He crossed the room and placed his meaty hands on her shoulders. "Have you already packed?"

"Yes, Shaina helped me."

Sloan could almost read the pastor's mind: *You didn't pack anything that comes in bottles, I hope.*

"Just two housedresses," Shaina said, "and one to wear to church on—" Eyes wide, she started for the hall. "I forgot to add a bonnet to your valise."

Once Shaina was out of earshot, Tillie said, "Meb, I want you to know that I'm going to pray extra hard tonight. And although we won't be together, I want you to promise you'll pray with me."

He looked as confused as Sloan felt.

"I *so* misjudged that sweet girl, and I feel just awful about it. So I need to ask the Lord for forgiveness."

And for the strength to overcome your addiction? Sloan asked silently.

"She's giving up her bed for me. I tried to talk her out of it, but Shaina insisted she'll be comfortable on the settee." Now, Tillie was the one who looked puzzled. "Can you believe it?"

As Sloan added another item to the growing list of things he didn't understand about Shaina, she rejoined them in the kitchen, this time carrying a suitcase of cloth and leather that looked like a cross between Doc's medical bag and a hatbox.

"I'm glad I went back for the bonnet," she said, setting the valise near the back door, "because if you decide to get some fresh air, you'll need gloves and a scarf. At the ranch, there aren't any buildings to protect us from the wind like there are here in town."

"As thoughtful and organized as you are," Tillie said, "I can't help but wonder if you really need me at the ranch at all." Hands on her hips, she faced her husband. "Meb Truett, you put her up to this, didn't you?"

She'd put the man in a tight spot. If he admitted that he had, Tillie would probably refuse to go. But, as a man of the cloth, he couldn't lie and deny it.

Shaina extended both hands, palms down. Why did it take Tillie's wide-eyed shock to make Sloan notice the broken fingernails and rough, red knuckles?

"If we alternate chores involving water, neither of us has to look this way."

Tillie worried her lower lip, but whether she was trying to make sense of the situation or too much time had elapsed since her last drink, Sloan couldn't say.

Shaina picked up the suitcase. "How selfish of me to take you away from your husband. Mable will understand why you couldn't come, once I explain it to her."

"Yes, perhaps it's best that I stay here." She relieved Shaina of the valise. "Can you forgive me? And tell Mable that I tried? That I'm sorry?"

"There's nothing to forgive," Shaina assured her. "I'm sure Mable will agree."

Now, Sloan added a line to the list of reasons to admire Shaina. And because he appreciated the way she filled out the simple white shirt and blue-gray skirt, he added another. The wide black belt accented her tiny waist, and the tiny red bow tucked under her collar drew his eye to her lovely face.

"Well," Sloan said, shrugging into his coat, "I suppose we should head out."

"Let me just tidy up this mess I made," Shaina said, carrying the breakfast mugs and plates to the sink.

"Leave those," Tillie said. "I'll do them after…."

After you've hunted down a hidden bottle of whiskey? Sloan finished.

"Tillie's right," the pastor said, taking her hands in his. "Leave the dishes. It'll give us something to do to pass the time together."

Guilt pulsed through Sloan's veins when he saw Shaina hide her chafed hands behind her back. When they returned to the ranch, he'd bring her a tin of Vaseline. He'd never cared for the greasy stuff himself, but the ranch hands claimed it relieved the drying effects of hay baling and rounding up strays during dust storms and blizzards.

"Besides, you've already done enough," the pastor added.

"But I didn't—"

"You were willing to," Truett said, "and in my book, that's the same thing."

She slipped into her short-waisted jacket, then hastily tied the black hat ribbon under her chin.

They said their good-byes to the Truetts, then followed the path back to the church. "I hope Tillie won't be upset with me," Shaina muttered.

Penny snorted and bobbed her head, clearly glad to see him. He stroked her withers, chuckling as she nuzzled his neck. "Why would Tillie be upset with you?"

Shaina hugged herself to fend off the chilly wind. "Because I emptied three bottles of whiskey out her bedroom window."

"Makes me wonder who buys the stuff, and why Truett hasn't told everyone in town they're not to sell her anything."

"He can't."

"Why not?"

"Because if he does, everyone will know their dirty little—" She pressed her gloved fingers to her lips.

"What now?" It riled him slightly that Shaina sided with Truett's decision to prize his reputation over a method that might help curtail his wife's addiction.

"They took the wagon," Shaina pointed out. "Abe and James, I mean, when they drove Mable home."

Now he understood: The only way to get back to the ranch was if she rode behind him on Penny.

"Well, look at it this way." He hoisted himself into the saddle, then held out his hand to her. "Since I'll be up front, blocking the wind, maybe you'll stop shivering."

She sighed resignedly and let him help her up. Without being told, she leaned in close and slipped her arms around his waist. Halfway home, the wind kicked up, and Shaina snuggled even closer, her cheek pressed against his back.

And the gap between care and love grew a little smaller.

Chapter Twenty-one

January added two feet of snow to the amount that had already blanketed Denver. Hundreds of the county's horses and cattle starved, stranded in wind-whipped drifts. Hundreds more froze to death in the subzero temperatures that imprisoned people in their own homes. But when the weather finally broke, folks took full advantage by attending an impromptu winter hoedown.

The walls of the community center pulsed with the lively music of the jug band. Two lines—men in one, women in the other—faced each other in the center of a huge circle. Clapping their hands and tapping their toes, they waited, some in fancy party garb, others in the clothes they'd worn to work that day, to follow the caller's instructions.

Shaina had never attended a function like this, not even back in Missouri.

"Oh, how I wish I could get out there on the floor," Mable said.

Shaina patted the older woman's knee. "Maybe they'll do this again next year. You're sure to be good as new by then."

The woman shrugged. "Maybe." She brightened to say, "Would you just look at Elsie and Abe! I have a feeling we'll be goin' to a wedding before summer's out!"

"I wonder why they haven't joined the dancers."

James laughed. "Because they'd have to quit holdin' hands, that's why."

"And dance with other people," Sloan added.

"And pay attention to what their feet are doin'," Mable pointed out, "and they can't do that, all goggle-eyed like they are."

When Shaina and Harper had first met, they hadn't been much older than Abe and Elsie. But they'd never looked at each other that way.

"Hey," James said, "there's Del Peterson over there. I hear he's fixin to buy some bulls from a rancher in Boulder."

Sloan had just come inside after securing the team. "Starting to snow again," he said, brushing flakes from his shoulders. "I hate to say it, but we shouldn't stay long."

James shook his head. "Ain't gonna be easy breakin' the news to Mr. Sweet-on-Elsie over there."

Sloan followed his gaze to the far corner, where Abe and Elsie stood hand in hand. His expression softened as he said, "Yep, that boy's a goner, all right."

In the months she'd spent at Remington Ranch, Shaina had seen how well Sloan treated his employees. He kept the bunkhouse equipped with every creature comfort, never asked the men to perform any chore he wasn't willing to do himself, and commanded their respect…even that of shifty-eyed Leo. But there was something different in the way Sloan interacted with Abe, something closer to a relationship between big brother and little brother than boss and ranch hand. Over the years, James and Mable had become substitute parents. Did Sloan see Shaina as part of his makeshift family, too?

He looked mildly surprised to catch her staring, and to hide it, Shaina pretended to straighten his string tie. "There. Much better."

One side of his mouth lifted in a tender grin, and for a moment, she thought he might just lean in and kiss her. But all too soon, he blinked, as if realizing where he was and what he'd almost done. He ran a finger inside his collar, then drove his hand through his hair as he turned to James.

"So what's this I hear about Del Peterson buying cows closer to home?"

"Don't know any of the details."

"I say let's ask him. I've been dealing with Lem Bedford in Wyoming, and I like the man. But getting to Boulder would be a whole lot easier than making a trip to Cheyenne."

As the men crossed the floor, Mable tapped Shaina's arm. "You gave me a chill just now, breathin' that big old sigh."

Were her feelings that perceptible? "Of course I'm relieved, but only because Sloan's right. Boulder is a lot closer to home than Cheyenne. Why, a trip like that would—"

"You can fool James, and maybe even yourself, but you ain't foolin' *me*. I see the way you look at him when you think nobody's paying attention." Mable pointed at Elsie and Abe. "Just. Like. *That*."

It took every bit of self-control she could muster to keep from burying her face in her hands. Because if she did, Mable would have proof that she'd been right.

"Tucker and his wife seem happy, don't you think?" Shaina said, trying to change the subject.

Mable shook her head, clearly recognizing the distraction for what it was.

"The children look happy, too."

Mable snorted. "Well, Sarah's still barely more than a bride. Let's see how things shake out after the newness wears off." She shook her head again, and this time, she added a frown. "Never did understand all that mail-order bride business. I mean, honestly—how'd Tuck know it wouldn't be a gorilla in a sunbonnet that he'd meet at the train station?"

"He probably didn't. But after everything he and the boys have been through, losing Lizzie so suddenly and all, I suppose Tucker felt he had no choice but to step out in faith."

"I suppose." Mable was quiet for some time, and then she said, "He would've lost the house, too, you know, if it weren't for Sloan."

Shaina dragged a chair closer to Mable's and sat. "What do you mean?"

"Lizzie had been gone, oh, no more than a month when Sloan heard about the dire straits that poor man was in. So he gave Tuck a promotion over at the plant. Said he needed someone with a sharp eye to make sure the right steam engine parts got shipped off to the right customers in a timely manner. Wasn't long after that he sent away for Slim Sarah, there."

During her years of marriage to Harper, Shaina hadn't paid much attention to what they produced at Sterling Manufactory. The fact that Sloan had created a position so that Tucker could keep a roof over his sons' heads—without feeling like a charity case—didn't surprise her in the least. She couldn't resist looking over at the man who'd rescued her, too. How many others had there been?

"I've seen twigs with more meat on their bones," Mable was saying, still speaking of Sarah. "Frail-lookin' as she is, how's she gonna keep them young'uns in line once they stand eye to eye with her?"

"Oh, I'm sure she's far sturdier than she looks," Shaina mused. "Besides, by the time the boys have grown that tall, they'll love her so much, they wouldn't dream of being disobedient or disrespectful."

"The eternal optimist, eh?"

Shaina shrugged. "You know what they say—you'll never see a rainbow or a sunrise if you're always looking down."

"Would you bring me a cup of water so I can rinse the sugar out of my mouth?"

The friends shared a moment of laughter, which drew the attention of Molly Vernon.

"What's so funny, you two?"

"Oh," Mable said, sobering at the sight of the reporter, "I just shared a little joke with Shaina, here."

"I love jokes. Tell me, too!"

"Why are lawyers like restless invalids?" Mable asked.

Molly dutifully responded, "I have no idea."

"Because first they lie on one side, and then they lie on the other."

Molly managed a thin smile. "It doesn't take much to entertain you two, does it?"

"Well, poor Mable has been cooped up inside for an awfully long stretch, so she takes full advantage of every opportunity to enjoy herself," Shaina put in.

The reporter all but ignored the explanation. "I haven't seen you since the earthquake, Shaina. A dozen times, I've wanted to ride out to discuss the fire, but there always seems to be a wedding or a funeral or some social event that Father wants covered for the newspaper."

Pausing, she cast a fleeting look toward Sloan. "So tell me," she said, wiggling her eyebrows, "is he a benevolent employer?"

Shaina didn't appreciate the position Molly's question put her in, and she saw no reason to pretend otherwise. "Oh, but aren't you the tricky one."

Molly made an expression of feigned innocence as Shaina continued, "If I make up some tall tale about Sloan's tyrannical management style, it'll result in an ugly rumor. And if I tell the truth, gossip of an entirely different nature will circulate."

"Frankly, Shaina, I'm surprised you think I'm that type of reporter." Molly stood up straighter. "I follow the facts. Period."

"It wasn't my intention to insult you or your work, so if I did, I apologize," Shaina said. "But I'm sure you can see the spot you put me in. Sloan is kind and fair, but he *is* my boss." Shaina gave the reporter time to process the information before adding, "And, as you're no doubt aware, I need that job."

She could almost hear Molly thinking, *What do you mean, as I'm no doubt aware?*

"It's snowing again," the reporter said instead. "Isn't that just awful!"

Shaina nodded in agreement. "We've all spent entirely too much time cooped up inside. But that's winter in Colorado for you!"

"Yes, it most certainly is." Molly scanned the room. "Oh, look," she said, pointing to Tucker and Sarah, who stood near the punch bowl. "It's the newlyweds. I've been dying to get a moment alone with the bride, to find out what it's like to travel hundreds of miles to marry a complete stranger."

"Hmm. Sounds like material for a novel, not an article for the society page," Shaina murmured.

"Why, Shaina Sterling," Molly said with a wink, "I have absolutely no idea what you're talking about!" With that, she turned and headed for the couple.

Mable waited until Molly was out of earshot to say, "Putting that old adage to the test, are you, missy?"

Shaina watched Sloan and Molly exchange polite hellos as he and James made their way across the room.

"What adage?"

"'Keep your friends close and your enemies closer.'" She grinned.

"So, Mable," Sloan said, joining them, "you've been reading those books I put in the parlor, I see."

She shrugged. "What else is there to do between darnin' socks and sewin' on buttons?"

Abe and Elsie joined them, arm in arm, both beaming.

"You saved me a trip across the floor," James said to Abe. "We need to bring the buggy round front and get Mable loaded up." He nodded toward the windows. "Snow's comin' down hard and steady, and we want to beat the storm home."

The younger man's smile didn't fade in the least as he said, "Sure, sure. Of course. But first…." He drew Elsie into a sideways hug. "We want you to be the first to know. I asked Elsie to marry me, and the fool girl said yes."

"Congratulations!" Sloan exclaimed, embracing the bride-to-be. "He's a good man, and he'll make a good husband."

"And a good father?" Elsie asked with a smile.

Sloan held Elsie at arm's length. "Well, I wouldn't trust him with the diapers and soakers. At least, not at first." Laughing, he shook Abe's hand, then patted his shoulder. "Leave it to you to find a woman who can stitch you up next time you handle barbed wire without gloves on."

If anyone else noticed the small group of men near the door, watching the revelry, he showed no signs of it. Shaina had hoped that her mistrust of Leo would ebb once she'd gotten to know him better, but it had not. If anything, he unnerved her even more. Whether it was the cold, hard glint in his dark eyes or the smirk that never left his face, she couldn't say. God willing, she'd never figure out why he looked so familiar, because something told her it could be dangerous information.

Abe and Sloan went outside to fetch the wagon while James helped Mable into her coat. She looked tired, even more than she should, considering all the rest she'd been getting since her fall. Shaina spotted Doc Wilson across the way, chatting with Deputy Bowen, and she made her way through the crowd to ask his opinion.

The deputy uttered a quiet greeting, then left them to rejoin the sheriff at the food table.

"So," the doctor said, "I take it you've heard the good news about my sister and Abe?"

"Yes, they just told us. I'm so happy for them!"

He leaned back slightly to get a better look at her face. "Why do I get the feeling you didn't come over to wish me well now that I'm finally getting the whole house to myself?"

"Because, wonderful as the news is, I came to talk to you about Mable." She held up one hand. "Don't look over there, because I know she's watching."

"What seems to be the problem?"

"Isn't it obvious? Her leg still hasn't healed! I'm afraid something serious might be wrong. Something more than the broken bones caused by her fall."

"Something like what?"

Shaina shrugged. "I don't know. The cancer, maybe, or some other bone disease."

"She's not a young woman," Doc Wilson said. "Not a small woman, either. The bones of someone her age never heal as quickly as a young person's." He squinted one eye. "She's one of the most stubborn patients I've ever treated. I wouldn't put it past her to get up in the middle of the night and hobble around when the rest of you are sleeping."

Shaina shook her head. "I sleep right down the hall. The parlor floor squeaks something fierce, and as you pointed out, she isn't a small woman. She couldn't take two steps without my hearing her." Frowning, she added, "Besides, Mable isn't a fool. Why would she deliberately do something that would jeopardize her health?"

"I'm only suggesting the possibility."

"Well, you are the doctor...."

He laughed quietly. "I'll try not to take offense at that." Sobering slightly, he added, "Let's give her another few weeks. If she's still unable to put weight on the leg, I'll look into the possibility of surgery, to see if there's more going on than meets the eye."

He'd said as much before, and it was a relief to hear him repeat it. Shaina glanced toward the door, where James and Mable were waiting. "Well, Sloan is eager to get home before the snow builds up, so I'd better get over there." She gave his arm a little squeeze. "Thanks, Amos, for taking me seriously."

He raised both eyebrows. "Why wouldn't I?"

"Because I have absolutely no medical training, for starters."

"But you spend more time with Mable than anyone else. And let's not forget what you did for Harper, and also for Mason before he passed. I respect your opinion, and I promise that if she's not getting around in a week or two, we'll have a closer look. Meanwhile, keep doing what you're doing."

Shaina sighed. "You don't think she looks tired? And maybe a little too pale?"

He glanced over at her. "She isn't accustomed to being out and about this late. Thanks to the leg and all these back-to-back snowstorms, she isn't getting much fresh air, either. And I'll wager she hasn't been taking her laudanum at bedtime."

"She says it makes her fuzzy-headed."

"Well, that's the idea. Whatever it takes to help her get a good night's sleep." He exhaled a sigh of frustration. "Tell you what. If the weather isn't too foul, I'll ride out tomorrow and give her a quick examination. When I have a look at that medicine bottle, I'll know if she's been taking enough."

"Thank you," she said again. "I won't let on that you might stop by."

Shaina buttoned up her coat as she made her way to the door. She didn't make it even halfway there before Leo blocked her path.

"Good evening, Miz Sterling."

She clutched her coat tighter around her throat. "Why, hello, Leo."

"I thought sure Mr. Remington would ask you to dance."

"Why would he? He's my employer, not my suitor."

"Seems a shame to waste all this"—he glanced at the band—"*music.*" He smirked.

"It's just as well. I'm a terrible dancer, anyway."

"Now, now. We both know that isn't true. Many a time I saw you gliding across the floor in the arms of your adoring husband."

She couldn't think of a single time when he'd been present at any event that involved dancing.

He stroked his chin, as if summoning a memory. "Of all your pretty dresses, I think I liked that shiny red one best." One eyebrow lifted slightly. "Though how you managed to look more beautiful than any other woman in the room without wearing gaudy jewelry and furs and ridiculous bustles, I don't know."

A good three feet separated them, so why did it feel as though he'd violated her space?

"I'd better go," she said, taking a step to the side. "Mable is fading fast, and it's a long ride home."

He moved closer, then leaned down to whisper near her ear, "Perhaps one evening you'll do me the honor of sharing a meal with me."

She wanted to shout, *"Perhaps on the second Tuesday of next week!"*

Instead, she replied, "Have a safe ride home."

It was all she could do to keep from running to the door.

Chapter Twenty-two

Ten minutes into the drive home, Sloan nodded toward the back of the buggy. "Well, that didn't take long."

Shaina smiled. "I think they were fast asleep even before you prodded the team forward."

She hoped that she'd merely imagined the quaver in her voice. She'd gone out on her own at an age when most young girls still dreamed of seeing the world, and between Missouri and Denver, only two men had made unwelcome advances—one with a tobacco-stained beard and no teeth, the other with the look of an outlaw on the run. She'd slipped away from both feeling anxious and vulnerable. Yet neither incident had rattled her the way her encounter with Leo just had.

"You're mighty quiet," Sloan said. "Something bothering you?"

If she answered truthfully, Sloan would confront Leo, and that would only invite all manner of trouble.

"I'm a little worried about Mable," she whispered.

"So am I."

"You are?" She scooted closer on the padded leather seat.

"It isn't like her to give up without a fight. A big one."

She peeked over her shoulder to make sure Mable was still asleep, then told him, "I talked to the doctor, and while he isn't completely convinced that there's something else amiss, he said he'll stop by tomorrow, weather permitting, and have another look at her leg."

Sloan nodded. "Good. Glad to hear it."

"So," Shaina said, "what do you think of Abe's news?"

"Doesn't surprise me. He's been pie-eyed since the first time he met Elsie. Pestered the poor girl at Sunday services and church socials and just about every other get-together you can name." Laughing now, he continued, "At the Doogans' wedding last summer, he followed her around like some lovesick pup, and she tried to clean his clock with her parasol. Lost her balance and would have fallen in the creek if Abe hadn't caught her."

Shaina laughed, too. "Literally and figuratively, I take it."

"Yeah, you could say that."

A moment passed, and the only sound was the quiet huff of the horses' breaths and the steady *thump* of their hooves on the snow-packed road. Every now and then, the moon peeked out from behind wispy clouds, its light glinting off the harness buckles and hames. It illuminated Sloan's profile, too. The slightly furrowed brow, strong cheeks and jaw, and aristocratic nose reminded her of the bust of Michelangelo's *David* that had once sat on Mason's credenza. Except that if ever she mustered the courage to trace those rugged contours, her fingertips would most definitely *not* come away cold.

"I wonder if Abe has given any thought to where they'll live," she said, mostly to herself.

"They'll stay with us, of course."

Shaina pictured the sprawling, two-story log home. Sloan's suite took up most of the upstairs, and there wasn't an unused space on the lower level.

"I'll set up a cot in my library, and they'll move into my suite. Just until...." He moved the reins to his left hand and thumbed the Stetson higher on his forehead. "Let me run an idea by you," he said, meeting her eyes, "and I don't want you to hold back. If you think it's plain loco, say so, all right?"

Shaina nodded, though she had no idea what she'd just agreed to.

"I'm thinking of giving Abe and Elsie that tract of land down below the road—the one that runs alongside the creek. I figure it'd make a right nice wedding present."

Since she'd never seen it, what could say but, "What a generous gift"?

"It's almost five acres. Flat as a griddle cake. Perfect for a house and a barn, a couple of outbuildings and corrals...." He hesitated. "Wait. You think it's too much? Might make 'em feel beholden to repay me or something?"

"I don't think anything of the kind. It's a lovely gift. And it sounds to me like you've been thinking about this for a long time."

He smiled at her, and the expression set her heart to thumping against her rib cage.

"Yeah, I guess I have. Abe's been with me since he was just a pup. I'm glad he chose Elsie, don't get me wrong; but, whatever woman he chose, that land would have been his one day. Couldn't save my brother, Pete," he said, "but maybe I can make up for it by helping Abe."

She could tell from his tone of voice, and by the way he'd straightened his back, that this wasn't the time to ask how he'd lost his brother.

"Someday, maybe you'll tell me all about how Abe came to live with you and James and Mable." *And how you came to live with Simon….*

"Someday. Maybe."

They didn't talk for another hundred yards or so of travel, and then he said, "So, what did Leo want earlier?"

Shaina hesitated. She hadn't thought Sloan would have known about the encounter, since he'd been outside.

"You seemed to be holding your own, so I kept my nose out of it." He paused before adding, "Couldn't see his face, but I could see yours. You looked mighty uncomfortable."

Shaina reminded herself that she didn't want to cause trouble. He'd been right in perceiving that she had held her own, and she would continue doing just that. Even if it meant taking a broom or a skillet to the loathsome man.

"He startled me, is all. One minute, I was rushing to the door, thinking about what Doc Wilson had said, and the next…." Shaina swallowed, remembering that smirking face and those dark, emotionless eyes. "Leo appeared from out of nowhere."

Sloan only nodded. "What did he want?"

"He wondered why you hadn't asked me to dance."

She could see him working his jaw and nodding ever so slightly. Had it been a mistake to share that small piece of information? Leo's sneering face appeared in her mind's eye again. If there was a face-off when Leo rode in from town, he'd probably win, just out of pure meanness. And whatever happened to Sloan would be her fault!

Shaina could scarcely believe what happened next. Sloan started to laugh! It started like distant thunder, slow, quiet, and deep in his chest, then rolled out and filled the cold air with a mellow, melodious sound that surprised and excited and even started her laughing, too.

He wiped tears of mirth from his eyes, then wrapped his big, leather-gloved hand around hers. "Ah, Shaina," he said, squeezing her hand, "you are a joy to—"

"What in tarnation is goin' on up there?" James groused from the back of the buggy. "Man tries to steal a few winks and starts dreamin' a pack of hyenas is on the attack. And is it any wonder?"

"Oh, James, just leave them young'uns be, you hear?" Mable put in. "Don't you remember when we used to laugh like that?"

A quiet rustling caught Shaina's attention, and she peeked back in time to see James reach around his wife to tidy the quilt they'd draped over her legs, which were stretched out across the buggy seat. Such a simple gesture, yet it was so sweet and affectionate that it brought tears to her eyes. She and Harper hadn't shared tenderness like that, not even when they'd been courting.

"Still do laugh like that," James said, draping an arm over Mable's shoulder. "Not so much since you busted up your leg, but you haven't lost your knack for coaxin' a snicker outta me."

The snow kept falling in big, quarter-sized flakes that piled up fast, squeaking in quiet protest as the buggy rolled over the ground. The wind picked up, too, whistling through the cab and forcing the foursome to duck deeper into their coat collars. They discussed the hoedown—the music, the sour punch, and the poor souls charged with cleaning up the mess. And then, finally, the ranch house came into view.

"Oh, my," Shaina said, "but isn't that a welcoming scene."

"Sight for sore eyes," Sloan agreed.

"Which of the hands stoked the fires and lit the lamps?" Mable wondered aloud.

James rubbed his palms together. "Don't rightly know, but whoever it was deserves a raise." He grunted. "Unless it was that odd-talkin' Blevins."

By Shaina's count, three people had now openly expressed an aversion to Leo. No doubt if she asked Mable's opinion, she'd agree. So why did Sloan keep the man around? The memory of him was enough to send tremors up and down her spine. He wouldn't be a bad-looking fellow if he didn't always look like he was cooking up some evil scheme. For an instant, she wondered what devious thoughts had painted that wily expression on his face. On second thought, she didn't want to know, and thanked the good Lord that he slept in the bunkhouse.

Abe and James got Mable inside while Sloan took care of the buggy and the team.

Shaina put the teakettle on the stove, thinking she'd fix them all a cup of hot tea to warm them, then helped Mable get ready for bed.

"You might want to rustle up some sticky buns with breakfast," the woman said as Shaina tucked her in.

She was fluffing pillows when Mable added, "Doc Wilson loves 'em. I'm sure he'll appreciate somethin' warm and sweet when he stops by tomorrow."

So, she'd overheard her quiet conversation with Sloan, had she? Shaina decided to go along with her.

"Whether or not he comes is entirely dependent on the weather. But I'll make them, anyway. It's been weeks since last we had them."

The woman smiled knowingly. "They're his favorite, you know."

Shaina uncorked the bottle of laudanum. "No, I didn't. But that's no surprise. I'm fairly healthy, so my dealings with Doc Wilson have been limited."

"I'm talking about Sloan, you silly girl. Put a pan of those things in front of him, and he's like a little boy in a candy shop, I tell you!" Her laughter quickly waned when she saw Shaina pouring the drug onto a spoon.

"Don't need that stuff," she said, turning her head away.

"Yes, you do. After being shuttled in and out of the buggy and bouncing over those bumpy roads, you'll find that your leg gives you fits tonight." She held the spoon near the woman's lips. "You *do* want to get better, don't you?"

Frowning, Mable met her eyes. "Well, 'course I do. What kind of harebrained dolt would want to lie around, helpless as an infant, all the livelong day?"

Shaina only raised her eyebrows, and Mable took her medicine.

Then she grinned. "If you tell anyone I said this, I'll deny it, but I'm plumb tuckered out."

"Don't worry," Shaina said with a wink. "Your secret is safe with me."

After stoking the fire and adding a few logs to the grate, she turned down the bedside lamp to a low glow. Mable was fast asleep when she tiptoed from the room.

James met her in the hall. "She's asleep? Already?"

"And she took her medicine, too!"

"Thanks, kid. Don't know what we'd do without you."

Shaina knew it was high praise coming from this man of few words.

"I only wish I could do more." She must have said it a dozen times since moving to the ranch, but that didn't make the phrase any less sincere. "I'm making some tea. Would you like a cup?"

"Nah, I'm dead on my feet. But thanks." He leaned forward and pressed a quick kiss to her cheek before heading to his room.

"What's wrong?" Sloan asked when she entered the kitchen.

"Nothing. Why?"

"Well, you have tears in your eyes...."

She touched her cheek, and smiled. "I'm just..." Shaina grabbed an oven mitt and lifted the kettle from the stove. "I'm just feeling very blessed." Filling a big mug with steaming water, she asked, "Can I pour a cup for you, too?"

In place of an answer, he stepped up beside her. "Are you happy here, Shaina?"

Memories flashed through her mind—her parents sending her and her brothers out to earn money; the scary trip west, ending in Denver; marrying Harper and then losing him to suicide, of all things; the destructive fire....

"Happier than I've been in a long, long time."

He hadn't asked for tea, but she poured him some, anyway, then carried the mugs to the table. When Sloan sat down beside her, she said, "More important, I feel safe." She touched her cheek again, remembering James's little kiss. "And wanted."

"I'm glad."

Knowing that her time here wouldn't be permanent, she hadn't wanted to grow too comfortable. But everything about this place, from the mountain vistas visible from every room to the rugged, overstuffed furniture and floor-to-ceiling fireplaces that warded off winter's chill, had lulled her into feeling that the big, sturdy house was *home*. When Mable's leg healed, Shaina would be forced to return to Denver to find a job and a place to live. What kind of selfish, self-centered person had she become that she was in no hurry for her friend to get better as quickly as possible?

"You're going to think I'm an insensitive clod," Sloan said, taking her hands in his, "but I'm in no hurry for Mable to get back on her feet."

How had Sloan so accurately read the words written on her heart?

He let go of her hands, and instantly she missed his warmth, so she wrapped her hands around her steaming mug of tea. "Will you and Abe wait until after the wedding to go to Cheyenne?"

"Next chance I get, I'll ride over to Boulder to check out some bulls there. If they look half decent, we won't go to Wyoming at all. As for the wedding, I don't think they've set a date."

"Based on the way they were looking at each other, I'm guessing they won't put it off too long."

"I'm guessing you're right." He downed a swallow of tea. "Can I ask you a question?"

"Of course."

How odd that Sloan's expression had changed from curious to skeptical. What reason would he have to doubt her?

"Have you answered your mother's letter yet?"

Shortly after her family's troubles began, she'd seen a hot air balloon in the sky above her house near St. Charles, and the very idea that people could float away from all their worries and problems had buoyed her sagging spirits. All too soon, the beautiful float had hurtled back to earth, shattering its gondola and injuring its pilot. The quiet, intimate chat with Sloan had been much like that...lifting her hopes at first, then dashing them with the mere mention of her mother's note.

"No," she said, staring at her hands. "I need to pray first, so I'll know what to say."

He took another swig of his tea. "About whether or not to send more money."

She nodded.

"I don't remember seeing them at your wedding."

Shaina had almost forgotten that Sloan had been there that day. *Almost*. If she closed her eyes, she could picture him in the receiving line, standing tall and handsome in his fine black suit—with a beautiful redhead on his arm—as he shook Harper's hand and then hers.

"I sent them money for the train, but...." It riled her every time she thought about the letter that had arrived while she and Harper had been away on their European honeymoon: *"We're so sorry about missing your special day, Shaina dear, but your father and I needed the money for rent."* She'd sent more than enough to cover that, in the same envelope as the train fare. Clearly, she hadn't mattered enough to them to warrant spending even a dollar on a token gift to commemorate the day.

She shook off the ugly memory. "So," she said, smiling at him, "how many calves have been born so far?"

He studied her face, his grin telling her he'd taken the hint to stop pressing the issue. "Last week, Abe and the boys rounded up four pregnant cows and put 'em in the calving barn," he began. "Those newborns are way better off than the ones born out there." He pointed toward the window, where wind-whipped snowflakes pecked the panes. "Poor, wet li'l things have enough to contend with, just trying to survive in the cold until we find them—hopefully before the coyotes do."

Shoving back from the table, he stretched both legs out in front of him and proceeded to tell her how, during past calf roundups, he and the hands had built huge campfires and wrapped the calves in their bedrolls to keep them from freezing. They'd taken turns standing guard, he explained, to pick off predators while the others slept.

He crossed one booted ankle over the other and slouched in the chair, fingers linked behind his head. "Worst year ever," he continued, "was when one of the hands lost his way during a blizzard. We found him in the spring, way up on the bluff, hugging that li'l cow like it was his own baby." He frowned and closed his eyes. "Thank God nothing like that has happened since."

"I'm ashamed to say I never gave much thought to how dangerous ranching can be," Shaina admitted. "I just enjoyed my steaks and leather satchels without considering the cost to men like you."

Sloan sat up straighter and studied her face for what seemed like a full minute before saying, "There isn't another like you, Shaina Sterling."

A compliment? Or a commentary on my self-centeredness?

"I should let you get to bed," she told him. "The sun will be up before we know it."

"Quoting James, now, are you? I don't know whether to applaud you…or pity you." He laughed. "Besides, I'm wide awake. No chance I'll get to sleep any time soon."

Shaina rose to her feet so quickly, she nearly overturned her chair. "I know just the thing for sleeplessness." She grabbed a saucepan from under the sink, placed it on the stove, and filled it with milk. "My grandmother used to make this for me when I couldn't sleep, and it always worked like a charm. Gran had a cure for just about anything, from warts to bloody noses to chapped hands."

"That reminds me…I've been meaning to get you some Vaseline." He started to stand. "Slather some on and go to sleep wearing gloves, and by morning, your hands will be as soft as a baby's bottom."

"How would you know what a baby's bottom feels like?" she teased.

"I…well, I don't have firsthand knowledge, but I figure if a thing gets said enough to become an old saw, there must be some truth in it."

Shaina smiled. "Gran swore by udder cream to treat dry skin, but I hated the sticky, greasy feeling. Hated the way it stained my best Sunday-go-to-meeting gloves and my bedclothes, too." She inspected her hands. "If they start to crack and bleed, I might take you up on your offer. Meanwhile, if it's all the same to you, I promise not to complain about my red knuckles."

"So," he said, "something else we have in common, then."

"Red knuckles?"

"No," he said, doing his best to stifle a chuckle, "the cure!" He paused. "You know, I don't think I've ever laughed more than I have since you moved in."

He sent her an alluring smile, and she wondered if his lips felt as soft and gentle as they looked. One thing was sure: If he kept looking at her that way, she might just have to stop wondering and find out!

The quiet sizzle of bubbling milk drew her attention to the saucepan. She poured the liquid into two mugs, then topped each one off with a pat of butter and a spoonful of sugar.

"Speaking of cures," she said as she set Sloan's mug on the table, "this one is guaranteed to make you yawn."

Right on cue, Shaina yawned.

This time, he didn't try to suppress his amusement. "There isn't another like you," he said again.

She'd never been overly fond of the phrase, which her ma had often spouted to discourage her from pairing floral blouses with striped skirts.

Sloan drew her into a hug so tight that she could feel his heart beating hard against her chest.

"Not another like you in the whole wide world."

And that was all it took to turn it into her favorite phrase in the whole wide world.

Chapter Twenty-three

So tell me, Mable...when do you intend to confess?"

"Heavens to Betsy, Amos Wilson—you scared me half to death!" She flapped the covers over her legs and smiled sweetly. "'Confess'? I'm afraid I don't understand."

He set his medical bag on the chair beside her bed and branded her with a stern stare. "Oh, don't play the innocent with me. I know *exactly* why you're all red-faced and out of breath. I saw you standing there in the window. Saw you race across the room when you heard me coming down the hall. *And* heard the bedsprings squeal when you climbed onto the mattress just now."

She waved both hands as if she'd walked into a swarm of bees. "Hush! You want them hear you?"

Wilson sat on the corner of her bed. "Who, James? Sloan? Shaina? Abe?"

"*All* of them! But it's for their own good." She exhaled an exasperated sigh. "James couldn't keep a secret if his life depended on it, and Abe's too young and naive to understand."

"Well then, why don't you help *me* understand why you're faking."

"For the love of Pete, need I remind you that you swore an oath to keep patients' secrets...well, secret?"

He folded both arms over his chest. "I'm well aware of what I swore on the day I became a doctor. And you can be sure that anything you tell me will remain in strictest confidence."

"Then keep your voice down, will you?" She reached toward the nightstand for her cup of water, took a sip, and set it down again. "Now then," she said, clearing her throat. "The reason I'm faking is... Sloan hasn't admitted it yet, not even to himself, but he's in love with Shaina. And once I'm better, she'll leave. He needs time to realize what a treasure she is. Time, because he's stubborn and proud, and if she goes away, he'll let her. Even though it'll break his heart. He won't admit he's heartbroken, of course. Oh, no. He'll just bury his head in his work, same as he did when Simon died."

Wilson grinned. "My, my. That was some speech. Have you been rehearsing it?"

She gave him a dirty look.

"This is quite a sacrifice you're making."

"It's worth it. I love Sloan like a son."

"What makes you so sure Shaina will leave once you've healed up?"

"If she isn't taking care of the house and nursing me, what's to keep her here? Besides, you know how those uppity folks in town can be. If she's here without a good excuse, why, the breeze from their waggin' tongues will blow the leaves clean from the trees." She aimed a frown of disappointment at him. "Frankly, I'm surprised."

"Surprised…?"

"Surprised that, with all your book-learnin' and schoolin', I have to explain this to you!"

The doctor laughed quietly. "Mable, sometimes, I just don't know what to say to you."

"Say you'll keep my secret."

"Of course I will. Now, why don't you tell me how long you've been putting on this act?"

She shrugged. "A couple of weeks, give or take."

He got up, grabbed the laudanum bottle from the mantel, and frowned. "Well, that explains why you've been refusing your laudanum. But it doesn't explain why you haven't been sleeping well."

"I remember when my sister had her young'uns, one of 'em got his nights and days mixed up. He snoozed all day and caterwauled all night. It's the same for me! Shaina won't let me do anything but eat and read and nap during the day. Oh, she gives me some mending to work on now and then, but I've been doing that for so long, I can sew on buttons and darn socks in minutes. There's not much else to do but sleep! So at night, when I'm sure everyone else is fast asleep, I get up and walk around—I know how to avoid every creak and squeak in this house!—to keep myself limber. I'm no spring chicken, as you well know. Last thing I need is to get all fat and flabby, lying around like a lady of leisure."

"So, tell me…when do you plan to let *them* in on our little secret?"

"Oh, I don't know. Maybe in a week or so, I'll get up and limp around for a few minutes at a time. Then, in another week, I'll hobble for five minutes. And in the meantime, God willing, Sloan will realize that he can't live without Shaina."

"But what about *Shaina*? How can you be sure she wants to spend the rest of her life with Sloan?"

"You need only to see them together once, and you'll have your answer. Believe me, she's crazy about him."

"I really wish you'd reconsider telling the truth and letting the chips fall where they may."

"Amos, you know I can't do that. Like I said, I love that boy as if he were my own. And I'm not gettin' any younger. I want to see him settled and happy before—"

"You're a long, long way from meeting your Maker, you big faker. But all right. I'll go along with it."

"Ain't like you have a choice," she said with a wink, "on account of your oath and all."

On his feet now, Wilson grabbed his doctor's bag. "Very well, Mable. I'll trust you to do what you think best. And I'll pray it's what the good Lord thinks is best, too."

"Oh, fine," she said when he disappeared around the corner, "leave me with *that* to think about." She threw her bedroom slipper at the door. "I won't sleep tonight, for sure!"

❧

"But…but I don't understand."

Shaina gripped the back of the chair so tightly, Sloan worried she might hurt herself.

"Didn't you say, just last night, that you'd operate?"

Wilson looked to Sloan for help, but what could he say?

"If memory serves me right," the doctor said, "I said I'd assess her condition, and if I found anything that concerned me, I'd consider exploratory surgery." He buttoned up his coat. "I saw nothing worrisome during the examination. And as I explained last night, bones don't knit as quickly when you're Mable's age and size."

Grasping his medical bag by its leather handles, he walked to the door. "Let's give it a few more weeks. If she's not up and about by then, we'll—"

"But how do you explain that, sometimes, she's red-faced and breathless, and other times, she's as pale as Caesar's ghost? Surely, those aren't symptoms of size or age!"

"Mable told me just now that, whenever possible, she does... exercises."

"Exercises." Shaina's left eyebrow lifted. "What kind of exercises?"

Sloan would have liked to ask the good doctor why he looked so guilty all of a sudden.

The doctor donned his bowler. "She didn't elaborate, and since all her vital signs are normal, I saw no reason to press her for details." Wilson paused, then held his forefinger aloft. "Aha, I think I understand." Now his expression turned empathetic. "You've put your heart and soul into this job. You're young. Unmarried. Unaccustomed to the hard work that's involved with caring for Mable, with taking care of this *house*." He emphasized its size with a grand sweep of his arm. "Perhaps you'd rather move back to town, try to put your life there back together. I'm only too happy to ask around and try to find someone suitable to replace you until Mable can fend for herself—"

Shaina gasped. "You couldn't be more wrong, Doctor! I'm not tired of the work. In fact, I love it here. Why, I'd stay forever, if—"

If what? Sloan wondered.

"My mistake, then," Wilson said. He glanced at the wall clock. "Well, I'd best be on my way. I have several stops to make before I can call it a day." Turning to Sloan, he said, "I've hired an architect, and just as soon as he delivers the building plans, we'll put our heads together to see if you have any suggestions or ideas for improvement."

"What do I know about things like that?" Sloan asked as he walked him to the door. "This is your project, Doc."

They exchanged parting pleasantries, and then the doctor was gone.

One hand on her hip, Shaina stared after him. "There's something rotten in the state of Denmark."

"You must have some serious doubts," he teased, "to quote Shakespeare."

"If the shoe fits...."

"*That* wasn't written by the bard. Methinks the lady doth protest too much. I believe the good doctor is in trouble."

She grinned. "Suspicion always haunts the guilty mind."

Sloan laughed.

"I don't know about you," she said, "but I'm impressed with us."

"Impressed? How so?"

"We live in a log cabin on a ranch at the foot of the great Rocky Mountains. We raise cows and horses. And we can recite classic literature from memory. How many people can say that?"

She'd said *we*, and it had sounded so good that Sloan didn't know how to respond. And the memory of the way she'd felt in his arms last night wasn't making it any easier to think of a clever retort.

"Exercises," she said with a scoff. "I'm not buying it, are you?"

"I've never known Amos to lie."

"Oh, I'm not saying he's lying. He might have misunderstood Mable. Or maybe he was pestering her to get out of bed more often, and she told that story to quiet him."

"I've never known Mable to lie, either."

She held his gaze for a moment. Oh, what he would give to read the thoughts that caused those huge blue eyes to flash like diamonds!

"Dr. Wilson didn't put any doubt in your mind with his nonsense about my being tired of all the hard work, did he?"

He'd heard her singing as she went about her chores, and humming as she prepared trays to carry in to Mable. Would she have walked around looking so merry if she didn't want to be here?

"No," he said with a shake of his head.

He watched the worry lines etched into her forehead fade into a relieved smile. "Good. Because nothing could be further from the truth."

He took a small step closer. "So, you meant it, then—what you said about loving it here?"

Her cheeks flushed, and she stared down at her shoes. Why the sudden shift in her mood? Was it because she couldn't bring herself to admit that Doc had been right, after all, and she wasn't happy here? Or did the change in her demeanor have something to do with the secrets still closed in her heart?

"I've lived in a lot of places," she said, "some hardly better than hovels. Others, like Sterling Hall, were quite grand. But not one of them—not even the house where I was born—ever felt like *home*."

"And this does?"

She answered with a sweet, calm smile that warmed him to his toes.

Two steps forward, and he could take her in his arms again. Just two steps to assure her that she could stay forever, if that was what she wanted.

But a quiet suspicion seeped into him. There were still too many things he didn't know about her, about her past. And until she stepped out in faith and trusted him with those secrets, what choice did he have but to guard his heart?

He took those two steps...toward the hall.

"There are some papers in my office that need my attention."

She flinched, every bit as visibly as if he'd struck her.

"Oh, of course." A nervous giggle punctuated her comment. "Just listen to me, chattering like a chipmunk, when you have work to do."

Yet again, Sloan had an urge to hold her—this time, to offer assurances that he hadn't meant to hurt her feelings. Or to insult her. Or to make her feel like an ordinary employee who'd been summarily dismissed. Had he ever felt more confused?

"I'm glad you're here," he said simply.

A small step, he told himself, *but a step in the right direction.*

Chapter Twenty-four

Leo Blevins believed that if a man wanted to keep a roof over his head and his belly full of food, he'd better know how to read and write. If he wanted to get those things without working for them, he'd better know how to read *people*.

He pressed the sole of one boot against the edge of the table, tilted back his chair, and squinted over the top of his hand of cards through the haze of his cigar smoke. Any minute now, Bud would fold and then stomp off in a huff. Sam McCloud would stay but wish he hadn't, and the same was true for that bearded, smirking idiot Joe Michaels. And Rafe Preston? He probably held the jack of diamonds Leo needed to complete his royal flush.

Every man at the table had, at one time or another, run with a gang of outlaws. Everyone but Leo, that is. He'd done his killing at Apache Canyon, Glorieta Pass, and Peralta, when he'd served under Colonel John P. Slough of the 1st Colorado Infantry in 1861. In '67, he'd hooked up with Bill Cody, this time killing buffalo to feed the Kansas Pacific Railroad crews. When Cody had pulled together his Wild West show in '83, Leo's skill with revolvers and rifles had made him a natural choice. If he hadn't put the moves on Cody's lady friend, he'd probably still be there, competing in shooting events. After being issued Cody's ultimatum of "Get out or get dead," Leo pulled his share of one-man robberies, surprising stagecoach drivers and relieving the passengers of their rings and watches. Before long, he'd tired of small stuff and small people and of looking over his shoulder. So, in '86, he'd adopted a Bill Cody-like persona—sans the beard and mustache—and fooled Remington into hiring him as a scout during a trail drive to Kansas City.

"Hello, Leo. How's my favorite fellow tonight?"

He wished she'd go back to her piano. Even the cacophonous plinking was easier to listen to than her high-pitched, nasal voice. "Alice," he said, smiling. "I'm good, real good. And how's that gorgeous sister of yours?"

"She got home day before yesterday, and all she's talked about is Leo, Leo, Leo!"

Abby had been in Littleton, helping their elder sister with her newborn baby. For the infant's sake, Leo hoped she hadn't inherited her aunts' annoying, clingy personalities.

"I'm looking forward to seeing her, too," he lied. Well, it wasn't a *total* fabrication. Abby's job as secretary at the smelting plant had provided all the information he'd needed to plan the robbery. A few dinners at The Windsor, a steady supply of wine, and some voice-induced ringing in his ears had been small price to pay for details like that.

"Tell her I'll stop by tomorrow to—"

"You gonna play cards," Rafe interrupted, "or sit around jabberin' all night?"

The look on Alice's face matched what Leo would have said if he hadn't required Rafe's cooperation.

"I'll tell her," Alice assured him. She flicked his cards and, glaring at Rafe, added, "I hope you win the whole pot, *Leo*."

Michaels watched her walk away, then grimaced and poked his forefinger in one ear. "Thought for sure I'd find blood," he said when he pulled it out again and inspected the tip. "If y'ask me, there's only one use for a voice like that. First chance I get, I'm gonna write a letter to the mayor, suggest he give her a job as an alarm bell up on the courthouse roof."

"Is he serious?" Rafe wanted to know.

Sam snorted. "Apparently."

"Didn't realize jabberin' was contagious," Sam grumbled.

Snickering, Michaels ignored him and leaned forward. "Think about it. Two birds with one stone: We wouldn't have to listen to that awful piano, and when she spots a fire or a tornado, she can cut loose with a piercing squeal and alert the whole town. It's the perfect plan!"

The men exchanged bored glances while Michaels rolled a cigarette.

"Speaking of plans," Rafe said to Leo, "we need to talk."

Leo nodded. "We will. Tomorrow."

"Where?"

"At the café."

"What! Why not here?"

"Because we need to stay sharp and pay attention." Leo stared at the tip of his cigar. "Can't do that guzzling whiskey and beer."

"What time?" Michaels asked.

"Noon."

"Tarnation!" Sam thundered. "Are we gonna play cards or sit around cluckin' like a bunch of old hens?" He swallowed a mouthful of beer and put his glass down with a loud thud. "Joe, it's your deal."

Michaels' eyes narrowed menacingly, prompting Leo to say, "Aw, don't mind him, Joe. He don't get out much." Leo fanned out his cards, then collapsed them again. By this time tomorrow, they'd have the basics ironed out. And the morning after that, he'd show the guys the abandoned miner's shack he'd come across while scouting out the area a month or so back. There, they would store the wagons, mules, weapons, and ammunition, as well as hole up between practice runs—two or three, if that's what it took to get the job done in the allotted time. If everything went according to plan, they'd complete the mission with a minimum of bloodshed.

Abby had come home just in the nick of time. A juicy steak, some pie, and a bottle or two of port wine would help him learn when the Andrews and Meeks Smelting Company planned to load the shipment of gold and silver into a boxcar on the Denver & Rio Grande train. Thanks to the Bland-Allison Act, the federal government was now required to buy $4,000,000 worth of silver, which they'd turn into coins at the mint in Carson City. A very bad deal for taxpayers, and a very good deal for Leo and his men.

The bonus—as if he needed one—was that Sloan Remington had purchased tickets on that same train. With him out of the way....

Michaels threw down his cards. "That's it, boys. I've had it."

Leo followed him, ignoring their protests and reprimands. What did he care if they kept the few paltry dollars he'd added to the pot?

A week from now, he'd be well on his way to Juárez, with saddlebags stuffed full of crisp bills—the reward for delivering his share of the gold and silver to Leadville. It wasn't likely Michaels or Preston had planned that far ahead; but even if they had, they weren't likely to meet up on the road south.

Should that happen, though, Leo intended to make sure they never crossed paths again.

⤴

"I can hardly believe my good fortune," Elsie said to Shaina. "If I hadn't run into you at the hoedown, I'd be doing all this by myself. Honestly, I don't know how you planned a wedding as grand as yours with no help from a mother, sisters, or aunts. How will I ever repay you?"

Shaina smiled. "There's absolutely nothing to repay. Things like this are fun for me, and since Harper died, I haven't had any parties to plan. Besides, it's a lovely change of pace from laundry and cooking and cleaning."

Goodness, Shaina thought, looking around, *I hope no one heard that!* After what she'd said to Sloan and Elsie's brother about loving her work here at the ranch, the last thing she wanted was for anyone to think she hadn't meant it.

"I've been dreaming of this day since I was ten years old," Elsie gushed. "It's like I've been granted a wish from a fairy godmother, and my dream is finally coming true." She blushed and giggled. "Just think of it—in a few weeks, I'll no longer be known around town as Doc Wilson's sister. I'll be Abe's wife!"

"And I have a feeling you'll be a very good one."

Elsie bit her lower lip. "Do you really think so?"

"Of course I do! Abe is one lucky young man. Why, he's not just getting one of the prettiest girls in all of Denver; he's getting one of the sweetest girls, too."

"Oh, I hope he feels that way. I *so* want to make him happy."

"I can almost see him now, all starry-eyed as he watches you walk down the aisle toward him."

Elsie giggled again. "Tell me, Shaina, what sort of dress do you see me wearing in your lovely vision?"

Shaina scanned the pictures Elsie had torn from catalogs and magazines. She chose a wedding gown from one pile and a veil from another, then set them aside. Next, she went through the satchel of fabric samples and placed a swatch of Spanish lace and another of white satin beside the pictures.

"We could layer your dress with the lace and make a veil from the same bolt," she mused aloud. "Why, I'll bet there will even be enough to make you a shawl, in case it's chilly on your big day."

"Yes," Elsie said, nodding, "I think that'll be just lovely."

Elsie had been keeping a wedding journal of sorts, where she'd jotted things down as they had come to mind. On the page titled "Gown," Shaina made a note of Elsie's choices, then turned to the page marked "Guests."

"Now then, have you given any thought to who you'll invite?"

"Oh, mostly people from church. A few neighbors. Molly Vernon, of course. And everyone here at Remington Ranch. Nothing ostentatious." Elsie grinned. "I wouldn't want Abe thinking he's marrying a spendthrift!"

The next page bore the heading "Flowers and Decorations," and the one after that said "Honeymoon." In less than an hour, they'd filled each sheet with Elsie's ideas, leaving only one decision.

"Have you and Abe talked about a date?"

Elsie shook her head. "Not yet. When I said good-bye to him at the train station this morning, he promised we'd choose one just as soon as he got home." She giggled again. "How silly am I? He's been gone only a few hours, and already I miss him to the moon and back!"

"You aren't the least bit silly," Shaina assured her. Because she'd been feeling much the same way since Sloan had left for town.

⌒

Nestled against a backdrop of snow-covered mountain peaks and towering pines, the smoking chimneys of farmhouses and cabins hurtled past the window. The rhythmic *clack-clack-clack* of the train's iron wheels grinding along the tracks might have soothed him to sleep—if Abe, seated across from him, hadn't been in the mood to talk.

"It's a rotten shame those Boulder bulls were so scrawny," he said.

Sloan nodded. "The winter was as hard on them as it was on our herds."

"Think those Cheyenne cows are really hardier?"

Sloan had read everything he could get his hands on, and he believed the Belted Galloway could withstand Colorado's rugged winters. "Yeah, I do."

"Sure would be nice not havin' to worry they'll all freeze to death, wouldn't it?"

"Oh, I reckon we'll still lose a few, if the weather turns ugly enough. But, God willing, the losses will be fewer and farther between."

Sunlight slanted through the window, and Abe lowered the shade. "Never been on a train before," he said. "Ain't what I expected at all."

Most of the time, Abe conducted himself like a man far older than his years. No surprise there, taking into account his rough beginnings. But once in a while, he let down his guard and allowed the young, full-of-life fellow shine through. This was one of those times.

Sloan took off his hat and hung it on one knee. "I've been meaning to run an idea by you."

Abe mimicked his movement. "Oh?"

"Have you and Elsie settled on a wedding date yet?"

"No, but I promised her this morning that we'd pick one when I got back."

"You'll need a place to stay—after the wedding, that is—so, unless you object, I'd like you two to take my suite at the ranch. Just until you get a place of your own, mind you."

Abe's brow furrowed slightly, and Sloan had a feeling he knew why: It had probably dawned on him, suddenly, that marrying Elsie came with certain duties and responsibilities, such as providing a home for her.

"You know that tract of land that crosses the creek?"

"Yeah...."

"I've already drawn up the papers. It's all yours. I've also ordered the materials you'll need to build a house—my wedding gift to you and Elsie."

"Sloan. I don't mean to sound ungrateful, but that's…that's way too generous."

"Why don't you let me be the judge of that?"

He decided this might not be the best time to tell Abe that he planned to give them some cows and horses, along with the nails and boards required for a barn and a corral. *All in good time*, he thought as the train rattled northward. *All in good time.*

Chapter Twenty-five

You two sounded like a couple of magpies," Mable said when Shaina brought her lunch.

Shaina laughed. "I know it's normal for a bride to get excited about her wedding, but I don't think I've ever seen anyone more wound up than Elsie!"

"Not even you?"

"*Especially* not me."

"Well now, that's odd. As I recall, yours was one of the biggest shindigs Denver ever saw."

"That's because I had very little to say about it." Shaina remembered pleading with Harper for a small, intimate ceremony and an even smaller reception. But he'd refused to take the chance that his customers and clients might see it as the sign of an ailing business.

"I didn't want the gown with the train that dragged behind me for miles, or the pearl-encrusted headdress that weighed a ton. I hated the enormous bouquet of orange blossoms, and those ridiculous satin shoes rubbed blisters on my toes that took weeks to heal."

Mable chuckled. "But you were a sight to behold!" She paused. "Do you think you'll ever remarry?"

"I'm not opposed to the idea." Shaina pictured Sloan in a dark suit and white shirt, waiting at the altar for her. Blinking, she shook her head. "But first, a man would need to show some interest."

"I've said it before, but it bears repeating, especially now: You can't fool me, Shaina Sterling."

She had a fair idea what Mable meant but had no intention of pursuing the line of thought.

"That portrait of Simon in the library," she said, hoping to change the subject, "how long ago was it painted?"

"Two years before he died, almost to the day."

"And he never married?"

Mable shook her head. "Said he had neither the time nor the inclination. I imagine that made sense, given the hours he devoted to the ranch."

Shaina's heart sank. Sloan had three times the responsibilities of Simon, what with the hotel and the manufactory to run in addition to the ranch.

"Well, it's a shame he never married," Shaina said, "because I think Simon would have made a wonderful husband. He did an amazing job raising Sloan."

"I can't very well argue with that," Mable replied. "Sloan is a good man—one of the best I've had the pleasure of knowing."

Someone rang the front bell, and Shaina went to answer it.

"Jennie," she said as she opened the door. "What brings you all the way out here?"

The woman leaned forward and gave Shaina a big, warm hug. "You, of course. I haven't seen you in months, and I miss our little chats." Stepping into the foyer, she removed her gloves. "You're one of a handful of people I can name who treat me with respect, despite what I do for a living. I've missed that, too."

"There's coffee on the stove, or I can brew you a cup of tea. You don't mind if I peel vegetables for stew while we talk, do you?"

"Of course not. Time is the one thing that, once spent, can never be retrieved. And coffee sounds delightful," Jennie said as she followed Shaina into the kitchen. "So tell me, how are things here at Remington Ranch?"

"Things are fine." She handed Jennie a mug of coffee. "Why do you ask?"

"Because you spent years in Denver, both before and after you married Harper. Don't you miss the hustle and bustle of the city?"

"Absolutely not. I enjoy the peace and quiet, as well as the clean air. And it's refreshing not having to worry about what certain people think of my hats and dresses."

"Ah, still bristling over the little tête-à-tête with Priscilla in church, are you?"

"That happened weeks ago. How did you know about it?"

"Oh, I have my ways." Jennie winked. "So, tell me, what do you *do* around here all day? No, let me guess. You do it all—the cooking, the baking, the cleaning, and"—she took Shaina's hand in her own—"the laundry, if these rough, red knuckles are any indicator." She released Shaina. "But you know what? I'm not really surprised that you love it here. You're too nice to rub elbows with those high-and-mighty snobs."

Shaina grabbed a bunch of carrots and began peeling them. "How have *you* been? Is everything going well?"

Jennie told Shaina how she'd bought a new house and was in the process of decorating it. And when she'd heard that Sloan had loaned Dr. Wilson the money to expand and renovate his clinic, she'd tossed a few of her own dollars into the pot.

"So where is Mr. Generous?" she asked.

Shaina smiled. "On his way to Cheyenne to buy new bulls."

"Oh, my."

Shaina looked up from the chopping board. "Oh, my?"

"*Now* I understand why you stay here. It has very little to do with the views or the crisp mountain air. Am I right?"

What could Shaina say to that?

"I'm reminded of a night years ago, when you and Harper attended a play at the Tabor. I had the privilege of sitting in a box seat, and, thanks to my trusty opera glasses, I could see quite clearly—you in your pretty blue dress, and Harper in his tailcoat—with Sloan sitting behind you." Jennie laughed. "He saw even less of the performance than I did, because his eyes were on you the entire evening!"

"On…on *me?*" Again, Shaina stopped chopping. "You mean, he didn't escort a young lady to the opera that evening?"

"Oh, he most certainly did. She was a rare beauty, indeed…but she wasn't *you*. And he was positively mesmerized."

Shaina laughed as she scraped bite-sized vegetable pieces into the pot. "The lenses of your glasses must have been smudged."

"He took her home early," Jennie went on. "The next day, I ran into him in the bank, and I asked him why." She helped herself to a peeled carrot and waved it like a wand. "Seems she made a rude comment about your lack of a pedigree, and he decided his time was too valuable to spend it with a snob."

"I don't even know who Sloan was with that night. How could a perfect stranger have known anything about my background, when I've never shared anything about my life before Denver with anyone?" Well, she'd told Sloan, but not until very recently.

Jennie shrugged. "Seems he was also perturbed with Harper for paying more attention to just about everyone else than he paid to you. Said that husband of yours left you alone no fewer than half a dozen times that night. If you were *his* wife, he said, he wouldn't have let you out of his sight."

Jennie took a bite of the carrot, and when she'd finished crunching, she said, "I wish I'd told you all this after Harper died. Not right away, of course, but after a suitable mourning period had passed." She took another bite, then paused her munching to add, "Bet you didn't know he promised Harper that he'd watch over you."

Shaina turned from the stove so quickly, she nearly overturned the pot.

"As God is my witness, I saw the whole thing. Sloan was down on one knee, trying to make Harper comfortable in those last moments. 'Don't tell her,' he said. 'Take care of her,' he said." She inspected the carrot. "Something to that effect, anyway." She met Shaina's eyes. "You don't mean to tell me you never noticed Sloan watching you from a distance."

"Well, of course I saw him." In the bank, at the café, at the grocer's…. "But he always seemed to have a legitimate reason to be…well, everywhere, so I never gave it a second thought."

"My advice? Before he gets home, give it a second thought. And a third," Jennie said before popping the last of the carrot into her mouth.

Then she got to her feet and gave Shaina a sideways hug. "Stay where you are. I'll see myself out."

Shaina heard the front door open, and before it closed, Jennie gave a merry giggle, followed by, "Maybe even a fourth thought!"

Chapter Twenty-six

According to Abby, the company would load $100,000 worth of gold and silver into one car, positioned two back from the engine. They'd hired three Pinkertons, one to stand on the porch of the caboose, one to ride with the gold and silver, and one in the cab to guard the coupling between the between the engine and the coal car.

Leo's crew had prepared well, and he'd been pleased with both practice sessions. But then, there hadn't been any intrusions during the timed dry runs. He'd warned them that during the actual raid, they'd have to neutralize the detectives, the engineer, the fireman, the conductor, the flagman, and any number of passengers with a hankering to put their six-shooters to the test. "Be confident, not cocky," he'd drilled into their heads.

He didn't have to worry about Sam or Rafe, at least not during the heist. Joe Michaels, on the other hand—despite the fact that Rafe Preston had vouched for him—made Leo's gut ache. *Too late now for second thoughts.*

Leo held his stopwatch in one palm, his pocket watch in the other. It had cost him nearly ten dollars to buy the others timepieces exactly like his own, telling himself it would be worth the investment once the job was done. Early that morning, they'd huddled in the mining shack and synchronized their watches. If they failed, it would be because one of the men forgot his signal, allowed his mind to wander, or got distracted by the sight of a moose in the clearing beyond the tracks. If they failed, Leo thought, the man responsible would die.

He could hear the distant whistle of the 9:10 to Greeley. By his clock, it should have been here twenty minutes ago. Any number of things might have slowed its progress, from beef on the tracks to a hitch in the rails. *Relax*, he told himself. *It doesn't matter if the train is on time, as long as we stick to* our *schedule.*

Leo had sat up here on this ridge nearly fifty times, measuring how long it took the locomotive to get from the gulch to the tunnel. By now, Michaels should have loosened the rail and fastened a rope around the tie. When the train was five minutes out, Leo would flash his mirror, Michaels' signal to urge his horse forward and dislodge the tie.

At three minutes out, Michaels would gesture to Sam, already in place on the old wagon road below. When Rafe saw Sam move the mules to the mouth of the tunnel, he'd crouch in the underbrush on the north side of the tunnel, directly across from Leo. The instant the train began to veer off course, they would pounce.

And there it was, in all its steaming, smoking splendor, sunlight glinting off the cowcatcher and the smoke-blackened brass stack. Heart beating hard, Leo put his thumb on the button of his stopwatch and willed his hands to stop shaking.

Click….

Five minutes: He flashed his mirror.

Four minutes: He heard the faint echo of Michaels' horse whinnying as the rope tightened around the tie, followed by the faint squeal of metal dragging over gravel.

Three minutes: By now, Michaels would have signaled Sam.

Two minutes: Sam, seeing the red flag, moved the mule-drawn wagons into place.

The 9:10's whistle blew, startling Leo so badly that he almost tumbled from the hillside.

One minute: Pebbles rained down, and he knew Rafe had moved into place above him.

Thirty seconds: Leo squatted, because he couldn't afford to be spotted by anyone in the engine's cab.

Fifteen seconds: Iron pistons and rods pumped up and down, up and down, as the train's wheels churned over the polished steel tracks.

In twenty feet—five seconds, at most—the train would enter the tunnel.

One final, shrill blast of the whistle sounded as the engineer's white sleeve, balanced on the open window, and the fireman's sooty, whiskered face disappeared into the blackness.

And then came an ear-piercing screech as the mammoth steam engine scraped the tunnel's stone and wood interior walls and came to a grinding, squealing halt.

Amid the violent chaotic madness, Leo had dropped the stopwatch, but he didn't need it in order to count the fractions of seconds that passed before the frenzied shouts of men mingled with the terrified screams of women.

It had begun.

~

"Everyone stay calm!" the conductor roared. With his hands extended like a blind man, he stumbled down the aisle, doing his best to keep his balance—not an easy feat, with the car tilting precariously to the left.

Sloan had counted nine people in the passenger car, including Abe and himself. Mostly businessmen in stiff-collared shirts, and a pair of elderly ladies. Except for wide-eyed fear, it appeared they'd all survived the crash unharmed.

One of the women clutched her knitting to her chest. "What happened? Are we being robbed?"

"Of course not," the conductor said, adjusting his jacket. "Just a minor mishap, ma'am. We're looking into it."

Sloan jerked the window shade from its roller and peered outside. "Minor mishap, my aunt Mary," he muttered. "Can't see a thing but the tunnel wall."

Abe looked over his shoulder. "I smell trouble, and it's comin' soon."

"Gentleman, I must insist that you remain in your—"

"What are you carrying back there?" Sloan demanded of the conductor.

The man straightened his lopsided hat. "That's really none of your concern. Now, please sit down, or—"

Abe blocked his path. "Or what? You'll throw us off the train?"

Guns drawn, they made their way to the back of the car and onto the gangway. Even after slamming the door behind them, they could hear the conductor shouting, "Sirs! Gentlemen! Come back here and sit down, I say!"

Sloan entered the dining car, which was empty, save for the broken cups and saucers scattered across the floor. The door to the boxcar behind it was bolted from the inside.

Abe was right on his heels. "We'll have to go round to get in through the side—"

A single gunshot echoed in the tunnel.

Anyone who could read a newspaper knew about the Bland-Allison Act. "Gold," Sloan whispered, using his chin as a pointer.

"Think that shot was for the Pinkerton?"

"Don't rightly know. But the government doesn't believe in doing anything small. I'm betting that car is fully loaded, meaning there are two, maybe three, detectives on this train to protect it."

Abe licked his lips. "What kind of ammunition do you reckon they're carrying?"

"Don't know, but between us, we've got twelve shots. More in our belts. How fast can you reload?"

"Real fast, if there's a loaded pistol aimed at me."

Sloan frowned and held up his left hand.

"What…?"

"It's too quiet. I don't like it."

"How many of 'em you figure there are?" Now it was Abe who held up his hand. "Let me guess—you don't know."

"Don't know what's out there, either," Sloan said, "so as soon as our boots hit dirt, shoot anything that isn't wearing a badge. I'll step out first, and you cover—"

"Hands up, boys, and turn around nice and slow."

"Leo Blevins," Sloan said. "I might have known."

"Toss those guns over here," Leo said, "and, like I said before, do it nice and—"

Another shot rang out, followed by two more in quick succession. Leo looked over his shoulder just long enough to give Sloan time to shove Abe to the floor. Both men ducked behind overturned tables.

Now it was the train's fireman who thundered down the aisle, a revolver in each hand, and more steam in his eyes than he'd built in the firebox. Leo spun on his heel and dropped the man before he could get off another round.

A Pinkerton appeared in the gangway, and in the moment it took to decide which car to enter, Leo had dropped him, too. Gunfire and fierce shouts erupted around them.

And suddenly Leo was nowhere in sight.

"What're the chances one of them dandies up there is carryin' a gun?" Abe hollered.

"Miracles happen," Sloan shouted back, "but I'd be less surprised to see one of those old ladies pull a Derringer out of her sewing bag."

Then it got real quiet, real fast. A second later, another Pinkerton crawled onto the floor of the gangplank. He flashed his badge, then met Sloan's eyes. "What's the head count in here?"

"You lost two, and the railroad lost a fireman."

"Lost the engineer and the conductor, too, I'm sorry to say." The agent shook his head. "Where's the fourth man?"

There wasn't time to ask how he knew about Leo. "In the passenger car, hunkered down between two seats. Which two, I couldn't say."

"The flagman's out back, guarding the ones we caught," the Pinkerton said. "That means there's three of us and just one of him. Here's what we're gonna do...."

He lifted his head just enough to start filling them in on his plan when Leo stood up and started blasting. The Pinkerton put a stop to it, but when the smoke cleared, Sloan saw that the man had taken a fatal bullet....

...and Abe lay spread-eagle in the middle of the smashed dinnerware.

The businessmen crowded the gangway. "He's still breathing," said one.

"Is it over?" asked another.

"Looks that way," said the first.

"Hard to believe all this madness and mayhem could happen in the span of three minutes."

When all eyes turned to him, the man held up his watch. "The lady across the way asked the time only seconds before it started."

And from the other end of the car, one of the women called, "What's going on? Will someone please tell us *what's going on!*"

The fellow with the watch said, "We've been *robbed*, you old fool. Now will you please hush?"

"No need to be rude," Abe rasped.

And Sloan nearly wept with relief.

Chapter Twenty-seven

Shaina stood at the window, watching night turn into day at Remington Ranch. The entire width of the horizon was awash with wispy of clouds that changed from lilac to pink, salmon to yellow, coming to rest on the horizon in a shimmering white splash. The magnificent, majestic mountains reached toward the pastel sky. Snow gleamed on high peaks that were peppered with ragged cliffs and boulders that supported thick rows of fir, pine, and spruce. In the shadows of the Rockies, the recent early-spring snowfall had painted the earth white, making it easy to see the cattle meandering toward food and water exposed by yesterday's sunshine. The big barn, silhouetted by daybreak, seemed small and unimportant against the grandeur of morning.

So beautiful and calm, she thought, turning to look at Abe, whose young face seemed frozen with pain as he fought for his life.

Long after Doc Wilson had cleaned and stitched and bandaged the near-fatal wounds, Sloan stood watch, and the signs of fatigue were beginning to show. He'd been shot, himself, yet he sat at Abe's bedside, watching and listening for a sign that his young friend, surely having touched the gates of heaven, had chosen to return to earth.

When Shaina moved into his line of sight, he glanced up.

"You look exhausted," he said.

"Am I the pot or the kettle?"

The feeble smile proved he'd gotten the joke, but he hung his head. His voice was thick with anguish when he said, "Has anyone told Elsie?"

"When Doc left, he promised to come straight back with more supplies and morphine. I'm sure she'll be with him."

Sloan only nodded. Her heart ached for him, sitting there looking so weary and weak. She adjusted his sling, then let her fingers linger on his injured shoulder. He laid his hand atop hers as she said, "Let me help you change into a clean shirt. I brought one from your room, and it's right there on the doorknob."

He looked at it, then shook his head.

If she'd ever seen anyone look more sad or lost, she didn't know when or where. On her knees beside his chair, Shaina said, "It wasn't a suggestion."

Sloan met her eyes. "Oh?"

"You don't want that dirty, bloody shirt to be the first thing Abe sees when he wakes up, do you?"

He looked down, taking stock of his attire for the first time since arriving home.

"All right," he agreed, standing.

Shaina got to her feet, too, then fetched the clean shirt and laid it at the foot of Abe's bed.

"How like you to give up your room," she said as she undid the knot of the sling.

"It's where he'll be soon, anyway, while he and Elsie build their house."

He winced slightly as she slid the fabric from his shoulder.

"Soon as we get you cleaned up, I'll bring you some breakfast." Shaina held up a finger to silence his protest. "You won't be any good to him if you fall over from exhaustion."

She proceeded to unbutton his shirt, struggling to keep the tears at bay at the sight of all the blood—Abe's, mostly—that stained the shirt. Letting the soiled linen fall to the floor, Shaina dipped a clean cloth in the basin of water on the bedside table.

"It'll be cold," she warned.

He emitted an involuntary gasp when the cloth met his skin. "Whoa. You weren't kidding, were you?"

"If I hurt you, you'll tell me, right?"

Eyes closed, he exhaled a ragged sigh. "Ah, Shaina. Don't you know by now what I'd...."

What would he have said if she hadn't asked the question?

She tossed the rag into the bowl, dried her hands on her apron, and picked up the fresh shirt. "Doc said to keep that arm immobile for a day or two," she told him, "so we're not going to worry about putting it into this sleeve." After buttoning him up and getting the sling back in place, she draped a lap quilt over his shoulders.

Sloan started to protest, but she hushed him with a stern look. "You lost a lot of blood, and you're cold. And is it any wonder, since you insist on sitting in that chair instead of lying down like the doctor told you to?" She smoothed the quilt, as if to keep it in place. "You'll just have to put up with this."

Until that moment, she'd thought she could read all his moods—worry when a calf came breach. Defeat when he couldn't prevent the cattle from freezing to death. Appreciation when she served his favorite meals. Frustration when Mable refused to take her medicine. Joy as he saddled or brushed Penny. Fear when he stood by, helpless, as Doc Wilson worked on Abe. But this? This was a look she couldn't define.

"And just what are *you* gawking at, Sloan Remington?" she teased. "Have I sprouted a mustache or something?"

Now, that is a look I recognize, she thought. She called it "affection," because her heart would break if she called it something more, only to have him prove her wrong.

Sloan drew her close and rested his chin on top of her head. He'd hugged her before—several times, in fact. But there was something different about the way he held her now.

"For a little thing, you sure throw off a lot of heat."

He lifted her chin on a bent forefinger, and when she met his eyes, he pressed his palm to her cheek. A time or two, when he'd studied her face this way, Shaina had thought he might kiss her. His face blurred slightly as it moved close, closer, and she closed her eyes. She felt his breath, warm against her lips. Every muscle tightened, every nerve tingled, as she waited.

And then, finally, he kissed her...

...on the forehead.

Before going downstairs to start breakfast, Shaina had opened the window blinds, inviting a sunbeam inside. "Maybe Abe will see this as an invitation," she'd said, "sent straight from God, to wake up and bask in its warmth." Then she'd drawn her hand through it, stirring dust motes…and his heart.

Now, Sloan stood in the same shaft of light, hoping she'd been right, because he sure could use a reason to believe in God's mercy right about now.

He was in awe of her ability to believe, unquestioningly, after all that she'd endured. If he asked, would she share her secret?

Standing beside the bed, Sloan watched the steady up-and-down rhythm of Abe's raspy breaths. He wrapped his fingers around the young man's wrist and gave it a gentle shake. "Don't you dare die on me, you hear, little brother?"

For an instant, Abe didn't breathe at all. Braced by one tightly clenched fist pressed into the mattress, Sloan leaned closer, listening, waiting, hoping. And then, as if in answer to a prayer he hadn't even prayed, Abe's chest rose, then fell. Sloan hadn't realized he'd been holding his own breath, and he exhaled slowly. He hadn't realized his grip on the boy's wrist had tightened, either. Forcing himself to relax, he let go and stepped back to the window.

Doc's empty buggy was parked in the drive. Any minute now, the telltale thud of footsteps would precede the doctor's entrance. No doubt, Elsie would be with him this time, and Sloan didn't want to be here when she caught sight of her husband-to-be, lying pale and still against the pillows.

He made a beeline for the door. *Too late*, he realized when they met him in the hall.

Elsie grabbed his hands. "Is he—?"

"He's unconscious," Sloan said, "but he's tough. He'll pull through, even if he does look a bit rough around the edges."

Nodding, she sucked in a great gulp of air, then stepped into the room.

Doc Wilson waited until his sister was out of earshot to whisper, "Has he shown any sign of coming to?"

"Just now I was in there, muttering to myself, and he seemed to react to something I said."

"React? How so?"

"His breathing stopped, just for an instant, like he was thinking up a typical Abe retort. Then it went back to normal."

"Might be a good sign."

"Might be?"

"Could mean he's coming around." He lifted one shoulder in a help-less shrug. "Could mean nothing at all, too. Only time will tell."

Sloan peeked inside the room at Elsie, who stood chewing one knuckle as her free hand brushed back the hair from Abe's forehead.

"How'd she take the news?" he asked the doctor.

"Not well at first. But she pulled herself together." Wilson smiled a little. "She's a strong woman, that sister of mine."

She'll need to be strong, Sloan thought, *to weather the storm she's about to face.*

"Well, Doc," he said, "I'll leave you to your business. I'll be in the kitchen if you need me."

With that, he headed down the stairs, hoping *he'd* have enough backbone to weather the upcoming storm.

He found Shaina at the sink, scrubbing an iron skillet.

"You keep that up, you'll rub a hole clean through the bottom," he said. The way she was going at it, he expected to see a burnt-on mess when he stepped up beside her instead of a smooth, food-free surface.

"Taking your frustrations out on the pan, are you?"

She dried her hands on a towel. "I was just about to bring you a tray."

"If it's all the same to you, I'd just as soon poke at the plate, right here." He took a seat at the table while she slid a platter of meat gravy and biscuits in front of him. "Doc and Elsie are up there," he added, picking up his fork.

Her lower lip quavered, but she quickly got ahold of herself. Sloan thought Doc's comment about Elsie's strength could just as easily apply to Shaina.

"Better eat up," she said, flapping the towel over one shoulder. "Gravy tastes awful once the grease congeals."

The ranch hands had eaten hours ago and were outside somewhere, performing routine chores. She hadn't saved this food from their breakfast. He knew, because he'd seen warmed-over gravy plenty of times, and it didn't look anything like this. He wasn't the least bit hungry, but since she'd gone to all the trouble of making it just for him, he felt obliged to choke down a few bites.

He patted the tabletop. "Won't you sit with me?"

Sloan could see that she had more dishes to scrub, as well as a basket of freshly laundered clothes near the door, ready to be hung on the line. And from the looks of the chopped vegetables and meat on the cutting board, she had a ways to go before the big midday meal was ready.

"I know it's a selfish request, but I hate to eat alone," he added. "I'll make it up to you later. That's a promise."

"Do you mean it?" Shaina asked as she sat across from him and folded her hands on the table.

"'Course I do."

"Then I know exactly how."

"Long as it isn't hanging socks on the line...."

She rolled her eyes. "No, you're not getting off that easy."

He couldn't imagine what chore she might assign him.

"When Dr. Wilson and Elsie leave, you must lie down and at least *try* to get some sleep. I've made up a cot in your room."

So, she'd anticipated his excuse that he didn't want to leave Abe alone.

He patted her hand. "All right. I'll try."

She'd worn a plain white apron over her simple blue dress, but there wasn't anything plain or simple about that beautiful face. Why hadn't he kissed her when he had the chance?

"Well," Mable said, hobbling into the kitchen, "just lookit the two of you, chatting like an old married couple."

Chapter Twenty-eight

What are you doing up?" Shaina asked. "I would have helped you, if only you'd called me!"

"Helped me?" Mable chuckled. "I suppose you were probably too busy ogling *that one*," she said, pointing at Sloan, "to notice I walked in here all on my own, without limping, I might add."

Sloan crossed both arms over his chest. "Yes, you did, didn't you? Not even the trace of a limp." Eyes narrowed, he added, "How long have you been up and about?"

Embarrassment colored her cheeks. "Long enough."

"If you wanted a holiday from your work," he said, "all you had to do was ask."

Mable wagged her forefinger at him. "This is *not* the time to get into it with me, Sloan Remington. You should be focusing on poor Abe, who's upstairs fighting for his life, not on an old lady who hates to be in bed."

"You hate to be in bed, eh? Then why did you keep your recovery a secret?"

The flush in her cheeks deepened as the doctor joined them.

"Any change?" Shaina asked him.

"No, but he's a strong young man. I have every confidence he'll rally."

"How soon?" Sloan wanted to know.

"I wish I knew."

The four of them stood around, looking at everything but one another. Abe meant a great deal to everyone in the room...and to the young woman who stood at his bedside right now. Shaina wanted desperately to comfort them all. If only she knew how!

"Well, don't we look like a gaggle of simpletons." Mable pulled out a chair and sank into it. "Sit down, everybody." She waved the men to the table. "Shaina, pour these sour-faced fellas some coffee so we'll have something to do while Sloan, here, tells us all about the robbery."

The men did as they were instructed, and so did Shaina. But she could tell by the look on Sloan's face that he wasn't ready to talk about the ordeal.

"Maybe we should wait," she said, "and give him time to get things straight in his head."

"Nonsense. The sooner he gets things out in the open—and off his chest—the sooner he'll be able to sleep at night." Mable leaned closer to Sloan. "You may have put it out of your mind, but *I* remember how it was after Simon died, when you paced the dark house like a circus tiger in its cage."

Oh, he remembered too. Shaina could tell, because she read the pain glinting in his green eyes.

"Mable, please," she said. "I'm sure Dr. Wilson needs to get back to town. You and Abe aren't his only patients, you know."

"Is that right, Doc?" Mable tilted her head. "You have other patients to see when you're done here?"

Wilson stuttered and stammered and shrugged.

"See there? He can stay." She faced Sloan again. "Go ahead. We're all ears."

"Please, Mable!" Shaina cried. "Can't you see he's tired, and in pain, and…." *And you interrupted the only meal he's had since yesterday's breakfast!* "Can't it wait a day or two?"

He reached up and gently grasped her wrist. "It's okay, Shaina. She could be right."

"Only one way to find out." Mable raised one eyebrow. "Start talkin', mister!"

Sloan recited the events as though reading from a book: There were gunshots. He and Abe went to check them out. The robbers shot the Pinkertons, but not before the detectives stopped the outlaws in their tracks. Abe was hit. Sloan brought him home. Doc Wilson patched him up. End of story.

"And now we wait," he added. "And pray."

"How many bad guys?" Mable asked.

"Four." He might as well have been reading a grocery list as he named them: "Sam McCloud. Rafe Preston. Joe Michaels. Leo Blevins."

Shaina gasped. "Leo, a train robber?" And then she knew why the man had seemed so familiar. "He…he was one of the gunmen who robbed the bank the day Harper was shot!"

"I remember that holdup," Wilson said. His brow crinkled with confusion. "But the newspaper said the men all wore masks."

"Yes. Yes, they did. But I would know that voice anywhere. Leo was the one who told everyone to get down, and when Harper didn't move quickly enough…."

Mable clucked her tongue. "Well, I wish I could say I'm surprised, but that one always did rub me the wrong way." She faced Sloan. "So he's dead, then?"

He nodded. "They all died trying to get the gold that was headed to Carson City."

Wilson shook his head. "The things some folks will do for money."

A moment of edgy silence punctuated his statement. Then he stood and said, "I'm going to get Elsie. We should head back to town and let you good people get back to…."

Only Shaina had something to do, but no one seemed compelled to point it out.

"Elsie may not want to leave, so I'll go up with you and tell her she's welcome to sleep on the cot in Abe's room," Shaina said, then turned to Sloan. "I just put fresh sheets on my bed. You can sleep there, and I'll—"

"Out of the question. I can sleep on the sofa in my office."

"That scratchy old thing? Why, even with two layers of linens on the cushions, you'll probably break out in hives. And how will you scratch them with your arm in a sling?"

One side of his mouth lifted in a flirty grin.

"If Elsie stays, you'll sleep in my room."

"And where will *you* sleep?"

"On that lovely settee in the library."

The last thing she heard him say as she followed the doctor from the kitchen was, "Bossy little thing, isn't she?" and then he and Mable shared a good-natured laugh.

Chapter Twenty-nine

That evening, after everyone had turned in for the night, Sloan wandered the quiet, darkened house. His arm ached from the shoulder all the way down to his fingertips, and even though Shaina had insisted that he sleep in the big, cushiony bed in the room she'd been using, he just couldn't get comfortable.

Head down, he paced the perimeter of the kitchen, trying to figure things out. If he'd fired Blevins the very first time his suspicions had been aroused, the man might have taken another job in Denver. If he hadn't hired Leo at all, the man might have kept moving west. Chances were good he would have hooked up with shady characters and left a trail of widows and orphans in his wake. But then, maybe Abe wouldn't be upstairs, fighting to avoid the Pearly Gates.

A flash in the sky caught his attention, and he walked to the window in time to see another. He'd been a mere boy when he'd last seen a shooting star that bright. It had been on that cold April day he'd first come to the ranch. Everyone, especially James, Mable, and Simon, had tried hard to make him feel welcome, to make him believe the ranch was his home, too. But the loss of his brother—the only one who'd shown him kindness since his adopted mother had dragged them both to her ramshackle house—had been too new, too raw; and this big old house had felt like anything *but* a home. He'd waited till everyone was asleep before coming downstairs, where he'd stood at this very window, marveling at all that was Simon's.

When that star had sliced the inky sky, he'd told himself it was his real mother, waving a hand across the heavens to let him know that everything would be all right.

And it had been.

In time, he'd grown to love Simon and to think of this place as home.

Sloan grabbed his jacket, grimacing as he slung it over his injured shoulder. The instant he stepped outside under that umbrella of stars, he forgot about Leo and Rafe, the Pinkertons, and the train crew. *It'll be all right, Abe,* he thought. One day, the young fellow would stand outside on a dark spring night like this, looking up at his own piece of sky. It would happen. It *had* to happen.

He rested an elbow on the top corral rail, and Penny sauntered over.

"Hey, girl," he crooned. "Did you miss me?"

She put her nose near his bum arm and, with a snort, nodded.

"Aw, it's no big deal," he told her. "I'll be good as new before you know it."

And as if to underscore the truth of his statement, another star streaked overhead.

Soft crunching sounds caught his attention. Penny noticed them, too. Head bobbing and ears swiveling, she nickered quietly.

Shaina stepped up and held out a steaming mug of coffee. "Thought you might need a little something to warm you."

She'd accomplished that just by showing up. "Thanks," he said, accepting the mug.

Then Shaina began shrugging out of her coat.

"Are you crazy? You'll freeze—"

"Bend your knees, will you? Otherwise I'll have no choice but to climb up on this fence to put this on you."

He did as she'd asked, and noticed that she'd worn her coat under his jacket. "You put it on just to get it warm, didn't you?"

"Did it work?"

"It did."

"I brought something for Penny, too."

At the sound of her name, the horse moved left, positioning herself directly in front of Shaina. And while Penny contentedly munched carrots, Shaina looked up at Sloan.

"What are you doing out here? You promised to at least try to get some sleep."

He pointed. "Zenith." His arm moved down and left. "And Virgo. And see there, just to the right of it? That's Leo."

"I didn't realize you knew so much about constellations."

"When I was about sixteen, I thought maybe I'd get into the weather business. Simon bought every book he could find—they're in the library, still—and I ate 'em up like most kids ate candy. The Nemean lion myth is one of my favorites. The way the story goes, the Greeks believed Leo was an indestructible man-eater with a hide so tough, not even Hercules' weapons could penetrate it. After breaking all his spears and swords trying to kill Leo, ol' Herc got so mad that he strangled that big cat with his bare hands, then put it up there in the sky like a trophy for all to see."

"A man of many talents," she mused. "Your coffee's getting cold."

He took a sip. She was right, but he drank it anyway.

"So what are *you* doing out here?"

"I couldn't sleep, and when I saw you out here...."

Shaina shrugged. "An experience like that...so much death and destruction...I imagine it'll stay with you for a very long time, and it'll never be easy to talk about." She laid a hand on his arm. "But if ever you want to talk about it, I'm right here."

But how long would she be here, now that Mable was back on her feet?

"Dr. Wilson said that when Abe comes around, he'll need a lot of tending. Mable might be getting around, but she's in no condition to run up and down the stairs or carry trays of food. And then, there are the usual chores. You know, cooking and tidying up and what have you." She grinned. "And keeping you in clean shirts, of course."

He remembered how gently she'd helped him out of the bloody one, how tenderly she'd washed spatters from his chest. "Of course." And how he'd pulled her to him and, like a fool, let her go again.

"Do you think maybe we should go back inside?" she asked.

Sloan nodded. "Yeah. I can barely feel my toes."

When they entered the kitchen, they found Elsie hunched over the table, sobbing.

Oh Lord, no, Sloan thought. *Abe can't be gone!*

Shaina went to her and knelt beside her chair. "How is he?"

Elsie blotted her eyes with a napkin. "The same," she said, her voice thick with tears. "No worse, but no better, either."

"Your brother is a good doctor, and he says Abe's being unconscious is his body's way of keeping him still so that the internal injuries can heal from the inside out." Shaina put her arms around Elsie and rhythmically patted her back. "Don't you worry. He'll be awake and on his feet and driving you mad in no time."

"Driving me mad? Impossible!"

"Just you wait and see. Men like the idea of getting married and having a wife, but they *hate* planning a wedding. He'll be no help whatsoever, and that will drive you mad!"

Elsie sniffed and studied her. "But I thought you said Harper completely took over the planning of your wedding."

"He did, because I didn't want any part of it. But I'm not normal that way, and you are. So, at the risk of being redundant, Abe will soon drive you crazy!"

Elsie had stopped sobbing. Better still, she was smiling. And Shaina was responsible for that. *She has that effect on people*, Sloan thought.

"I think we should go back upstairs and get you tucked in for the night," Shaina told her. "You'll need your sleep if you plan to help take care of him. And, more important, imagine what a lovely surprise it'll be if he wakes up in the middle of the night and sees his pretty bride-to-be right across the room!"

"Yes. Yes, of course." She got up and held out her hand to Shaina. "You're coming too, right?"

Shaina nodded, taking her hand, then turned and extended her other one to Sloan. "You're coming too, right?"

He put his hand in hers and climbed the stairs, feeling like a giant accompanied by two tiny women.

Sloan didn't know what they expected to see as they rounded the corner into the semidark room. Certainly not Abe, groggy but awake, looking directly at them.

"If y'all aren't too busy playing Ring Around the Rosie," he said around a weak grin, "I sure could use a sip of water."

Chapter Thirty

Every time the doctor stopped by the ranch to check on Abe, Shaina invited him to have a slice of pie, a honey biscuit, or a cup of tea, but he was always too busy to accept. So it surprised her when he sat at the kitchen table and devoured a bowl of soup.

"Is there somewhere on the first floor where Abe might rest, or even take a nap?" he asked between spoonfuls.

Shaina slid two loaves of bread dough into the oven. "No one uses the parlor much, now that Mable is back in her own room...."

"I'd like Abe to start getting back to his normal routine. Moving around will send blood to his wounds and thereby advance the healing process."

"That makes perfect sense. And you know I'm happy to do anything I can, for his sake and for Elsie's!"

"Speaking of Elsie, I want to thank you for convincing her to move back to town. Folks were beginning to talk about the goings-on in this house."

"Goings-on?" Shaina frowned. "Whatever do you mean?"

"Oh, just the typical low gossip. Unmarried men and women under the same roof."

"Who's saying these things?"

"The usual gossipmongers. No one pays them much mind, really."

Evidently, the good Dr. Amos Wilson did. Why else would he have broached the subject? She warned herself to take care in responding. He'd been Elsie's sole caretaker for decades, and in his mind, his little sister needed his protection, even if she was old enough to take a husband.

"I'm sure you're right about no one giving much credence to ugly rumors," Shaina began, "but I'm going to pray for those gossipmongers, because *God* is paying attention."

Wilson set down his spoon. "If I could have found someone like you when I was of a marrying age," he said, a timid smile slanting his mouth, "I wouldn't be a crusty old bachelor today."

The perfect example of a loaded statement, if ever she'd heard one. Wilson couldn't be more than forty years old, certainly not past the age to take a wife and raise a family, if that's what he wanted to do. The comment had probably just been his clumsy way of paying her a compliment. But if it wasn't, sending him the wrong message would be unfair and unkind.

"I'm sure that if you pray on it, the good Lord will introduce you to the right woman." Shaina was quite pleased with the way she'd matched his loaded statement with one of her own. "So, has Elsie finished sewing her wedding dress?" she asked, changing the subject.

Wilson groaned. "I have no idea. The parlor, the dining room, and even the foyer are filled with wedding paraphernalia. Hard to tell what's finished and what's left to be done!"

Shaina smiled. "Well, the wedding is just a few weeks away. It'll all be over soon."

"Yes, I know." He frowned. "I've never lived alone. It's going to be quite a change."

"I understand completely." Shaina topped off his coffee. "When Harper died, the house felt twice as big. Every footstep seemed doubly loud. I found myself going into his office or the parlor to get his opinion on something or ask what he'd like for supper, and my voice just bounced off the walls."

And the echo had gotten worse when she started selling things to pay the bills.

"But you're blessed to have such a busy, meaningful life," she continued. "Before you know it, you'll wonder how you ever abided all the chatter and clutter!"

He nodded slowly. "I pray you're right."

"More soup?"

"No, thank you. It was delicious, but I'm stuffed." He carried his bowl and spoon to the sink. "Sloan is a very lucky man, and if he doesn't wake up soon, I think he'll have serious regrets."

Shaina ignored his last comment. "I'll get the parlor ready for Abe this morning. As it so happens, when I was dusting the other day, I found Mason's old cane tucked behind some books on a high shelf. I'm sure it'll make Abe feel more confident as he starts moving around on his own."

Wilson grinned. "Leave it to you to think of something like that." He put on his hat and coat. "Will I see you at church this Sunday?"

"It'll depend on Abe. And Mable."

"Why Mable?"

"She's returning more and more to the woman we all know and love, but she still isn't fully her old self."

"Well, she isn't getting any younger. And I'm sure it wasn't easy being confined to your bed just so she could play matchmaker."

"Matchmaker!"

"Uh-oh." The doctor gave a sheepish smile. "It seems I've unintentionally let the proverbial cat out of the bag."

"The cat, eh?" Shaina planted her hand on her hip. "Well, now that it's running free, you might as well tell the rest of the story."

He opened the door. "Sorry, can't do that. Gave my word. Doctor-patient confidentiality, you know?" He grinned. "Until I see you again, be well, Shaina."

She didn't need to be a genius to decipher the implications of his statement. The clues had been there, all along. Why hadn't she pieced them together on her own? She hoped no one else had picked up the hint. Even more, Shaina hoped Mable hadn't shared the details of her matchmaking scheme with anyone other than Dr. Wilson.

But she couldn't be bothered with that right now. A long list of chores awaited her, among them, readying the place for Abe's reintroduction to the first floor.

Tonight, Shaina would prepare a special supper to celebrate his ongoing recovery. She had all the ingredients for his favorite meal—fried chicken and mashed potatoes. No one needed to know it was Sloan's favorite, too. Or that the pie she planned to bake, using canned peaches from the root cellar, was his preferred dessert.

Several weeks later, Remington Ranch had all but returned to normal.

After church one Sunday, Shaina started fixing the customary big meal.

"I'd help," Mable said, "but I'm feelin' a mite woozy today."

Shaina had noticed the beads of perspiration on the woman's brow of late, and she'd chalked it up to the sticky summer weather. Now, she wasn't so sure.

"Why don't you take one of your novels out onto the porch?" Shaina suggested. "It's nice and shady there, and you might just get lucky and catch a breeze."

It wasn't like Mable to so quickly agree, and the fact that she did so raised Shaina's level of concern.

"I'm going to make a pitcher of lemonade," she said. "When it's ready, I'll bring you a tall glass."

Mable started to protest, but Shaina wouldn't hear of it. "Sloan paid top dollar for all those lemons. Wouldn't it be awful to let them go to waste?"

The always practical woman shrugged, and then, mumbling something under her breath, she shuffled toward the front of the house.

"If I didn't know better," Shaina said to herself, "I'd say the old dear has been nipping at that bottle of laudanum."

Hours later, after the table had been cleared, Mable joined her at the sink.

"That was one of the best dinners we've had in ages," she said, giving Shaina a sideways hug. "Thanks, kid."

James had said as much while eating his pie, and it had pleased Shaina no end. What pleased her more, however, was the warm look of approval on Sloan's handsome face.

"If you don't need a hand, I think I'll head up to bed." Mable punctuated her sentence with a silly wink that looked more like a twitch.

Better check that medicine bottle, Shaina thought, *and put it in a safe, out-of-the-way place.*

"Sweet dreams," she said as Mable toddled from the room, "and I'll see you and James in the morning."

Half an hour passed as Shaina swept the floor and put away the pots and pans. With her chores finished for the day, she filled a tumbler with lemonade and carried it to the front porch. Maybe *she'd* get lucky and catch a well-timed breeze.

Eyes closed, Shaina listened to the flutelike song of the Swainson's thrush, competing with the coo of the common whip-poor-will. When a nighthawk called out, silencing the other nocturnal birds, Shaina sighed. "Go and hunt somewhere else," she told it. "You're destroying the peaceful—"

"You know what they say about people who talk to themselves, don't you?"

Shaina's heart fluttered at the sound of Sloan's voice. She didn't move, except to smile. "I thought you'd gone up to bed with the rest of them."

He sat beside her on the porch swing.

"So, what *do* they say about people who talk to themselves?"

"That they can always be certain at least one person is listening."

Shaina laughed softly. "Couldn't sleep?"

Sloan shrugged. "Something's been bothering me." He planted both of his big hands on his meaty thighs. "I wanted to run it by you, see if you've noticed it, too."

She knew in an instant what he was going to say. Turning slightly to face him, Shaina said, "Mable?"

He nodded. "Is it just me, or has she been...*different* lately?"

"It isn't just you. I thought maybe she'd gotten addicted to the laudanum. Doc Wilson said it happens sometimes."

"Sure would explain why she's been quieter than usual."

"I checked the vial, and it seems just as full as when she stopped taking the medicine."

"But addicts have been known to get sneaky about their habit. Maybe she's adding water to the bottle, to make it seem it's just as full."

"I hadn't thought of that." She sat up straighter. "But I've hidden the stuff, so if that's what Mable has been doing, she'll have to come right out and ask me where I've put it."

"Good for you."

"It's what I had to do when Harper grew dependent on the drug."

"I hope he knew how lucky he was to have you in his life."

"I hope he didn't know how I came to hate him...for a time."

"For a time?"

"The laudanum was one of the few addictions he didn't seek out on his own. Doc Wilson prescribed it, and I administered every dose." She heaved a breath of frustration. "Or so I thought. Neither the doctor nor I knew it—until it was too late—but he'd stolen a vial right out of Doc Wilson's medical bag." She released another sigh. "Harper had always been weak, but never weaker than when it was time to wean him from the drug. It was sad, really, watching him struggle with right and wrong."

Penny whinnied, drawing their attention to the corral.

"You've spoiled her," Sloan said, chuckling. "She's waiting for you to deliver apple slices or carrot sticks."

Shaina grinned. "I can't help myself. She's such a sweet animal. Spending time with her helps me miss Flame less."

"Flame...the horse you sold to Jennie?"

Shaina nodded. "I never miss the clothes or the jewelry, the art or the furniture. But Flame? Oh, how I regretted having to let him go. Still regret it, sometimes."

"Only sometimes?"

"Penny makes it easier." She adjusted her skirts, crossing one ankle over the other. "So, tell me, why is Abe going with you to Cheyenne?"

"Because, eager as he is to learn what it takes to run a place like this, he's young. Easy pickin's for shrewd salesmen. I want him to watch and listen, see for himself how fair and honest deals are struck." And then he yawned.

"I'm guessing that if you went up to bed right now, you'd fall straight to sleep."

He got to his feet, stretched, and yawned again. "You know, I think you're right." Sloan started for the door but stopped halfway there. "You should turn in soon, too. Your day starts as early as mine."

Shaina nodded. "I'll be up in a bit." She gazed toward the Front Range.

"Sleep well, Shaina," he said before disappearing into the house.
"Oh, I will," she whispered, "because I'll be thinking about you."

Chapter Thirty-one

It was June 2, 1883, and the good ladies of the church had decorated the altar and the aisle for the most anticipated wedding of the year.

Elsie had insisted on arriving early to make sure everything looked just right. Once she'd given her decisive approval, she joined Shaina in the suite Sloan had reserved for them at The Remington.

"I know it seems silly," Elsie said, tightening the belt of her dressing gown, "but I want this to be perfect."

Shaina didn't have the heart to point out how impossible perfection was.

"I'm determined to make this day one that neither Abe nor I will ever forget. Not just the date, mind you, but all the old traditions people have been celebrating for generations."

"Oh, I have a feeling everyone in attendance is going to remember this day," Shaina said as she fastened the clasp of Elsie's pearl necklace. "You'll be the most beautiful bride ever married in Denver."

"Only Denver?" she teased.

"In all of Colorado, then!"

Elsie beamed. "I'm so pleased you're my maid of honor. I can't think of anyone I'd rather have at my side than my dearest, most treasured friend."

Drawn together, first by Mable's accident and then by Abe's injuries, they'd grown closer than most sisters.

"It's truly an honor," Shaina said, "but I think I'll forgo fulfilling the original purpose of bridesmaids."

"Which was…?"

"Ah, they were a superstitious bunch, those ancient ancestors of ours. They believed there were evil spirits floating about, just waiting to descend upon the bride. So they dressed a group of handmaids in similar gowns to confuse the spirits."

"Thank the good Lord those pinched-faced old crones in the choir don't know about that! They'd have bridesmaids banned from wedding ceremonies in perpetuity!"

"Thank the good Lord *Jesus* freed us all from fallacies like that!"

"Amen," Elsie said. "It makes me all the more grateful you agreed." A sweet, loving smile lit her face. "I'm sure Abe feels the same way about Sloan's agreeing to be the best man."

"I'm sure." Shaina leaned forward and whispered, "We won't tell him how much the role has changed from the days of the Huns and the Visigoths!"

"I'm almost afraid to ask you to explain," Elsie said, sitting on the tufted footstool in front of the vanity.

Shaina took a seat on the chaise longue. "Well," she began, "in those days, the main role of a best man was to stand guard, his saber at the ready to protect the groom from marauding enemies. He would quite literally have died protecting his friend, if need be."

"Ironic, isn't it, that Sloan actually *did* risk his life for Abe that day on the train?" Elsie said.

"What do you mean?"

"When Sloan saw that Abe had been shot, he lay across him and took the final bullet. It's true. Abe told me it's the last thing he remembers before falling unconscious."

Shaina shook her head in admiration. "I'm not surprised he did something so brave. Not surprised that he never told anyone about it, either."

"So tell me," Elsie said, "what's the legend and lore of the phrase 'something old, something new, something borrowed, something blue, and a silver sixpence in her shoe'?"

"I'm so happy you asked!" Shaina clapped her hands. "'Something old,' you see, links the bride to her family. What's something old that you're wearing?"

"These pearls," Elsie said. "They were my mother's."

"Perfect! And 'something new' represents hope in the future."

Elsie held out her hand. "Abe bought me this pretty silver ring."

"'Something borrowed' is to remind the bride that her friends and family will always be there to lend a hand when she needs it. That's why I want you to wear these." She pressed a pair of pearl and silver earrings into Elsie's hand. "They were my grandmother's. If I hadn't been wearing them when the fire destroyed Sterling Hall, I couldn't loan them to you today."

"Oh, Shaina! They're beautiful." She leaned into the mirror and put them on. Then, facing her friend, she said, "You've lost so very much. I'll take good care not to lose them. You have my word."

"I know you will."

"And 'something blue'? What's the significance of that?"

"The color blue is a symbol of faith and loyalty. What marriage could survive without those?"

Elsie sighed.

"And the 'silver sixpence in your shoe,'" Shaina concluded, "represents security—a home built on a solid foundation, food in the pantry, enough money to get by on, and so forth."

Elsie dug through her purse, her brow furrowing slightly. "Oh, bother! I don't have any coins."

"But I do," Shaina said. She dropped one into Elsie's right slipper. "Consider it an early wedding present."

"Oh, Shaina, it's going to be a beautiful day, isn't it?"

"In every way."

The clock sounded a quarter after the hour.

"Time to get into your gown!"

Pastor Truett took his place in the center of the altar and faced the congregation. "Shall we begin with a prayer?"

All present rose and bowed their heads.

"Dear heavenly Father, we stand before You on this wonderful, joyous occasion, thankful for the blessings You have bestowed upon us. We ask that You would bless this day and everyone gathered here as Abe Fletcher and Elsie Wilson are united in holy matrimony.

"To this moment, Abe and Elsie bring dreams and hearts filled with love to share and bind together. We pray these proceedings will have Your blessing, and that their lives will bring You honor and glory.

"In the name of Jesus, we pray...."

And everyone joined him in a resounding "Amen."

"Please, be seated."

Once the church grew quiet again, he continued. "A wedding is a happy occasion. But marriage is not always filled with absolute joy." He glanced at Tillie, who sat stiff and quiet at the far end of the first pew, then returned his gaze to Abe and Elsie.

"I pray that you will both remember that marriage is a journey, and this beautiful day is but the first step. I also pray that when difficulties come—and they shall!—you will reach deep inside yourselves for reminders of the love that brought you here today. Make sacrifices for each other. Never let what you *want* become more important than what your mate *needs*. Let go of prideful needs. Above all, hold fast to the truth that love will prevail. As the apostle Paul wrote"—he placed one hand on each of their heads—"love *suffereth long, and is kind;...envieth not;...vaunteth not itself, is not puffed up, doth not behave itself unseemly, seeketh not her own, is not easily provoked, thinketh no evil; rejoiceth not in iniquity, but rejoiceth in the truth; beareth all things, believeth all things, hopeth all things, endureth all things.' Love 'never faileth.'* I pray God will watch over you always, that your life together may be long and happy."

Hands now clasped over his chest, Truett said, "Marriage is not to be entered into unadvisedly or lightly, but reverently and deliberately. Into this holy union, Abe and Elsie now come to be joined. If any of you can show just cause why they might not be lawfully married, speak now, or forever hold your peace."

Shaina struggled to recall her own wedding day, when the pastor had spoken those same words to her and Harper. *What a silly, immature little fool you were*, she thought, because not one of those words had sounded as meaningful as they all did now.

She watched Abe's face, shining with pure and complete love for his beloved, and Elsie's tear-misted eyes, returning that love in equal portion.

Neither she nor Harper had looked at each other that way, on their wedding day or any time thereafter. Had they just been better at masking their emotions? No. What better place to admit the truth than here in church, standing on God's altar? They'd exchanged vows not because they'd wanted to spend their lives together but because they'd wanted to be married, for secret reasons of their own.

She glanced at Sloan, looking dignified and regal in his black suit. He ran a finger around the inside of his starched collar, fiddled with the fussy black tie at his throat, and tugged at the cuffs of his stiff white shirt. He must love Abe a lot, to endure such discomforts!

"I pronounce you husband and wife," the pastor was saying. "Those whom God has joined together, let no one put asunder."

He looked at Abe. "Son, you may kiss your bride."

Sloan caught Shaina looking at him, and he grinned. Such a simple thing, really, to exchange smiles on such a happy occasion. Why, then, did she feel the urge to cry?

Because you want to stand up here beside *him, not across from him!*

Chapter Thirty-two

I'm not envious of much," Mable said, "but marching bands and fireworks? That's almost too much to bear!"

James shrugged. "Can I help it if people want to go all out for my birthday? This time last year, I wasn't at all sure I'd celebrate another."

"We're mighty glad your stroke last year was a minor one," Sloan said. "And it isn't every day a man turns sixty...on the Fourth of July."

"And works as hard today as he did at twenty-five!" James kidded. As if to prove it, he flexed his biceps.

"Be still my heart," Mable droned.

"Tease all you like." He tweaked her cheek. "You're one lucky old woman!"

"You know," she said, "this gets me t' thinkin'...."

"Uh-oh. Stand back, everyone. This could be dangerous!"

"Hush, James." And then she finished her thought. "Remember how Lloyd over at the tack shop let you trade in your old, worn-out saddle and gave you a whoppin' discount on the new one?"

He got the joke, even before she issued the punch line. "Aw, Mable. You can hardly keep up with me. What're you gonna do with some young whippersnapper?"

It had been a full day of enjoyment, and Sloan credited Shaina for planning the elaborate celebration. She'd put out the good dishes, and before long, there were so many serving bowls in the center of the dining-room table that he couldn't see the tablecloth—a tureen of soup, a platter of stuffed roast chicken, bowls of mashed potatoes and boiled beans, and a basket of golden rolls topped with sweet-cream butter, as well as a footed dish displaying the fancy layer cake she'd baked.

When she lit the candle in the center, James asked, "What in tarnation is that for?"

"It symbolizes life," she explained. "Now, close your eyes and say a silent prayer."

"Of all the...."

Despite his grumbling, James closed his eyes, and when he opened them again, Shaina said, "You prayed?"

"Call me crazy, but yes, I did."

"Good! Now, blow out the candle."

"What in tarnation for?"

"Because the smoke will carry your prayer to heaven."

Mable groaned. "Will you just humor her so we can have a slice?"

Hearty laughter made its way up and down the table, and right behind it were thick slabs of moist cake topped with jam.

Shortly after dessert, Sloan stood outside on the porch, waiting for a cool breeze. He smiled to himself, still thinking of how Shaina had gone overboard. But then, he'd never known her to do anything less.

The screen door opened with a creak, then closed with a soft thump.

"Ah, here you are," she said, stepping up beside him. "I'd ask if you were stargazing again, but you can't see the sky from here on the porch."

"But you can see fireflies."

She looked out into moonlit yard. "I didn't realize we had them here in Colorado."

"'Course we do. It's just that they're rare, like the green flash. It's mostly just by pure luck that mere mortals like us get to see them."

"Green flash? What's that?"

"Never saw one myself—I *have* seen a firefly or two, though—but I read an article 'bout the green flash a few years back. Apparently, in thirty-seven, a sailor by the name of Black wrote in his captain's log one morning that he spotted something he'd never seen before—a bright flash that sparked *just* as the sun disappeared into the horizon. He described it as 'the most brilliant emerald color.' The story got me curious, so I did some investigating. Found out the green flash is so rare, people who claim to have seen it are often called liars...or insane."

Shaina took a step closer. "What about you? Do you believe it exists?"

He looked over at her. "Just because I haven't seen it doesn't mean it isn't real."

Shaina nodded. "Like God."

Sloan thought about that for a moment. "Exactly."

Palms pressed onto the railing, she closed her eyes. "I love the fragrance of pines in the dew, don't you?"

"Yep." And he loved the crisp, clean scent wafting from her, too.

She leaned forward to get a glimpse of the sky. "And all those stars. Why, there must be millions of them up there, winking down at us. It's rather miraculous, don't you think?"

"Mmm-hmm." The bigger miracle, he thought, was that God had seen fit to put an angel right there beside him.

"Just look at the way the moonlight shines on the snow-covered mountain peaks," she said, pointing. "What a beautiful sight."

"Yes, beautiful." *But not as beautiful as you, Shaina Sterling.*

After James's stroke, Mable had asked Shaina to stay on. "I'm not gettin' any younger," she'd said, "and I find myself relying more and more on your help." Then she'd done something wholly out of character and pulled her young friend into a fierce hug. "Besides, the place just wouldn't be the same without you."

He'd agreed then, and he agreed now.

"Do you suppose it ever melts way up there?"

"Don't know."

But he knew she'd melted his heart, and that he had to find the courage to tell her before she slipped out of his grasp.

⁓

Shaina grinned. *If only Sloan could hear himself.* His one- and two-word answers didn't surprise her. She'd heard him leave the house that morning long before the sun came up. When he returned hours later, Sloan had explained that he'd ridden up to the south pastures to make sure the previous day's thunderstorm hadn't downed any fences. There'd been horses to feed and stalls to muck, all before driving everyone to town for the Independence Day festivities. After standing in the hot sun for over an hour to watch the parade, they'd gathered around the gazebo to listen as a brass quartet played patriotic songs. Sloan had disappeared for a time to check on things at the hotel and the manufactory, then had driven them all home in time for James's birthday dinner. So, if he seemed tired and distracted, he'd certainly earned the right to feel that way!

"Why are *you* so quiet all of a sudden?" he asked.

"I thought, after the noise and busyness of the day, the last thing you'd want to hear was me chattering away like a chipmunk."

"You're wrong. That's exactly what I need."

She feigned a pout. "You mean to say that I *do* remind you of a chipmunk?"

His quiet chuckle interrupted her. "No, what I mean is, your voice is...soothing."

"Hmpf. So now you're calling me *boring*, are you?"

"Ah, Shaina, I'll say it again—there's not another like you. And before you ask if that's good or bad, let me assure you, it's good. Very good."

He took a step nearer, close enough that she could see his day's worth of whiskers glinting in the moonlight. Harper had always worn a beard, so she knew well the coarse feel of a man's facial hair. What she didn't know was what compelled her to reach up and stroke Sloan's cheek, or why she allowed her fingertips to linger on his scar.

"Does it ever bother you?"

"What do you mean?"

"You know...does it itch or ache or feel taut when you smile or frown?"

She could tell by his relieved smile that he'd thought she was going to say something about the way it *looked*.

"Only if I nick it when I shave." He blanketed her hand with his own. "Does it bother *you*?"

"You're joking, right?"

His hand fell away, but she kept hers right where it was. "Why would it bother me? I think it gives you a certain"—she tilted her head to study him—"mystique. But, far more important than that, it'll always be there to remind me what you're made of."

"Made of? Now I'm really confused!"

At that moment, it seemed that Sloan was a six-foot-two inch magnet, and she was made of ore. She moved closer still.

"Then allow me to explain. You earned this scar defending Jennie." Now her hand covered the part of his shirt over the round, raised scar on his upper chest. "And you earned this one protecting Abe. That's bona fide heroism, not the kind people read about in dime novels."

Sloan shook his head. "You give me far too much credit. I did no more than any man would have done under those circumstances."

"You're wrong. I've heard what people say about Jennie…and anyone who befriends her. You've heard it, too, yet you saved her from…from only God knows what sort of horror at the hands of that awful Rafe—"

"Shaina, hush, will you? You're embarrassing me."

"I most certainly will not hush!" She felt his heart thumping beneath her palm. "You say there's not another like me. Well, *you* are one of a kind, too."

"I'm no hero. I stood by and watched my adopted ma and brother die, and then, six months later, I did the same thing when my so-called pa got sick. That's the opposite of a hero, if you ask me."

"You don't really believe that."

Based on the tight set of his jaw, he did.

"But what could you possibly have done to save them?"

"I could have given them my share of food and water. I could have sold something—my coat or my hat—to buy medicine. I could have…."

All these years, he'd blamed himself for their deaths? Shaina didn't know if she could bear it! "You were just a child, Sloan. A vulnerable, frightened boy." She cupped her elbows and faced front again. "I won't stand here and listen to you run yourself down."

"There's something you need to know about me, Shaina. I'm not who I pretend to be. All these years, only Simon knew the truth. When you hear it, you may not want to stay here a minute longer."

She waited, wondering what he could possibly say to change her mind about him. Even if he'd killed someone, surely there had been a good reason.

"When my *real* mother was barely more than a girl," he began, his voice low and gruff, "her family was slaughtered by the Dakota Indians, and she was taken captive." He turned to face her. "Black Eagle was a cruel and depraved man, and...."

Shaina thought she knew what he'd say next, and she held her breath.

"...and he is my father."

She learned that Black Eagle had tortured Sloan's mother, who had died of injuries and of near starvation when her only son was barely six years old. Terrified of what would become of him without his mother, whom he'd known only as "White Dove," to protect him, Sloan had slipped away in the dead of night. After wandering for days, he'd stumbled into a town, hungry, afraid, and exhausted.

"That's where Kitty found me," he continued. "She cleaned me up, fed me, and took me to the shack she and Ralph called home."

It hadn't taken him long to figure out that he and their young son, Pete, were little more than slaves to Kitty and Ralph. "I would have run off again, except I worried what they'd do to poor Pete.

"Somehow, Ralph got his hands on the claim to a gold mine, and despite all the whiskey he and Kitty consumed, they caught influenza. Pete died first, followed by Kitty. And because, no matter how hard I worked, I couldn't produce enough gold to suit Ralph, the man had little choice but to do some of the work, himself."

He stared off toward the mountains for a long time, then he expelled a ragged sigh.

"One day, Ralph was more drunk than usual. He hit a support beam instead of a vein of gold, and the mine caved in. I tried to dig him out, but all our tools were buried with him." Sloan shook his head, then drove a shaky hand through his hair. "I don't know how many days I walked, eating berries and roots and bugs. And then Simon rode into my life. Pulled me onto that big black stallion and rode for miles, talking without ceasing about Remington Ranch. I thought sure he aimed to make me into a slave, like Kitty and Ralph had done, but when I got my first glimpse of the place, I thought, *This is as good a place as any to die.*"

Shaina's heart ached for him. For the scared, orphaned boy he'd been.

"Simon warned me, almost daily, never to speak of my heritage. 'Ain't nothin' to be ashamed of,' he'd say, 'but what the Dakota did to folks in these parts is still too fresh in their minds.'"

In other words, Shaina realized, if anyone had found out about Sloan's secret past, he'd be ostracized as never before. She nodded, slipping her hand into his.

He gave it a gentle squeeze. "Abe and Elsie's house is coming along nicely, isn't it?"

Shaina smiled, just as ready as he to change the subject. "Yes. It's going to be a beautiful place," she agreed. "And if Elsie has her way, they'll fill every room with children."

Sloan chuckled. "She's an impatient little thing, isn't she? They haven't even gone on their honeymoon. They deserve more than one night at The Remington."

"I haven't heard them complaining."

"True." He paused. "Do you think Abe's strong enough to travel?"

Shaina shrugged. "He's been to town a few times with no ill effects."

"I don't mean riding into Denver and back. I'm talking about a longer trip. By train."

"If I were Abe, I know I wouldn't want to go anywhere by rail ever again!"

"Not even to San Francisco?"

She'd seen photographs of tall, narrow houses with dozens of steps leading to the brightly painted porches. "Especially not to San Francisco! Why, I've read stories about crime in the streets, and—"

"Like Denver, you mean?" he said around a yawn. "I ask only because I'm thinking they could use a change of scenery and some time all to themselves. Years ago, Abe saw a picture of San Francisco, and I'll bet he's talked about going there thirty, forty times. I'd really like to send them there."

"But it's thousands of miles away!"

"Just a little more than a thousand."

"Well, Abe is a grown man. A husband. And before you know it, he'll be somebody's pa. He'll have others depending on him. He can't just pack up willy-nilly and hop a train to California!"

Sloan didn't respond. In fact, he was quiet for so long that Shaina wondered if he'd fallen asleep on his feet.

Soon the clock in the hall struck ten. Placing his hands on her shoulders, he turned her around. "If you're even half as dog-tired as I am, it's time to turn in."

She wasn't the least bit sleepy, but something Pastor Truett had said during Abe and Elsie's wedding came to mind: *"Never let what you want become more important than what your mate needs."*

So she faked a big yawn and let him lead her inside. As he headed for his office/bedroom, she said, "Pancakes for breakfast?"

"James's favorite. He'll think it's still his birthday." With that, he disappeared around the corner.

How like him, to consider someone else's feelings above his own. It probably never entered his head that she wanted to make *his* preferred breakfast staple, not James's or Abe's or even her own.

Shaina blew him a kiss. "Sweet dreams," she whispered.

There must be something wrong with you. Other widows dreamed of their deceased husband, especially if he'd died by his own hand. Women who'd lost a lifetime of memories in a devastating fire would dream of favorite photographs and collectibles, gobbled up by greedy flames. *But not you, Shaina Sterling. Not you!* No, her slumbering hours were filled with images of Sloan, rising extra early to make sure every animal on the property had what it needed. Of Sloan, staying up later than anyone else to balance the books in order to secure the well-being of all who called Remington Ranch home. Of Sloan, who put great thought into protecting the people who ran his hotel, as well as the employees at Sterling Manufactory, which had nearly been destroyed by her late husband's greed and addictions. Of Sloan, who'd made such a habit of doing for others what, more often than not, he forgot to do for himself.

Perhaps she was normal, after all, because what woman *wouldn't* dream of a life with a man like that?

According to Jennie Rogers, he'd secretly watched over Shaina, too. Could it possibly mean he loved her, not simply as one of the many who counted on him, but her as an individual, as someone who held a special place in his heart? Oh, that would be the dream of a lifetime!

She hadn't knelt beside her bed for evening prayers since childhood, but tonight, after changing into her nightdress and turning down the lamps, she did exactly that.

As usual, Shaina thanked the Almighty for her many blessings and asked Him to watch over and protect everyone dear to her, including her parents and brothers, wherever they were. She closed with a special prayer for Sloan, who'd spent a lifetime under the crushing weight of guilt that wasn't his to bear.

"Father, touch him with Your loving hand, and bless him with much-deserved peaceful, restful sleep. Ease the burdens he's carried all these many years, and help him to realize that he couldn't have prevented the deaths of his loved ones. And if it's Your will, help *me* find a way to let him know how honored I'd be to share the rest of his life. In Jesus' name, amen."

Chapter Thirty-three

Sloan awoke later than usual, feeling rested and revitalized. His shoulder didn't hurt a bit when he slipped into his shirt, and he managed to shave without nicking his scar. Yesterday, he might have explained these as good things happening in their own good time. But he knew better.

Last night, he'd paced the length and width of the library, and when studying the Scriptures failed to calm his restlessness, he'd decided to fix himself a cup of warm milk with a pat of butter on top, the way Shaina made it. On his way to the kitchen, he'd noticed the sliver of light spilling out from under her door. He'd forgotten to say good night, so he decided to use that as his excuse to invite her to join him. Just as he'd lifted his fist to knock, he'd heard her soft voice, praying…for him!

He'd gone straight back to his room and fallen fast asleep; and, like every other night since Shaina's arrival, he hadn't had even one bad dream. And he knew why.

Sloan couldn't wait to see her.

He heard her happy laughter even before he walked into the kitchen. When he entered the room, Shaina was so busy serving the men that she didn't even see him there, leaning against the doorjamb. With every biscuit taken from the big basket hugged against her chest, she doled out a compliment: One man had parted his hair differently; another trimmed his beard; a blue shirt brought out the green in yet another's eyes.

Since her arrival, the men had changed. No one ever came to the table with dirty hands. They all said "please" and "thank you," and Sloan couldn't remember the last time he'd heard a big, gratifying belch…or even a small one.

It made him smile to consider the big changes that this tiny woman had brought to the ranch.

He loved Mable like a mother, but that didn't keep him from admitting to himself that while she'd always done what needed doing, she didn't put anything extra into the work. Why go to the extra bother of washing napkins, she'd once said, when the men use their sleeves? What sense did it make to put fork, spoon, *and* knife beside each plate when just one utensil would do? Flowers on the table? Pah! Vittles— that's all those men were interested in, so why bother?

Before Shaina, he'd blamed Mable's upbringing, devoid of formal education and lacking a mother to teach her how to behave like a lady. After Shaina, he realized he didn't know how to explain Mable's gruff manner, because Shaina had practically raised herself, supported herself, and educated herself. The comparison did nothing to diminish his affection for the woman who *had* gone the extra mile for him from the moment Simon brought him home.

Still, the comparison made him wonder: If Shaina would go so far to please men she barely knew, how much more would she do for the man who held her heart? He just needed to ratchet up the courage to let her know how he felt about her.

As promised, she'd made pancakes, and the ranch hands couldn't get enough. No sooner did she put a new stack on the table than they were clamoring for more.

"Where's Mable?" he asked, taking his place at the head of the table.

"Tackling that mountain of bedding," James said, sticking his fork into a sausage patty.

Shaina looked surprised, and Sloan understood why. The day before yesterday, he'd seen sheets and pillow slips fluttering on the clothesline out back. He could almost read the meaning behind her patient smile: "*If Mable needs a little rest and time away from the lot of us, she's earned it!*"

He and the other men discussed what needed to be done that day: Check the fences along the western border and make any necessary repairs. Roll bales of hay and deliver them to the fields. Grind feed. Groom the horses. And perform the never-ending task of mucking stalls.

"Soon as I hitch the horses to the wagon, I'm headin' into town," James said. "Anybody needs anything, speak up—or wait till my next trip."

After the men had listed their needs, Abe offered to ride along. "Unless you're lookin' for some quiet time," he added.

"Aw, you don't jabber all that much." The older man looked down the table at Sloan. "You still plannin' on ridin' in to check the hotel and the plant?"

"I am. But don't wait on me. I have some work to finish up here before I leave."

In truth, he'd need only tuck his ledger into a saddlebag. But he couldn't very well share the real reasons he wanted to stay behind. Not until the men headed out to dig into their chores.

When at last he and Shaina were alone, he refilled his coffee mug from the carafe. "Sleep well?" he asked her.

"Like a baby."

"Don't know as I'd say that's a good night. I overheard young Bailey down at the bank complaining that his newborn young'un woke the whole house every two hours like clockwork."

Shaina laughed and went back to stacking plates, leaving him to wonder whether she'd spent a fitful night. The last thought on his mind before dropping off to sleep, himself, had been her sweet, thoughtful prayer.

"Sit with me," he said. "Those dishes aren't going anywhere."

She gave his suggestion a moment's thought, then pulled out the chair nearest his and lowered herself into it.

"Heard from your folks lately?"

Her entire demeanor changed, from happy and relaxed to stiff and fretful. She shook her head. "I'm holding fast to the adage that 'no news is good news.'"

"What about your brothers?"

"Not long before Harper died, I received a letter from Ben. He was in Abilene, working for a farmer. He asked if I'd been in touch with Earl, because last he heard, Earl had enlisted in the army. I wrote back, but I haven't heard from him since."

"Sorry."

"It's strange, and it hurts, because the distance between us is so much more than just the miles. We were like three peas in a pod, climbing trees, fishing off the pier, playing hide-and-seek...." She sighed. "Once, Earl hid so well, it took Ben and me hours to find him."

"Where was he?"

"In the outhouse, of all places!"

It was good to hear her laugh. So good that Sloan decided he would do everything humanly possible to see that she had plenty of reasons to laugh, every day, for the rest of her life.

"Looks like we're in for some good weather. You told me once how much you love the wind in your hair when you ride. Why don't I saddle old Bernie for you before I leave?"

She patted his hand. "That's very thoughtful, but I really don't have time." She got up, went back to the sink, and said over her shoulder, "I'm sure someday I'll get over regretting having to sell Flame, but in the meantime, riding just isn't the same."

Sloan added his mug to the others waiting to be washed. "I should find Mable and see if she can help you."

"No, she has plenty to do, getting that mountain of bedsheets on the line…and back onto the beds."

He saw the twinkle in her eye, and knew the remark held no mockery. "Guess I'll be on my way, then."

"Can I pack you a lunch?"

There wouldn't be time if he hoped to accomplish everything on his mental list. He patted his stomach. "Thanks, but I'm sure that breakfast will stick with me clean till suppertime."

He leaned in, as if to kiss her cheek, the way a husband might when leaving for the day, but he stopped himself. *Bide your time, man.*

Sloan let Penny choose the pace, and she carried him to Denver at a steady trot. He got the most mundane tasks out of the way first: A stop at the bank to withdraw funds, then on to Sterling Manufactory to deliver the cash his bookkeeper would tuck inside pay envelopes for each of the plant's 174 employees, and finally a visit to The Remington to give the Sweenys their salaries.

When he walked into the Denver Pinkerton office, Jase Hough was snoring quietly, boot heels resting on his desk, fingers interlaced behind his head.

He started at the sound of the door closing. "Just restin' my eyes," he said, dropping both feet to the floor. "What brings you to my humble office on this fine day?"

Sloan sat in the chair facing Jase. "Got a favor to ask you."

"Well, a man can ask."

"I hear you. How would you go about finding two men who aren't wanted by the law?"

The detective rubbed his bearded jaw. "Well now, let me think on that a minute. You say they're not wanted?"

"Not that I'm aware. They're the brothers of my...." It seemed wrong to call Shaina his "housekeeper" and inaccurate to say she was his "woman." He cleared his throat. "Someone very dear to me was forced by bad circumstances to leave home at a very early age, and she hasn't seen either of her brothers in—"

"Very dear to you, eh?" Jase snickered. "In all the years I've known you, I don't believe you've ever referred to a woman quite that way."

Sloan had two choices: Bare his soul and risk a good ribbing, or let the comment slide.

"She had a letter from one brother, but that was nearly three years ago," he decided to say.

Jase slid open the narrow drawer near his belly and plucked out a pencil. "What are their names?" he asked, pressing its nib to the tablet on his desktop.

"Ben and Earl Brewster. I'm guessing they'd be in their mid- to late twenties."

The pencil scratched over the paper as Jase scribbled down the information. "Description?"

Sloan shook his head. Shaina stood no more than five feet two inches and likely didn't weigh over 105 pounds. She had the bluest eyes he'd ever seen, and hair as dark and sleek as a river otter's fur. But not all siblings looked alike. For all he knew, the boys were tall as trees, or maybe they resembled Swede Jenson, the portly fellow who ran the granary.

"Well," Jase said, drawing out the word, "that's a start."

Sloan held his breath, unable to believe that he'd said all that out loud. Maybe biding his time hadn't been such a good idea—it had turned him into a loopy chatterbox!

"Where did this, uh, 'dear friend' of yours last see these two?"

"They hale from St. Charles, Missouri. The one named Ben was in Abilene, last she heard, and she thinks the other one might have joined the army."

"The army, you say? Now, that's a right good place to start. It's been my experience they keep good records of soldiers' comings and goings." He put down his pencil and chuckled. "How else would they round up the deserters?"

Sloan got to his feet. "I don't know how to thank you."

"No thanks necessary. I was one of the investigators on that attempted train heist, and every passenger and crew member I interviewed claimed things would have been far worse if you hadn't been on board."

The image of Jase's comrades, falling one by one in their attempts to fulfill their duties, flashed in his mind. Sloan blinked away the bad memory. "I appreciate it all the same."

Jase shook his hand. "Can't guarantee I'll learn anything, but you have my word that I'll do my best."

Sloan was halfway out the door when the detective added, "Ain't been to a wedding in a coon's age...."

Good thing you don't play cards, he said to himself as he headed to Jennie Rogers' place. He didn't need a poker face to cut a deal with her. He'd need one once he got home, though, after buying Flame and getting Jennie to promise to continue caring for the stallion until he could deliver him to Shaina.

Chapter Thirty-four

With the table cleared and the breakfast dishes done, Shaina started supper. Stuffed roasted chicken and potatoes was always a crowd pleaser, especially if she served it alongside steaming bowls of boiled cabbage, corn, and hot biscuits.

She blamed her drowsiness on the long, sleepless night. How odd that not even her favorite Bible verses had delivered peace and contentment. But no matter. As her sweet grandmother used to say, "Time spent in prayer is never a waste."

Perhaps that was exactly what she needed to soothe her, now that Sloan's questions had raised new worries about her brothers. She missed her folks, but not half as much as she longed to see Ben and Earl, who'd taught her to bait a hook, shoot a gun, win at dominoes, and make a doll from an ordinary clothespin. Shaina would search for them if she had any idea where to start.

Feeling sorry for yourself never got you anything but puffy-eyed, she scolded herself, blotting tears from her eyes. If a reunion was in God's plan, it would happen, by His timetable and not a second earlier. And if it didn't? Then He'd provide the strength to bear up until she met them in paradise.

She put away the dishes and pots, then pulled back the curtains to allow the morning breeze into the kitchen.

How odd. The clotheslines should have been sagging under the weight of freshly washed sheets. What in the world could be taking Mable so long?

Grinning, Shaina dried her hands and headed for the porch. No doubt she'd find Mable out there, engrossed in yet another one of the romance novels that helped her while away the hours as she "recovered" from her accident. Were the heroes in the stories anything like her precious James?

But Mable wasn't on the back porch. Or in the parlor. Not in the library, either. Shaina headed up stairs, thinking the woman might still be stripping the beds. Or maybe she'd gotten distracted by some other chore while she was up there.

"Well, I'll be," she said, hands on her hips. Granted, it was a big house. But there were only so many places the woman could be, and she'd investigated all but the root cellar.

Moments later, emerging with jars of preserves and sprouting potatoes in the sack she'd made of her apron, she began to worry. What if Mable had fallen again, and lay helpless—or, worse, unconscious—somewhere?

Finally, Shaina found her, in the one room she'd never thought to search—Sloan's office. She'd turned his big leather chair around to face the window, so that only the top of her curly gray head was visible.

"Goodness," Shaina said, "you had me worried sick!"

She braced herself for the barrage of good-natured, sarcastic barbs that would surely follow.

But there was nothing.

"Mable Corrigan," she scolded, "I am not amused."

Still nothing.

The woman was a sound sleeper, as anyone at Remington Ranch could bear out. To this point, Shaina had been relatively quiet, so as not to startle the poor thing.

She walked up to the chair and spun it slowly around. There sat Mable, a Bible on her ample lap, a look of such tranquility on her wizened face that Shaina hated to disturb her. She reached for the Good Book, which was open to Psalm 119.

Why did Mable's hands feel cool to the touch? The temperature outside had to be 90 degrees, and here in Sloan's sunny office, the thermometer would likely register in the 80s.

And then she knew, and it put her on her knees: Mable was gone. All the ranch hands were in the fields and wouldn't return to the house until suppertime. Abe had gone into town with James, and Sloan was in

Denver, too. That left Elsie, but Shaina was torn between fetching the girl and leaving poor Mable alone.

She stiffened her resolve. This was no time for tears and weakness. Besides, she needed to practice fortitude, because James and Sloan would need her to be steadfast, not weepy and clinging.

She found Elsie out back, hoeing the garden. "You're just in time to help me pick a mess of beans for tonight's supper," the girl said without looking up.

Then she straightened, and by the look on her face, Shaina knew that her own attempt to keep her misery hidden had failed.

"What's happened?"

Shaina drew her friend into a fierce hug. "It's Mable. She's...she's gone."

"Gone? Whatever do you mean, *gone?*" Elsie shaded her eyes from the sun. "Surely, you don't mean...."

Several seconds of sickening silence passed, and then they allowed themselves a moment's worth of grief-stricken sobs. Shaina stepped back and said, "I need you to ride into town and tell the others. And your brother. And Pastor Truett. Tell one of them—Abe, I suppose— to notify Bass, the undertaker. And whatever you do, avoid Molly Vernon until we know more, all right?"

Elsie nodded. "I'll leave right this minute." She dropped her hoe and started for the barn.

"Do you need me to help you saddle a horse?" Shaina called after her.

"No, I'll be fine." She hesitated. "Are you sure *you'll* be all right, here all alone with...?"

"Of course. Now, you be careful," she added, turning toward the house.

"Shaina. Wait." Elsie ran back to her, wringing her hands. "What do I tell them?"

"Just tell them...." Shaina bit her lip to stanch the tears that burned behind her eyelids. "Just them to come as fast as they can."

⌇

Yesterday, Shaina had cleaned the place, top to bottom. She'd done the laundry, too. The bed linens Mable had claimed needed washed and dried now hung on the line, and she'd neatly folded Sloan's white shirts and stacked them neatly in his wardrobe. Supper was in the oven, and except for stoking the coals in the stove from time to time, there wasn't a single household chore to occupy her.

Shaina knew it would be hours before the others returned from Denver. How would she pass the time?

And then she remembered Mable's Bible, open to Psalm 119, her forefinger on verse 175.

She returned to Sloan's office, where the Good Book still lay open on his desk, and willed herself not to stare at her friend's face, frozen forever in an expression of what she could only describe as sweet serenity.

Carrying the Bible to the sofa, she sat as far from Mable as the cushions would allow, and began reading. Was it her imagination, or did the sun beating down on her back intensify when she got to the verse Mable had marked with her stubby finger?

"'Let my soul live,'" she read aloud, "'and it shall praise thee; and let thy judgments help me.'"

She'd hoped the Word would give her some idea of what had been on Mable's mind when she'd passed—what peace she'd received or guidance gleaned from that verse. Whatever meaning Mable had found eluded Shaina. She closed the Bible ever so gently and set it back on Sloan's desk. If the Lord intended her to understand, He would enlighten her in time.

She thought of James, and how lost and heartbroken he'd be when he heard the news.

And that's when she figured out how she'd occupy the hours until their return.

When her father-in-law passed, Shaina had helped the servants get him ready for his final voyage. After washing him, dressing him in his best suit, and tucking his pocket watch into one hand, they'd closed all the curtains, turned every photograph toward the wall, stopped every clock to mark the time of his death, and hung a wreath of black-draped boxwood on the door as a signal to passersby that someone inside had died. All this had been done in preparation for four days of wailing and a garish procession of mourners who followed the undertaker's ornate black carriage, pulled by horses wearing black plumes on their heads, from the house to the church, and then from the church to the graveyard.

When Harper died, Shaina had refused to participate in any of those superstitious traditions; and if she had anything to say about it, none of them would be observed for Mable, either. There should be light and joy in the house to remind everyone that while they'd lost Mable, she'd gained paradise.

Upstairs, she rummaged through Mable's wardrobe and pulled out all her favorite things: a bright blue skirt and matching jacket, a pair of low-heeled, high-button boots, and her mother's calico broach to affix to her collar.

It wasn't easy moving Mable from the chair to the leather sofa in Sloan's office, but by the grace of God, she found the strength. For some unknown reason, she took the time to heat water on the stove, then carried it to Sloan's office in a beautiful serving bowl instead of an ordinary pitcher and used a soft cloth rather than a regular washcloth to gently bathe her dear friend. She brushed Mable's hair and held it back from her face with tortoiseshell combs—a birthday gift from Harper that Shaina had been wearing the day of the fire.

By the time she'd changed Mable into her pretty outfit, Shaina was exhausted and all but cried out. But the result was worth every sweat- and tear-inducing moment. At least now, the two people who'd loved Mable longest and best wouldn't come home to find her posed in a chair like some dress-shop mannequin.

Next, Shaina cleaned herself up, mostly to spare them from thinking, *Oh, poor Shaina…just look at all the trouble she's gone to on our behalf!* Then she put the best tablecloth on the kitchen table, set out the good plates and the silverware, prepared enough bread dough for four loaves, and whipped up the batter for a spice cake. If someone didn't get home soon, she didn't know what she'd do.

Minutes later, she paced the length of the shaded front porch, praying that when James and Sloan showed up, she'd know the right thing to say—and the right time to say it. The sound of a horse's hooves caught her attention, and she stared hard at the far end of the road. It was Elsie, home after being away for hours. She must have alerted the ranch hands along the way, because they began straggling in from the fields. One of them led Shaina's horse into the barn while the others ambled into the bunkhouse.

Elsie greeted her with a quick, tight hug. "Take me to see her," she said. "The others are right behind me, and I don't want to be there when James walks in."

Shaina nodded and led the way.

"Why is the sofa out here in the middle of the room?" Elsie exclaimed.

"Two reasons," Shaina began. "First, they can't see her right off with it positioned this way. Every second they get to prepare themselves will make that first sight a little easier to bear. Second, the sun was beating down on the sofa, and in this heat...."

Hopefully, Elsie would figure out the rest on her own.

"Why didn't you just close the curtains?"

"Death itself is dark enough. We don't need the room to look gloomy, too."

Taking Shaina's hand, Elsie said, "Walk with me?"

Her parents were dead. Surely, she'd seen something like this before. But Shaina complied.

Fingertips pressed to her lips, Elsie said, "Oh, my. She looks...."

"Like she's sleeping. Yes, I know. And thank the good Lord for that."

The front door slammed, and the women headed for the hall.

Abe walked straight to them and took Elsie in his arms. "What happened?" he whispered to Shaina.

"I wish I knew."

"That's too bad. James is hot on my heels, and he's barely holding it together."

Oh, if only Sloan were here to help the poor man cope.

But what was she thinking? Shaina wished he was here to help *her* cope, too!

Chapter Thirty-five

Amos Wilson was in Sloan's office, but only the good Lord knew why. Mable had been gone more than twelve hours, and he failed to see what a doctor could do for her. It seemed to him that Marcus Bass, the undertaker, was the man who ought to be in there now. Instead, he was back in Denver, setting up the burial. Even Pastor Truett would have been of more use. At least he could offer solace and Scripture to help them all understand how a woman as hale and hearty as Mable could be talking about mountains of dirty laundry one minute, then gone from this earth the next.

He went to the kitchen, mostly to get away from the others. It didn't seem right, showing his own grief when James had just lost his partner of nearly forty years.

The minute Shaina saw him, she ran over and threw her arms around him. "I'm so sorry, Sloan. I know how much she meant to you."

He could barely manage to grunt a reply, so he buried his face in her hair and soaked up her sympathetic warmth. And before he knew what was happening, he broke down. His sobs shook them both, but she neither stepped back nor loosened her grip. When the tears subsided, he held her at arm's length and saw that she'd been crying, too. What a selfish lout he was, not realizing that Mable had also meant a great deal to Shaina.

"Forgive me," he croaked. "I didn't mean to—"

"Don't you dare apologize," she scolded gently. "I'm humbled to know you trust me with your honest grief."

She led him to the table and pulled out a chair, and he slumped into it. Then she slid out another and brought it so close to his that their knees were touching when she sat down.

"Elsie said you found her?" Sloan asked.

"I did."

He didn't know if he could bear to hear about it. Didn't know if she could bear to *talk* about it.

"I don't think I'll ever forgive myself," she murmured.

Sloan didn't understand, but if he knew Shaina, she'd soon explain.

"I should have checked on her sooner. I'm guessing it was more than two hours between the time she left to round up the laundry and when I...."

She'd been such a comfort to him just now. And when he thought about all she'd done, single-handedly, to spare others from having to do it, he put his forefinger under her chin and lifted until she met his eyes. "You know you're being ridiculous, don't you?"

She only blinked.

"Believe me, I know it's painful, losing her so suddenly. But you're not a doctor. And, as good as you are at looking after people, you're not a licensed nurse, either. What makes you think you could have done something to prevent—" He wasn't yet ready to say, "*Mable's death.*" "To prevent what happened?"

A tiny smile lifted the corners of her mouth. "Are you hearing what you're saying?"

At first, he didn't get it. And then he remembered that night out on the porch, when she'd quietly reprimanded him for carrying the burden of his surrogate family's deaths.

"Oh, you truly are one of a kind, Shaina Sterling." Someday, God willing, she'd be Shaina Remington instead.

"Yes, we've established that we're both quite unique." She stood up and held out her hand to him. "I suppose we should see if James needs anything."

Nodding, Sloan got to his feet and walked alongside her, thinking with every step that the only thing James needed was Mable.

Doc Wilson met them at the end of the hall. "I can't believe I was able to talk James into it," he said, "but he agreed to take some of this." He held out a bottle that resembled the one he'd left for Mable, only the label looked different.

"What is it?" Sloan asked.

"Tincture of opium. It'll calm his nerves and get him through the next few days." He handed the bottle to Shaina. "I'm putting you in charge of this, because I've read articles claiming it's highly addictive. Give him one spoonful if he looks jittery or seems inconsolable." Facing Sloan again, he added, "You should take some, too, just until...."

Until Mable was in the ground?

"Thanks, but I'll be fine." *Shaina is my drug of choice*, he thought, remembering how easily and quickly his crying jag ended when he'd taken refuge in her arms.

Wilson glanced into the library, where James sat in a chair beside the sofa, his elbows on his knees.

"If you can get him out of there, do it," the doctor said.

Shaina nodded.

Then Wilson took a step closer and lowered his voice to say, "I'd like to run something by you. I know it's standard procedure to wait three or four days, but in this heat, I think it's best for all concerned to move things along at a slightly quicker pace."

As hard as it was to hear, Sloan knew Wilson was right. He nodded.

"I'll have a talk with Bass, see if he can get things squared away." The doctor looked at James again. "I'll leave it to you two to help him through it."

Sloan walked the doctor to the door, and Shaina followed. "I appreciate your coming all the way out here on such short notice." As he shook the man's hand, Sloan pressed a wad of money into his hand. "That should be enough for Bass to start on the headstone. Tell him Mable wouldn't want anything fancy."

Then Shaina handed the doctor a slip of paper.

"What's this?" he asked, unfolding it.

"I had a lot of time alone today, and I remembered how difficult it was for Harper to come up with something suitable when Mason died. I thought...I thought if it was that difficult for him to write something for the marker, when he had months to prepare, how much more difficult would it be for James and Sloan, who had no time at all?"

Wilson's eyes misted with tears as he read aloud, "Mable, Wife to James, Mother to All. Eighteen twenty-three to eighteen eighty-three."

Shaina looked at Sloan. "It's not a final version. It's...you know, just to spark ideas, to give you and James a starting point."

"It's perfect," Sloan said, sliding an arm across her shoulders, "and I'm sure James will agree."

Wilson tucked the money and the note into his pocket. "If you like, I'll have a word with the pastor, too...save all of you an unnecessary trip to town and back." He opened the door. "Tomorrow? Day after?"

Sloan looked at James, who held Mable's hand to his lips.

"Unless you hear otherwise, tomorrow. The earlier in the day, the better."

Donning his hat and picking up his bag, Wilson stepped out the door and quietly closed it behind him.

"Do you think it's too soon?" Sloan asked Shaina.

"No, and I don't think James will, either. He's a practical man, if nothing else. He'll see the logic of putting her to rest sooner than later."

Sloan still hadn't removed his arm from her shoulders, and now he pulled her closer. "How long do you think we should let him sit there like that?"

"As long as he wants."

He turned her so that they stood toe to toe. "You know what this means, don't you?"

"What?"

"Losing Mable means you can't leave me." He held her face in his hands. "Ever."

She turned her head slightly and pressed a soft kiss to his palm.

And he hoped it meant she agreed.

〜

Shaina sat on the sofa between Sloan and James, keeping a careful eye on the latter. It seemed he was holding it together, but for all she knew, he'd mastered the art of pretense. The good Lord knew she'd grown good at it over the years.

He'd let her give him a spoonful of the opium tincture, and when she suggested he go up to bed, he went. Hopefully, he would manage to get at least a few hours' sleep before they woke at dawn. They needed to get Mable to Denver so that Bass could get her settled before folks began filing into the church.

The next morning, after Shaina padded the wagon bed with quilts and comforters and blankets, Sloan and Abe moved Mable to what would be her third-to-last resting place.

James told them where to sit—Elsie between Shaina and Abe, Sloan up front to drive the wagon—and talked incessantly all the way into town: Who'd show up in this awful heat? Had they given Bass enough time to carve the epitaph into her tombstone? Should they stop and pick wildflowers to lay on the coffin before it was lowered into the ground?

Once they arrived, however, it seemed James had been struck dumb. He stood, hands clasped at the small of his back, pacing around and around the hole the groundskeeper had prepared in the little grave-yard behind the church.

Somehow, Pastor Truett had talked his wife into greeting parishioners at the door. "It's too hot to gather together inside," Tillie said to each one, "so the pastor will meet you out back in the cemetery."

Shaina wondered who'd carried all the wooden folding chairs, usually reserved for church socials and meetings of the deaconry, to the shady knoll beside the parsonage. One by one, parishioners, neighbors, and friends filed through the wrought-iron gates; and when half the seats were filled, two men rolled the wooden box—Mable's second-to-last resting place—under the shade of a giant bur oak tree.

Looking around at all the people garbed in their mourning clothes, Shaina squirmed slightly as they took note of her pale blue shirt and matching skirt. *Let them stare*, she told herself. Even if she still owned a black dress, she wouldn't have worn it. Mable detested the color!

Pastor Truett stood front and center and raised his Bible high above his head. "Brothers and sisters," he began, "let us pray."

Even the birds in the trees seemed to obey, for they stopped their flitting and chirping.

"We now find ourselves in one of the most difficult moments that any church family faces—the death of a beloved member.

"Mable, like the finest diamond, had many facets. And just as the light passes through the stone and transforms into many colors and sparks in many different directions, Mable sent her unique style of love in many different ways to all those who knew her best. She never had children of her own, but she was a mother to Sloan and Abe, to Elsie and Shaina, and to every man who ever worked at Remington Ranch. She was a loving, dutiful wife to James, here. All facets in one beautiful stone.

"One of my favorite stories about Mable is the day we talked about the earth's great oceans and seas. She was born and raised in Kansas, so the biggest body of water she'd ever seen was the South Platt River. She often dreamed of one day traveling to California, just to see the blue Pacific. I think she would have liked this poem I found, written by the young writer, teacher, and clergyman Henry van Dyke."

He took a sheet of paper from between the pages of his Bible and read.

I am standing upon the seashore. A ship, at my side, spreads her white sails to the morning breeze and starts for the blue ocean. She is an object of beauty and strength. I stand and watch her until, at length, she hangs like a speck of white cloud just where the sea and sky come to mingle with each other.

Then, someone at my side says, "There, she is gone."

Gone where?

Gone from my sight. That is all. She is just as large in mast, hull and spar as she was when she left my side. And, she is just as able to bear her load of living freight to her destined port. Her diminished size is in me—not in her. And, just at the moment when someone at my side says, "There, she is gone," there are other eyes watching her coming, and other voices ready to take up the glad shout, "Here she comes!"

And that is dying.

Truett tucked the paper back inside the Good Book.

"And that is dying." He pointed at the coffin. "Let me remind you that Mable is not in that box. She is in heaven. She is with God. But even beyond that, she continues to live in our love for her and in her qualities that we have, over the years, adopted as our own. I am confident that if each one of us will take a close look, we will find aspects of what we love about Mable in ourselves and in one another. That is her true legacy, and the only one she herself would have wanted. Like an endless stream, our love and friendship for Mable will keep her alive in our memories forever. Because our love for her did not end when she left this life. Not even death can change that!"

A week passed, and gradually, things returned to normal at Remington Ranch. James rose with the rooster and led the hands into their workday with all the enthusiasm of a young cowpoke. During meals, they spoke often and fondly of Mable, laughing at remembered antics and comical remarks. Pastor Truett had been right: She would live on in their hearts and minds. Even Sloan, who'd lost his beloved mother; Pete, the boy who had been like a brother; Simon; and now Mable, joined in the revelry.

Shaina had decided that today, she would get him alone and tell him everything she'd been holding in for months. After supper, she got her chance.

A cool breeze blew down from the mountains—nothing unusual about that on an August night in Colorado—and he'd gone to check on Penny. The dishes could wait, she decided, racing after him.

He didn't seem the slightest bit surprised to see her, and he smiled when she joined him at the corral gate. By now, Penny knew to expect Shaina to deliver carrots, apples, or cabbage leaves, at the very least. While the horse munched contentedly on her treat, Shaina leaned against Sloan's side.

"It's quite chilly for an August night. Are you cold?" she asked him.

"Not anymore," he said, grinning down at her. "Are you?"

"Of course not. *I* had the good sense to wear a coat."

"And you didn't think to bring one for me?" He snorted. "I have to admit, I'm shocked."

She shrugged out of the jacket she'd worn over her coat and handed it to him. And when he laughed, Shaina admitted to herself yet again that she could not imagine spending the rest of her life without this man.

"So, are you here for another astronomy lesson?"

"Oh, I think there are already enough stars in my eyes tonight."

When confusion drew his brows together, she exhaled an exasperated sigh. "Oh, stop looking so perplexed. You know perfectly well how I feel about you. And unless I've lost all grasp of reality—and I honestly don't think that I have—I believe you feel the same way. Life is unpredictable, and far too short. If what happened to Mable isn't proof of that, I don't know what is." She was rambling, and she knew it, but she couldn't seem to stop herself. "If we don't grab hold of the good things when they come along, they might get away from us altogether. And then, who will we have to blame when we're old and gray and sitting all alone in some—"

"Shaina?"

"Sloan?"

"I'm about to haul off and kiss you like you've never been kissed, so if that makes you uncomfortable, you'd better hotfoot it back to the house right now."

"I see absolutely no reason to do that. I don't feel the least bit uncomfortable." Grinning, she tugged at her collar. "Because, as you can see, I'm wearing a nice warm—"

He hadn't exaggerated. She had never been kissed that way before.

Chapter Thirty-six

He'd threatened a kiss that she would never forget. Sloan hadn't considered the possibility that Shaina would return it with equal fervor.

And he should have.

Part of him was sorry when it ended, and part of him thanked God for the opportunity to look into that sweet, open face. Sloan still had questions about her past. There were quite a few years unaccounted for between her departure from Missouri and her marriage to Harper. He didn't know what secrets she'd locked up tight in her heart and mind, but they didn't matter anymore, because he knew without a doubt that she wouldn't hurt him. At least, not intentionally.

Besides, he had a few secrets up his own sleeves. Nothing as mysterious and intriguing as where he'd been and what he'd been doing for a sizable chunk of his life, but once his secrets were out in the open, she might be more inclined to answer his unasked questions.

And if she never came clean? *Well*, he thought, holding her tight, *what could be more exciting than life with a mysterious, intriguing, beautiful woman?*

"So tell me, have you been keeping a book like Elsie's, filled with pretty wedding gowns and bridal bouquets?" he asked her.

Shaina laughed. "No. I think it's sweet—for girls like Elsie—but I've never dreamed of a Cinderella wedding."

"What kind of wedding *have* you dreamed of, then?" It didn't matter what she answered—he'd give it to her in a heartbeat, as long as he was a part of her dream.

She leaned into him and sighed, then stood on tiptoe. Her lips were a fraction of an inch from his, close enough to kiss, if he had a mind to. And if she didn't answer his question soon, he definitely had a mind to!

"I dreamed of a simple white suit, not a ruffled gown made of satin and lace, and a jaunty little hat instead of a long, trailing veil. And if I'm going to carry flowers, I'd like them to be something that grows wild, like columbines. Or daisies. And my bridegroom will wear...." She glanced at his legs. "He'll wear ordinary black trousers with pointy-toed boots, a white collarless shirt, and—"

"No tie?"

She shook her head. "And a scar on his face that tells the world what he's willing to risk to protect the people he cares about."

"Hmm."

"Sound like anyone you know?"

"I believe I could convince Judge Honeywell to issue a license tomorrow. If you're free on Saturday, how 'bout we make your dream come true?"

～

"Oh, Shaina," Elsie gushed, "you look so beautiful!"

There hadn't been time to shop for a simple white suit or a jaunty hat, so Shaina happily borrowed a pink dress and matching hat from Elsie.

"But will *Sloan* think so?"

"If he doesn't, I'll have my brother examine his eyes. Now, we'd better get out there, or else...well, you know James."

"He'll start without us!"

Shaina saw him first thing upon opening the door. "You know it ain't polite to keep an old man waitin', don't you?"

She could have pointed out that they were five minutes early. Instead, Shaina linked her arm through his and said, "Sorry."

He winked. "It was worth it. You look purtier than a newborn pup."

Elsie took her other arm, and together, they walked toward the altar, where Pastor Truett stood tall and straight, with Abe on his left and Sloan on his right. Thanks to Elsie's frantic motions and facial expressions, he noticed the error and waved Sloan to the proper spot.

"Well," Truett began, "by my count, there are seven of us here today. Scripture is saturated with the number seven. It says in the second chapter of Genesis, '*And on the seventh day God ended his work which he had made; and he rested on the seventh day from all his work which he had made. And God blessed the seventh day, and sanctified it.*' In the Bible, the number seven symbolizes completion, or perfection, and what could be more perfect and complete than joining Sloan and Shaina in holy matrimony?

"I'll dispense with the usual 'enter this union reverently and soberly' and get to the crux. Who gives this woman to be married to this man?"

James put Shaina's hand into Sloan's. "I do, and by all that's holy, it's about time!"

Quiet laughter preceded Truett's heavy sigh.

"Now then, Sloan, do you take Shaina for your lawfully wedded wife, to be joined in matrimony?"

"I—"

"Not yet, son," the preacher said. "You have more promises to make first!"

"Oh. Sorry."

"Will you love, honor, comfort, and cherish Shaina from this day forward, forsaking all others, keeping only unto her, for as long as you both shall live?" Following a lengthy pause, Truett said, "*Now* you may respond."

"Oh. Yes, of course I do."

Truett rolled his eyes. "And Shaina, do you take Sloan for your lawfully wedded husband, to be joined in matrimony, and will you love, honor, comfort, and cherish him from this day forward, forsaking all others, keeping only unto him, for as long as you both shall live?"

"I do."

"Rings, please?"

James handed Truett a plain gold band, and the pastor continued. "May this ring be blessed so that he who gives it and she who wears it shall live joyously together and continue in love all the days of their lives." He handed the ring to Sloan. "Repeat after me: With this ring, I thee wed. Wear it as a symbol of our love and commitment."

Sloan echoed the words and, hands trembling, slid the ring onto Shaina's finger.

"And from the Song of Solomon," Truett said, opening his Bible. "*Thou hast ravished my heart, my sister, my spouse; thou hast ravished my heart with one of thine eyes, with one chain of thy neck. How fair is thy love, my sister, my spouse!*"

He paused and then, with a smile, said, "I now pronounce you husband and wife. Sloan, you may kiss your bride."

Following a flurry of congratulatory hugs and kisses, Sloan whisked Shaina off to the waiting buggy.

"We aren't going home?" she asked.

"I've reserved a suite at The Remington for our wedding night."

Shaina feigned shock. "The Remington! But it's the most expensive hotel in all of Denver!"

"Oh, don't worry. I'm well acquainted with the owner, and he quoted me a very fair price."

"But…you just passed it," she pointed out.

"Yes, I know. That's because there's something I want to show you first."

He slowed as they approached the gates of the former Sterling Hall, now standing wide open to expose a new foundation and mounds of construction supplies.

"Do you see that sign?" he asked, pointing to a four-by-eight foot white panel.

"Yes…."

"Can you read what it says, or are we too far away?"

Shaina squinted, then read aloud, "The Elbam and Aniahs Hospital." She looked at him. "Elbam and Aniahs? What language is that?"

"It's English, of course." He fished a small mirror out of his shirt pocket. "Normally, the boys and I use one of these to signal the men if I've found a missing cow. But I think it'll come in right handy to help you translate."

He gave it to her and said, "Now turn around and use the mirror to look over your shoulder and read the sign. Don't bother with the first and last words. Just read the middle two."

"Shaina and Mable." She faced him again, handing him his mirror. "Is this really how you want to start our married life—by confounding me with riddles?" she asked with a grin.

"Do you remember what Mable said just about every chance she got?"

Suddenly it made perfect sense to name a hospital after the woman who'd been like a mother to him—the woman who'd loved pointing out the oftentimes backward nature of life.

"And which two women in my life always made sure to take care of others?"

Mable and I, she thought. "But...the property taxes were in arrears. You don't mean to say...."

"I do." He winked. "Again."

Shaina could hardly believe that he'd put that once-beautiful estate to such good use.

"Are you ready to see the other surprise?"

"Another surprise? Sloan, if you keep this up, you'll spoil me!" She bumped him with her shoulder. "I hope you won't label me a frail sissy if I keel over in a faint. A wedding, a hospital, and now something else? I don't know how much more I can take!"

He steered the carriage into the narrow drive beside Jennie Rogers' residence and stopped out back, near the stables and other outbuildings. And just when Shaina was about to ask what they were doing here, Jennie walked toward them...leading Flame. As wonderful as it was to see him, she thought her heart might break, because she'd have to leave him yet again.

The horse recognized her immediately and leaned into the carriage to receive pats and kisses. "Oh, you are a sight for sore eyes, you big, handsome thing!"

"When we leave Denver tomorrow," Sloan said, "we're taking him home with us."

Shaina raised her eyebrows.

"Oh, don't look so surprised, sweetie," Jennie put in. "Yes, this big lug you married really does love you enough to buy back your favorite pony. But don't you worry—I'll keep right on taking good care of Flame for one more night."

"You'll have to come out to the ranch first chance you get so that I can see if you're as good a horsewoman as you claim," Shaina teased before they drove away.

When at last they arrived at the hotel, Sloan helped her down from the buggy, then told her to wait in the lobby while he took the horses around back.

"If you'll give me the key, I can—"

"What, let yourself into the suite? And deprive me of the pleasure of carrying you over the threshold?"

It was all she could do to keep from skipping up the front steps of The Remington, because she didn't see how this day could possibly get any better.

And then she walked into the dim, hushed lobby and realized in an instant that it *could* get better. Two times better!

She was so happy to see her brothers that she nearly bowled them over with a hug.

"I can't believe my eyes. How long have you been in town? How did you know where to find me? Where have you *been* all these years?"

"She sure hasn't changed much, has she?" Earl asked.

"Nope, she sure hasn't," Ben agreed. "She can still talk the ears off a hound."

"I—I don't understand."

"Your husband sicced the Pinkertons on us," Earl said. "Asked if I knew where to find Ben, and when I told him I did—and that my enlistment was up—he said there was work for us at the ranch if we want it."

"And you're here," she said, "so you must want it!"

Sloan entered the lobby just then, and by the way her brothers greeted him, it was clear they'd met before.

"I think my head might explode, it's so full of questions," Shaina told him.

"Well, they'll just have to wait," Sloan said. He took her elbow and started for the stairs. "James is waiting out front with horses. He'll show you around when you get to the ranch," he told the brothers. "I suggest you both get a good night's sleep, because I have a feeling your sister, here, is going to drill you so full of questions, we'll be able to read the newspaper through you."

Moments later, after he'd carried her over the threshold and locked the door behind them, Sloan took her in his arms. "So, tell me, Shaina Remington, did you get your dream wedding?"

She smiled. "*Shaina Remington*. I like the sound of that. And yes, I got my dream wedding—and so much more. It's been the perfect, most beautiful day. But what about you? Are you happy, too?"

"The happiest I've ever been."

Shaina crooked her finger, and when he leaned in close, she whispered, "I have a secret to tell you."

"Oh?"

"I love you. I've loved you from the moment you stood on my porch the night of the earthquake."

"A lot you know," he said, holding her tight. "That was no earthquake. It was my heart, beating with love for you."

Book Club Discussion Questions

1. Which character from *Currency of the Heart* is your favorite, and why?

2. Which character is your *least* favorite, and why?

3. What did you learn about Denver of the 1880s that you didn't know before reading *Currency of the Heart*?

4. What would you say is the main theme of this story?

5. Did you have a favorite scene? If so, which one, and why?

6. Could you identify with Shaina's behavior early in the story?

7. Which event would you cite as the reason Shaina grew as a person?

8. Could you identify with the type of man Sloan was when the story opened?

9. Do you feel he changed—and improved—as the story progressed?

10. Do you hope that any of the secondary characters will appear in books two and three of the series Secrets on Sterling Street? If so, which ones, and why?

From the Author

Dear reader,

Even the best of us have secrets—a forbidden cookie stolen before supper, a fib told to spare another's feelings—and some too dark and shameful to share with anyone.

Why is it so hard to confess these secrets? Could it be that, because we've harshly judged others, we fear that coming clean might separate us from friends and family, or, worse, from the Almighty Himself?

We needn't fear harsh judgment from our loving Father. Throughout the Bible, we read about His tender mercies. The trick, then, is convincing ourselves that we, the great secret-keepers, are just as worthy of His perfect love as any other sinner, from Eve to King David to Mary Magdalene.

Luke 7:47 says, "*Wherefore I say unto thee, [Your] sins, which are many, are forgiven.*" That is the promise I cling to when self-doubt darkens my heart, and it's the lesson Sloan and Shaina need to learn—individually *and* together.

If you enjoyed *Currency of the Heart*, I hope you'll let me know by dropping me a note c/o Whitaker House Publishers, 1030 Hunt Valley Circle, New Kensington, PA 15068.

Be sure to look for the next books in the Secrets on Sterling Street series, too!

Blessings to you and yours,
Loree

About the Author

Once upon a time, best-selling author Loree Lough literally sang for her supper, performing before packed audiences throughout the Midwest. Now and then, she blows the dust from her 6-string to croon a tune or two for her grandkids or to sing at weddings or funerals, but she mostly just writes. Over the years, her stories have earned hundreds of industry and Readers' Choice awards and 4- and 5-star reviews.

Loree has nearly five million copies of her books in circulation, and in March 2014, she added her hundredth published book to the shelves. She has written fiction and nonfiction for kids and adults (2,500-plus articles and 68 short stories), and four of her novels have been optioned for movies.

To date, there are almost 66,000 letters in her "Reader Mail" file, and she has answered every one, personally. (A carton of books is on its way to Corinna P. of San Antonio, Texas, for writing the 65,999th letter. Corinna said she plans to donate the books to her local library!)

Loree loves sharing learned-the-hard-way lessons about the craft and the industry, and her comedic approach to teaching makes her a favorite (and frequent) guest of writers' organizations, book clubs, private and government institutions, and college and high school writing programs in the U.S. and abroad.

A writer who believes in "giving back," Loree dedicates a portion of her income to Soldiers' Angels, Special Operations Warrior

Foundation, and several other worthwhile organizations (see the "Giving Back" tab at her Web site, http://www.loreelough.com, for a complete list). She splits her time between a tiny home in the Baltimore suburbs and an even tinier cabin in the Allegheny Mountains, where she continues to perfect her Critter Tracks Identification skills. She shares her life with her real-life hero, Larry, who rarely complains, even when she adds yet another item to her vast collection of "wolf stuff."

Welcome to Our House!

We Have a Special Gift for You ...

It is our privilege and pleasure to share in your love of Christian fiction by publishing books that enrich your life and encourage your faith.

To show our appreciation, we invite you to sign up to receive a specially selected **Reader Appreciation Gift**, with our compliments. Just go to the Web address at the bottom of this page.

God bless you as you seek a deeper walk with Him!

WE HAVE A GIFT FOR YOU. VISIT:

whpub.me/fictionthx

WHITAKER HOUSE